23/8/22

www.southdublinlibraries.ie
South Dublin Libraries

NOW THAT YOU'VE GONE

D1407523

ALSO BY FIONA GARTLAND

In the Court's Hands

Published by Poolbeg

NOW THAT YOU'VE GONE

FIONA GARTLAND

POOLBEG
CRIMSON

This book is a work of fiction. References to real people, events, establishments, organisations, or locales are intended only to provide a sense of authenticity, and are used fictitiously. All other characters, and all incidents and dialogue, are drawn from the author's imagination and are not to be construed as real.

Published 2019 by Crimson
an imprint of Poolbeg Press Ltd
123 Grange Hill, Baldoyle,
Dublin 13, Ireland
Email: poolbeg@poolbeg.com

© Fiona Gartland 2019

The moral right of the author has been asserted.

© Poolbeg Press Ltd. 2019, copyright for editing, typesetting, layout, design, ebook.

A catalogue record for this book is available from the British Library.

ISBN 978178199-795-6

All rights reserved. No part of this publication may be reproduced or transmitted in any form or by any means, electronic or mechanical, including photography, recording, or any information storage or retrieval system, without permission in writing from the publisher. The book is sold subject to the condition that it shall not, by way of trade or otherwise, be lent, resold or otherwise circulated without the publisher's prior consent in any form of binding or cover other than that in which it is published and without a similar condition, including this condition, being imposed on the subsequent purchaser.

Printed and bound by ScandBook, Lithuania

www.poolbeg.com

ABOUT THE AUTHOR

Fiona Gartland has been a journalist with *The Irish Times* for fourteen years and has covered many cases at the Criminal Courts of Justice and at Family Court. She was shortlisted for the Francis McManus Short Story Competition on half a dozen occasions, has had stories broadcast and has been published in magazines. Her first novel, *In the Court's Hands*, was published in 2018.

She lives in Dublin with her husband and four children.

Chapter 1

Wednesday, October 19th, 2016

I've witnessed many sordid things in my life. As a stenographer at the Criminal Courts of Justice, I thought I'd seen how low a human being might stoop. But one week into O'Malley v O'Malley and I'd decided there was nothing uglier than a bitter break-up.

I prefer criminal work – it's easier to tell right from wrong, good from bad. Family law is complicated, often dirty and at its worst has badness on all sides. As well as goodness, of course. I have to remind myself of that more frequently than I'd like.

I had no choice but to take on family law. Once solicitors and barristers became comfortable with digital audio-recording at the CCJ, they began relying on the work of stenographers and our meticulous transcription much less. And I have to earn my living somehow.

My colleague, Janine Gracefield, with whom I had worked for many years, opted out of stenography entirely in 2014. It was partly because of the downturn in demand for our services, and partly because her boyfriend Alastair McAuliffe had turned out to be a killer. She took a break from our little enterprise and got involved with a charity for street children in India. The last time we spoke, she was in Calcutta giving English classes to ten-year-olds. A part of me envied her, she was so engrossed in worthy work. But then I could never see myself being able to deal with ten-year-olds. Still, I did sometimes think about the possibilities of an alternative career, especially when sitting in Court 32, at the Dublin Circuit Family Court, Phoenix House, listening to the painful minutiae of the married life of the O'Malleys.

The courtroom looks like a large office. The judge's desk is on a modestly raised platform, with the registrar and myself to one side, only slightly below. One entire wall is obscure glass, facing out onto the street. The main body of the court is taken up with a large table – solicitors sit on one side with their backs to the judge and registrar, and barristers on the other facing toward the judge. There is only one row of chairs against the back wall for clients, who usually sit far apart from each other behind their respective legal teams. The public cannot attend the cases, so little additional seating is needed.

The O'Malleys were what lawyers liked to call a "medium net-worth couple", not so wealthy as to go straight to the High Court but wealthy enough to be worth fighting on their behalf. I had learnt that the greater the worth, the harder the fight. Their barristers had decided, given the funds at stake, that it would be best for everyone to have a daily transcript from the proceedings for their legal separation, so that every utterance of the estranged spouses could be parsed, analysed and twisted. And that was when my services were called for.

A week into the case, it was expert accountants who had been taking up the court's time. There was one hired by each side and both had diametrically opposing views of the value of what had been a family business and whether a trust in the Cayman Islands really belonged to Mr O'Malley or whether it belonged to his brother. Not for the first time, I was grateful I had never married.

"I'm looking at the time, Ms Hollister – are you almost done?" Judge Peter Hadley-O'Toole asked.

Úna Hollister, a barrister whose uniform of black skirt, white blouse, black jacket and robe which shone in places from overuse, shook her head.

"All right, two o'clock then." He put both his hands flat on his desk and heaved himself to his feet. He nodded at the O'Malleys, at Ms Hollister, and at her opposite number, Ruby Clements, a barrister in fresh black and white, with red high heels. Then he nodded at his courtroom assistant, who opened a door to the left of the bench, through which the judge eased himself.

I checked my watch. There would be time to go back to the little room they had rented to me in the Courts Service offices next door. I could eat the lunch I'd prepared and check over some of my notes before two.

I slipped my arms into the camel-coloured coat that I'd draped on the back of my chair, settling it over my plum suit and jacket. Though I was only going next door, I felt the need to wrap my scarf round my neck, button the coat up to my throat, firmly tie the belt and turn up the collar. October so far had been cooler than normal. Today, there was a raw wind blowing down the street, between the glass-fronted court buildings of Phoenix

House and the lower stone wall across the way, where a Luas stop offered minimalist shelter to those awaiting transportation.

I felt the air sting my cheeks as I walked briskly out one set of glass doors, turned left, and in through another set.

In my tiny office three floors up, with the half-light from Stable Lane supplementing my desk lamp, I took off my coat and opened the jacket button of my two-piece. A part of me still longed for the bright and spacious office that I'd had in the CCJ and that view of lush green over the Phoenix Park. Though this building had the name of Phoenix, it was actually in Smithfield and my view was not green, but the red and grey brick of solicitors firm Gore & Grimes.

I ate my carefully prepared sandwich and uploaded the transcript of the morning's hearing from a memory stick onto my laptop.

As I finished the food my phone pinged and I saw there was a message from Georgina, a friend I'd known for twenty years. She had responded to my earlier contact, sent before the court case had begun, enquiring about her wellbeing.

"I'm okay, thanks, but wouldn't mind company tonight."

I keyed in: **"I'll call by. Would six suit?"**

The response was swift.

"Yes. Thanks."

I put my phone into my bag, disconnected the memory key from my computer, stowed it and logged out of my laptop.

4

In the ladies' toilets near my office, I tidied my red chignon, dabbed at the foundation that disguised my freckles and, to some extent, my increasing wrinkles, and topped up my mink lipstick. I wondered what to take Georgina. Cake, perhaps? No, that would seem celebratory. Dinner? I would be hungry after work, but that might be insulting – it implied an assumption she wouldn't provide food and therefore was not coping. It would have to be a bottle of wine. Though I didn't drink alcohol myself, I knew she was partial to a good vintage.

Poor Georgina. It was three months since her husband, Andrew Dalton, died and it had been a nasty business. Violent attack, the gardaí had said. The papers described him as having had his head caved in before being dropped into the Blessington Basin. Some old man out walking his dog found him floating there in the city's old reservoir, green algae lapping around him. Dreadful.

At the funeral she was barely able to stand, and the children, two little things who adored Andrew, walked behind their father's coffin, as bewildered as shorn lambs. Georgina's Emma was there too, trying her best to support her mother. Georgina had told me Emma always refused to call Andrew "Dad", preferring "Andy" when she was in a good mood and "your husband" when she was in a bad one. The fourteen-year-old's own father was officially unknown – a brief relationship with an American student who had melted away when Georgina had refused to go to London to put an end to the pregnancy.

Andrew's death had seemed the cruellest of blows. Georgina had been a long time finding him and they'd seemed perfect for each other. She had told me many times how she adored him and, in their company, I had concluded that the feeling was mutual.

His killing made me hate the city a little, for enabling such a fate to befall a good man. He was walking upright one minute, going about whatever business he was going about in a park at night, and he was dead the next. I pictured him, his brisk, long-legged stride, as he passed through the gate at the top of Blessington Street, into the hidden garden that now surrounds the old reservoir. Where was he going? Taking the picturesque route to Phibsboro, perhaps. The papers suggested he was flattened by some mugger, desperate for drug money, and the gardaí hadn't contradicted them. It could have happened in any city. Anywhere there were humans together, rich and poor, fortunate and unfortunate, good and bad. It was foolish to think that Dublin should escape such things, just because it was Dublin.

Chapter 2

After work, I visited an off-licence in Smithfield and asked advice about buying a nice, classic red.

"It's for a friend who's had a terrible tragedy," I explained to the sommelier, as though wines were medicinal.

He nodded, recommended a Pomerol and I paid the €35 requested.

I hadn't driven to work, preferring to leave my car at the train station not far from home on Clontarf Road. There was next to no parking around Smithfield and what was there was too expensive to use regularly. I took a taxi to Donnybrook and thought about the first time I'd met Georgina. I had only just returned from London in 1995, where I'd trained and worked in stenography, and was determined to set myself up in business. I had found through trial and error that I worked best when self-employed and, with my own business, I could take up contracts with the Courts Service or with individuals who commissioned me. Back then, before the introduction of the dreaded digital audio-recording system in the courts, there were many more stenographers in the capital. I had rented a small office on Capel Street and I'd found Georgina through an acquaintance. She specialised in secure computer systems. And though she had been clear and straightforward with her advice when she set up my system, I had found I needed to contact her half a dozen times before I was comfortable with the security she had provided. I had emphasised the confidentiality required from stenographers and told Georgina if I was ever hacked I would never work again. I remembered her patient explanations and her earnestness. She was younger than me, by more than twelve years I reckoned, a pretty blonde who liked to visit the gym even then, before it became the kind of religion it is now. She had a steadiness and diligence that I'd admired. And I, so newly back in Ireland and unwilling to reconnect with the companions of my youth, had been grateful when she invited me to dinner at her home. I was not so grateful when I discovered an attempt at matchmaking and Georgina soon learned it was best not to go there.

The taxi pulled up at 21 Belford Avenue. I had always liked the house and had to admit it was partly because, on a street of red, it was one of the few made of butter-coloured brick. It had a decent driveway, with enough paving for two cars, and a pretty raised flowerbed. The black hall door had a polished brass doorknob and knocker, with a broad arch of glass above it on which the house number was painted in white. I paid the driver and got out, clutching the bottle.

Opening the door, Georgina managed a small smile. I smiled back and stepped over the threshold, taking in as I did her pale complexion, the taut skin over her cheekbones, her fair hair pulled back into an untidy ponytail and the glazing in her hazel eyes. Her blue trousers and white shirt looked as though she had slept in them. They also seemed too big for her and I was sure she must have dropped a couple of sizes since I saw her last. I handed her the wine and shed my coat, draping it across the banister, along with my handbag and suit jacket.

She led the way down the narrow wooden-floored hall to the kitchen, an extended glass-and-wood cathedral to cookery. The copper pots I remembered still hung from hooks over the island. There were none on the stove.

"I hope you don't mind, I ordered takeaway. I didn't feel like cooking."

I said I didn't mind at all and hid my disappointment when I noticed a Thai menu on the countertop.

"The children are with Andrew's sister Tracy for a couple of days."

"Distracting for her, I suppose."

"She says they give her comfort."

"Hmm." It was hard for me to imagine children as a source of comfort.

Georgina searched in a drawer, produced a complicated and expensive-looking corkscrew and wrenched the cork out of its resting place in the bottle I had given her with one strong movement.

"The food will be here soon, may as well." She poured herself a generous glass and found a bottle of sparkling water for me.

"How's Emma?"

"Fine once she got back to school. I think it helped her to get away."

I thought briefly of my own escape, all those years ago to England, after the death of my brother Laurence. Had that helped? In some ways, I supposed it had. But it had hurt too.

"St Columba's, is it?" I surprised myself by remembering. It must have stuck in my head when Georgina had told me they were sending Emma away for seven-day boarding. I'd been shocked. I'd thought people didn't do that anymore.

"It's a lovely place. It will give her a real sense of stability," Georgina had said at the time.

I'd wanted to ask why she couldn't find stability at home but thought better of it. Who was I to judge the domestic arrangements of others? And what would I know about raising a teenage daughter, especially for Andrew, when she wasn't his own? Maybe it was easier for everyone if Emma went away.

We made small talk about the weather, how it was exceptionally cold for October and didn't it feel like snow? We spent a while trying to remember a colder month.

When the food arrived, Georgina divided the green curry and rice between two plates.

"Do you mind if we go inside?" Not waiting for an answer, she picked up her plate, a napkin, a fork and her wine and walked through dividing doors into the living room. The fire was lit there, and its flames cast shadows across a blush-coloured rug and mocked the rigid pool of light cast by an art-deco floor lamp, positioned to the left of a cream sofa.

10

I put my drink and plate on the glass-topped coffee table, sat down on the sofa next to Georgina, spread my napkin across my lap and then picked up my plate carefully. An abhorrence of lemongrass forced me to separate out each cube of chicken, and dab each in turn at the edge of my plate, before putting it in my mouth. I ate only the rice untouched by sauce. When the food was finished, Georgina took the plates to the kitchen and returned with the bottle of wine in one hand and the water in the other. She filled up her glass and topped up my water before sitting down.

"Tell me, how are you doing?" I asked then.

"Honestly? Not so good – I'm finding it impossible to believe he's really gone." She began talking about their life together, like someone recalling an old familiar place that no longer existed.

"You know, the first day I met him I knew we were meant to be together."

I kept my eyes on my hands, afraid that a look of deep scepticism would leak out and make itself obvious to Georgina. I have never believed in that sort of thing, that love-at-first-sight notion that's peddled.

But she was not paying me any attention. She was talking about how Andrew swept her off her feet when he walked up to her desk at work and introduced himself.

"There was just something in his look, the way he held himself, you know?"

I didn't admit to having been worried the first time I met Andrew, a month after she began dating him. At forty-three, he was eight years older than Georgina, but seemed older still, weary even. Over the years, though, that weariness had disappeared and I believed they were happy together. He seemed to supply for Georgina the family support she had lost in her twenties when both her parents had died. Thinking of it now, that "orphan" status was something Georgina and I had in common, and I supposed it had helped to bond us.

"He was only back from London, you know – jaded with the music industry, he said. Just as well, I haven't a note in my head." Georgina laughed for a second then censored herself in the way that grieving people often do. "He was only here a couple of days when he picked up a job at Techworld, walked into it. They liked the cut of him. Of course, it was 2006 – so, you know yourself."

"It's getting a bit like that again."

"You think?"

"I do. You should see some of the cars pulling into the Four Courts these days." I had seen half a dozen Mercs parked in the cobbled courtyard of that 18th century building the last time I'd worked at the commercial court. There was more than one jaguar and BMWs seemed common.

She poured more wine, the bottle now three-quarters gone.

"This is nice," she said, holding up her glass, "Andrew would have enjoyed this – a good red."

I leaned forward to take my glass of water from the coffee table.

"He did so well in Techworld, didn't he, though?" She looked at me for approval.

"He did, but you did too. Sure, you were the perfect couple. Everyone said so."

She began crying then, head down, shoulders shaking. I handed her a napkin. She blew her nose.

"Sorry, it's just so hard sometimes."

"I know."

"You don't though, you don't." She began crying again.

I thought of Laurence and how much I'd cried after his death. He had ended up in the water too, but by his own hand.

"You're right, I don't know. It must be terrible to think someone could do such a thing to Andrew, a good man like that. Are the guards telling you anything?"

"Nothing, very little – ongoing investigation, that's all they'll say. There was no CCTV in there, so . . ."

She dried her eyes and swallowed the contents of her glass in one go.

"Do you know what the worst thing is? We had a row. I told him, Jesus, I told him to fuck himself." Her face contorted as she attempted to hold herself back from crying again. "What sort of a human being does that?"

I shook my head. "Every sort at one time or other. It's natural." I patted her arm. "Put that row out of your head. Think of all the lovely times you had together." How cruel it was for fate to ensure their last words had been bitter. What a sad burden to have to carry.

When she had composed herself, she told me about the knock on her front door the night Andrew was killed. She had told me many times before about getting the news – at the removal, at the funeral, on the phone when she'd called me late at night.

"They stood there – this was 2am – a young woman guard with her mouth open and this curly-headed, plain-

13

clothed, farmer type and the time between when I opened the door and when they started to speak went on forever – and then he said 'Ma'am' and I knew."

She drained the bottle into her glass. "What I thought was, he must have crashed the car, but then they told me what happened and where. I swear I couldn't make sense of it. I thought they must have got the wrong person."

"It's hard to believe really," I said. "Killing someone like that – for what? A few euro?"

She rubbed her forehead with the fingertips of her right hand. "They didn't even get his money. It was still on him when they – when they took him out of the water. They gave his wallet back to me with everything in it. All his cards. He had his phone even."

"It doesn't make any sense." Perhaps the attacker had not had time to get the wallet, maybe he wasn't meant to fall into the water. I didn't say those things out loud. It didn't seem right to be speculating.

"They've no answers, the guards, only questions. Did I think he was in some kind of trouble? Did he use drugs? Did he have enemies? I said no to everything."

She stopped speaking and, though I would have liked to ask my own questions, I held back and let the silence sit between us. After a while she began to talk again.

"What was he even doing there? Miles from work, miles from home, why would he be walking through that place?"

I thought of the Blessington Basin park. Its entrance was at the top of Blessington Street in the heart of the city – it exited at Royal Canal Bank, in Phibsboro. It was a forty-five-minute walk or thereabouts, from Techworld near the Grand Canal, to Phibsboro near the Royal. The breadth of the city at one time.

"Did they find his car?"

"Still in the underground car park at work. Wherever he was going, he meant to come back, he meant to come home to me."

I patted her arm again. "Of course he did."

"It's torture, the not knowing."

"It must be." At least my parents and I had been spared that when Laurence died.

"I wish the guards would tell me more." She looked at me and her eyes, though dulled from the wine, had a question in them.

Had this been the reason for her invitation, to see if I could get her some information? It must have been. She knew Gabriel and I were friends and that he had friends in the guards. I thought for a while before speaking and picked my words carefully.

"I'll see what I can do, Georgina, but I can't promise anything. Gabriel and I are a bit . . . out of touch."

"Anything, anything at all."

I would do what she asked. I would contact Gabriel Ingram. But it wouldn't be easy. How long had it been since that last hurried lunch? What was it that had brought the shutter down between us? I tried but I couldn't remember.

"It's yourself." Gabriel looked up and back down as quickly at his newspaper.

It was an inauspicious start to what I'd hoped would not be too awkward an encounter. I'd been impatient to complete the task once I'd agreed to it and had gone straight to Stoneybatter from Georgina's. I called first to Gabriel's house on Oxmantown Road and then to each of the local pubs. It was a quarter past ten when I found him in Hanlon's, a pub filled with dark wood, plum-coloured seats and posters for local sports clubs.

I stood before him now where he was seated in the corner, not knowing what to say.

"Can I get you a pint?"

"No, thanks – I've had my quota." He lifted up his half-empty glass.

"Well, maybe I'll just get . . ." I went to the bar, ordered soda water and lime, then went back and positioned myself on a wooden chair at Gabriel's table and put my coat and handbag on the chair that filled up the space between us.

The barmaid, a young woman with blonde hair in spikes too short for her oval face, placed the glass in front of me.

"Thanks, Billie," Gabriel said with a smile.

I thanked her and paid.

She smiled at Gabriel again before she left.

He had lowered his paper, like a sail at half-mast, to talk to her. Now he folded it and announced he would very shortly be going home.

"Just let me finish this and I'll walk with you." I took a long drink.

"What do you want?"

"Pardon?" His bluntness had caught me by surprise.

"What is it you want, Beatrice? You wouldn't be here if you didn't want something. And another thing, how

16

did you find me?" He scratched his iron-grey hair with his right hand, looking for a moment like a lanky bird beginning a mating dance.

"There aren't that many pubs within walking distance of Oxmantown Road." I took another drink. There was no point playing games with him. "And you're right, I do want something."

"I'm busy."

He was going to make this hard for me. He gulped the last of his pint, stood up and pulled on a navy donkey jacket. I couldn't help admiring the fill of him in it.

I stood and put on my own coat.

"Just let me walk along with you so, for a little while," I said.

He gave Billie a wave as we left the pub.

"I'm going the long way around," he said as he began his familiar, fast step up the North Circular Road toward the park. I matched his pace and we had passed the turn for Aughrim Street, and half a dozen of the Georgian houses, before I spoke again.

"It's like flat-land along here now," I said, beginning a conversation we'd had many times before.

Gabriel glanced in the direction of one of the three-storey houses with their fine granite steps and their garden basements. "They must have been lovely one time."

"Will you maybe hear me out, Gabriel?"

"I'm not stopping you."

I took a deep breath. "You remember Georgina O'Donnell, lives over in Donnybrook?"

He nodded.

17

"And you know it was her husband they found in the basin?"

"I read that all right, terrible thing."

"Only, the guards are telling her nothing, and I think it's Matt McCann on the case."

McCann was a former colleague of Gabriel's, now a detective inspector. Two years earlier, he had done all he could to help us, despite the mess we'd made for ourselves or, really, I had made for us, during the O'Farrell trial.

"Could be him. I heard he'd moved to Store Street," Gabriel said.

We walked through the iron gates into the Phoenix Park and I recounted all that Georgina had told me and all I'd read of the case in the newspapers. As I described the discovery of the body, the branches on the bare trees either side of us seemed to creak and moan in lamentation. The cold, damp air laced with a sharp odour of burning leaves enveloped us. As we passed the rose garden close to Parkgate Street the smoky smell dispersed.

"Any complications in the background? Drink problem or debt or anything, do you think?" Gabriel tried to keep from displaying his natural curiosity and failed.

"I don't know, but I doubt it." I couldn't imagine that. They were too happy together. "I've never seen Andrew drunk and I think Georgina would have mentioned it if she had money worries."

"Are you sure? You'd be surprised how blind women can be when it comes to their husbands."

Was I sure? Would she tell me?

"They have a lovely house, nice holidays, and Emma's in a private boarding school. That doesn't sound like money problems."

"Doesn't sound like it, no."

We reached the door of Ryan's pub and Gabriel stopped. He said he wasn't going home. He had promised to meet a pal inside before closing time.

"I'll make one phone call, that's it, that's all I can do," he said.

"Thanks. I know Georgina will be grateful. And I will too."

"You can keep your gratitude." He turned away from me and I could see him heading for the empty snug at the back of the room where we had often talked together, before the pub door swung shut.

Chapter 3

Saturday, October 22nd, 2016

I'd arranged to meet Gabriel in Hanlon's three days later. He had what looked like a fresh pint in front of him when I arrived just before eleven o'clock. I tried to remember if he'd always started drinking so early in the day. I supposed the longer he was retired, the more tempting it was for him.

"Morning." I unwound the yellow wool scarf from my neck and took off my pale-blue leather gloves and grey coat. I sat down and he immediately stood up.

"Sorry, I'll be back in a second."

I thought he might be about to order me something, but he headed for the gents'.

I went up to the bar myself to get some tea. Billie, the young woman who had served me before, was there, concentrating on pulling a pint of stout. She filled the glass three quarters and let it stand.

"Can I help you?"

"One tea, please."

She nodded and turned to a jug kettle behind her, standing amid the upside-down bottles of gin, vodka and whiskey. She filled the kettle and switched it on, then returned to the pint, tipped a little of the drink into the drip tray below the stout tap and then topped it up. She stood watching it settle for a moment then saw me looking.

"I love watching it. There's something soothing about it," she said. She laughed to herself, picked up the pint and handed it to a man sitting at the end of the bar.

"Barney."

"T'anks."

He pushed a pile of coins in her direction which she scooped up and, without counting, tipped them into the till.

The kettle was building up a head of steam and condensation had begun to form on the mirror at the back of the bar.

"You sit down and I'll bring the tea over to you when it's ready."

"Thank you."

I sat, and Gabriel returned.

"Sorry about that." He rubbed his stomach. "Must have eaten something off last night."

I was tempted to ask if by any chance he'd had too many pints, but knew he wouldn't like that.

"Is there no one else working here?" I asked instead.

"Too early. Billie usually opens herself or else the manager, but he's away at the moment. There'll be a few by lunch time though – there's a chef and a couple of other barmen."

"I didn't know they did food."

"They didn't always."

Billie arrived with my tea.

21

"Thanks. Billie, isn't it?"

She nodded and I paid her.

"Chilly out there," Gabriel said to her as he reached for his glass.

"I know. Are you sure you wouldn't prefer a hot tea? Warm you up?"

She grinned at him and he laughed.

Men of his age, I thought, like being gently mocked by young women.

Billie went back to the bar.

"Anyway, you were right about Matt being involved – he's heading the case."

"Good." I respected the detective inspector, though I didn't always approve of the way he went about things.

"Georgina needn't worry. He's a grafter – he'll get to the bottom of it."

There didn't seem to be much evidence of it so far.

"What did he say?"

"They think Andrew Dalton had been visiting a casino. Maybe owed money or something."

"Casino? Where?" Georgina had said nothing about that. She mustn't have known.

"A place in Phibsboro – Spin, it's called."

I recalled passing the place, on Phibsboro Road. It had seemed incongruous there among the ordinary shops and houses, a three-storey building, with a large sign in the shape of a roulette wheel, the name 'Spin' in gold lettering at its centre. The double-door entrance was shiny black. A gold sash hung from brass hoops across the door and the windows either side had heavy red drapes. There were half a dozen empty car-park spaces out front with VIP written on the tarmac in each space. The overall effect was tacky.

"So was he coming from there when it happened?"

"Seems so." He paused, tentative now. "Matt said – well, he suggested – since he's given you some information, you might be able to help him."

I couldn't prevent the displeasure from showing on my face and he laughed a little at me.

"And he wants what?"

"He wants you to talk to Georgina, find out if Andrew owed money – not banks – moneylenders or bookies, that sort. And find out if they were okay, together like."

Gabriel took a drink from his pint. He had been neglecting it and consequently it looked flat and more yellow than cream.

"So, in exchange for this titbit of information about the casino, McCann thinks I'll spy on a friend?" It didn't seem like a fair trade to me and would put me in a very difficult position. And Gabriel knew that. By the look of him, if he'd been wearing a shirt with a collar, he'd have run his finger around the neck of it. But, as it was, he could only pull absentmindedly at the place where the soft collar of his polo shirt met the V of his jumper.

"Forget about it, sure, just leave it alone. You don't have to do anything."

I poured tea, sipped and put the cup back into its saucer with a clink.

"I'm not convinced Georgina wouldn't tell McCann if he just asked her," I said.

"He said she was very defensive."

"Oh, right. So her husband gets battered, she gets the shock of her life and the guards are surprised she's defensive?" They could be unbelievable sometimes. "Have they no insight into human nature at all?"

He pulled at his jumper again. "You know how it is – they don't always have time for subtlety. You'd be helping her."

"There's something twisted about that logic."

Gabriel finished the pint, coughing at the last yellow sup.

"You started this, you know."

He had caught me there – there was nothing I could say to that.

"Sorry, back in a minute." He jumped up out of his seat and made for the gents' again.

When he returned I asked him more about what McCann had said.

"Well, his first reaction when I turned up in Store Street station was 'There you are, Gabriel, what ails you?'."

I could picture that: McCann after a long shift, hoping to get straight to the point, avoiding any small talk.

"Wouldn't come for a pint, only sat into my car for a few minutes. When I told him what I wanted to know and who I wanted to know it for, well, you can imagine."

I imagined McCann's red, round face turning redder, making his mass of black curls seem even darker.

"He said to me 'Lookit, this isn't on – you should know bether'."

Gabriel was doing his best to imitate the inspector's Cavan accent, which seemed to surface more when he was angry.

24

"I said, 'You know Bea – she's just trying to help her friend. Anything at all you can tell me – a word of comfort?'."

I nodded. Those were the right words to say to the detective.

"He said he'd be back to Georgina himself soon enough."

I felt a little sorry then, for putting Gabriel in an awkward position.

"So then I suggested you might be able to help."

He gave me a cautious look, wary of my reaction. I waited.

"He admitted he was under a bit of pressure with resources – too few guards and too much work to do. So he told me about the casino and said the lads are questioning all the staff. He can get the bank accounts as well but needed to know if Dalton had any unrecorded debt. That's where you come in."

I nodded again.

"I asked him if there was anything else and he asked could you let him know what they were like as a couple and . . ."

He paused and I knew there was something more.

"And?"

"He said to tell you you're not to lose the run of yourself." He picked up his glass then and tried to hide his laugh behind it.

"That's rich. He wants me to help, but he doesn't." Well, he couldn't have it both ways.

"I'll talk to Georgina, but you can tell McCann from me, if he wants help he can take what goes with it."

I finished my tea and prepared to leave. I wound my scarf round my neck and did up my coat.

"I'll give you a ring after I talk to Georgina," I said.

I had turned away when Gabriel called me.

"Don't forget these!"

He picked up my gloves from the chair beside him and held them out to me. I reached over, he held them for a moment longer and then let go. I thought I noticed his cheeks flush and put it down to the three pints he'd had on his upset stomach.

"I hope you'll feel better."

"What? Ah no, I'm grand now."

Chapter 4

Sunday, October 23rd, 2016

I drove to Georgina's on Sunday afternoon through slanting rain that required high-speed wipers. As they whipped back and forth across the windscreen, I fretted over what I was about to do. I was her friend and I wanted to help her. Friends didn't ask questions and then go running to the guards. Yet if giving McCann some information about Andrew would progress the investigation, I would be helping her, wouldn't I?

By the time I pulled into the drive at Belford Avenue the rain had eased off and I was able to pause and admire the bare, delicate curve of the weeping willow in the front bed. When Georgina answered the door, I told her how lovely it was, but she shrugged as though she couldn't see it.

The house was quiet and Georgina explained the children were with Andrew's sister again for a couple of nights.

I followed her into the kitchen where, to my surprise, the table was laid with cups and saucers and a plate of sandwiches. I felt Georgina had made a special effort and

I thought that must be a good sign. We sat and she poured tea into my cup.

"You shouldn't have gone to so much trouble," I said.

"It kept me busy."

She'd put some make-up on too, though the dark circles still showed through a little. When I told her about the casino she looked more bemused than shocked.

"He never said a thing about it, ever."

"He was a regular visitor, apparently. Did you know he gambled?"

"No. No, I didn't." She looked past me over my shoulder as though she could see him standing there.

I bit into one of the sandwiches – it was filled with spiced chicken.

"This is delicious, Georgina." I hadn't meant to sound so surprised, but it pleased her.

"I'm glad you like it – it's a recipe I picked up when Andrew and I were in Mexico. It's the freshly ground spices that do it." She nodded toward a granite mortar and pestle.

"*Mmm*," was all I could manage. When I'd finished chewing, I went back to the subject I'd come over to talk about.

"You never had any strange callers to the house or anything before Andrew died, did you?"

"No. Not when I was here anyway."

"Or since? No one ever came to the door looking for money? Or phoned the house?"

She shook her head and pushed hair behind her left ear. "Never. Why?"

"It's just one of the possibilities they're looking at,

that Andrew might have owed someone money. They look into everything, you know, otherwise they wouldn't be doing their job right."

She nibbled at a sandwich and then put it down on her plate and sighed.

"You must think I'm stupid, do you, Bea? My husband was gambling in a casino and I didn't know about it. I thought he was working too hard or even, maybe, there was some woman." She looked astonished at herself for having said that out loud. "I never asked him, of course – there was never anything to ask really. It's just ..." She shook her head. "Never mind, I let my imagination run away with me sometimes, that's all."

"He never struck me as the type to stray – he was mad about you." I was eager to console her. "You know that, don't you?"

"Do you know the way a man can stare sometimes?" She was watching me as she spoke, gauging my reaction.

I nodded.

"I saw him staring at this young woman who was working at the afterschool club where James and Milly go. March, I think it was. Normally I'd drop them off on my way to work, but this time we were both there – I think his car was in for repairs or something. Anyway, there was this young woman, in her twenties I'd say – long hair, tied back, smiling at the children, really lovely, you know?" She paused for a breath. "It was just the way he stared at her – there was something in it. It's hard to explain, a kind of hunger or something."

"And?"

"That's it. He did the drop-off once or twice after

29

that, but only because I couldn't. We never talked about it. Just silly really."

"I'm sure it was nothing. Is she still there? You could always ask her."

"She is but what would be the point now?" Georgina stood up and crossed to the fridge.

"It might put your mind at rest."

She took out a white cardboard box, used a scissors to cut through the twine and lifted four cream cakes onto a plate. I chose the smallest éclair. She sat down again but didn't take a cake herself. She played with her spoon, stirring her tea though she took no sugar. I noticed a small tremor in her hand. Then the tears began.

"I'm struggling, Bea." She put her left elbow on the table and covered her eyes with her hand. "This morning, I just sat on the edge of my bed and stared at my bare feet on the floor for an hour. I couldn't move. I could see my toenails needed trimming – I could see the traces of red polish on them. I couldn't do anything."

"Ah, Georgina."

"I put it on, that nail polish, the morning Andrew was killed. I was happy then, you know?"

I said I did, but I mustn't have sounded convinced because she shook her head again and said, "Never mind. Now it's as though that was someone else, someone younger, still in love."

"But you don't stop loving him just because he's gone." I didn't think it worked like that. "The life you made together, the children, it's all still here."

"All I seem to feel now is this molten heat at the pit of my stomach." She pushed a clenched fist under her ribs.

"You know, I almost went back to bed? I only managed to move because you were calling."

"But you did move, that's the main thing." And I had thought she'd improved. But the tea, the sandwiches had been a colossal effort for her.

"I still have a vision of him coming out of the bathroom that morning, freshly shaved for work. I wish to god that was the last time I saw him. I think I'd feel better if it had been."

"It wasn't?"

"We rowed." Her voice had a tremor in it.

"You told me. Everyone rows."

"Not like this. We never rowed like this."

I wanted her to change the subject. I didn't want to hear about the inner workings of their relationship. It was impossible to understand those complexities, like expecting to understand the culture of a foreign country never having lived there. But I made encouraging noises, knowing she needed to talk.

"I'd taken my holidays a day early, you see, to get everything ready. The children were at summer camp and Emma was shopping. She'd said she desperately needed a new swimsuit, that she couldn't possibly wear the bikinis she had. Teenage stuff, you know?"

"Yes."

"Anyway, if I hadn't taken that day off, Andrew wouldn't have dropped home at lunchtime." She rubbed her temples. "I know it's no use, going over and over it in my head. No matter how much I want it, I can't undo that row."

I topped up her cup with tea. She didn't notice.

"Do you remember that story? HG Wells, I think – with the man who so longs to save his dead wife that he builds a time machine?"

"Yes." I wanted to say that the film added the wife and she wasn't in the book.

"I understand that now. I want to be able to go back and it exhausts me, the longing for it."

"I think that's normal, Georgina." I knew it was. It had gnawed at me like hunger after Laurence died.

"Is it?" She dropped her gaze. "I've lost weight. Look, I have cheekbones." She put her hands to her face.

"You always had cheekbones."

"I nearly had all the packing done and I was searching for Andrew's jacket, a beige one, he likes it for travelling." She looked at me as though she expected I would recall it.

"Oh, yes."

"I finally found it in a ball at the bottom of his wardrobe. I brought it downstairs to the kitchen to see if ironing might resurrect it. I spread it on the ironing board, lining side up, and I was just getting started when Andrew arrived. He took one look at me and the jacket and said 'What the fuck are you doing?'."

I winced at the harshness of the words.

"Then he crossed the room, pushed me away from the ironing board, pulled the jacket off it and went out the door to his car. I heard him open it and lock it again, then he came back inside and went upstairs."

"That's very strange." I found it hard to imagine it of him.

She took a breath. "I know, and I was so stunned I

just stood there for five minutes. He came back into the kitchen and said 'That's suede, you can't iron it. I'll drop it in to the dry cleaner's', as though his reaction had been reasonable. I was so angry, Bea, I just let fly. I told him how hard I'd worked to organise the holiday, how he'd done less than nothing and hadn't even helped pay for it. God, I called him a lazy, arrogant pig." She wiped tears away from her cheeks. "And he started shouting and said I was always throwing money around. He was purple, you know, like he was about to burst. *'How do you think that makes me feel? And did you even ask me what I wanted before you booked this?'* He shouted it right into my face."

"That must seem awful to you now, Georgina, but you would have made up."

She continued as though she hadn't heard me. "I thought he'd be delighted when I booked the holiday and he never said anything when I told him. I couldn't figure it out, I couldn't figure out why he said I threw money around. I never did that."

"Of course not."

"So then I noticed the bag he'd put down on the table – it was lunch from our favourite deli, Bea – and he realised I saw it, and just for a moment I thought we'd make up. Then he gave me the coldest look and said 'You are a stupid, selfish bitch!' and went out and I shouted after him 'Go fuck yourself!'. The last words I said to my husband were 'Go fuck yourself'." She let go then, sobbing and shaking.

I fetched a glass of water and put it on the table at her elbow. After a while she stopped shaking, wiped her face and took a gulp of the water.

"He mustn't have been himself, Georgina. It wasn't normal for him to behave like that, was it?" I felt myself blush as I spoke. I was supposed to be consoling her, but what was I doing? Gathering information for the guards?

"No. We had our rows, but they always made sense before. That's what shocked me about it. I was only trying to do something nice for him." She drank more water. "I never thought of it before, but I don't think I've seen that stupid jacket since."

"He left it in the car, you said. Maybe he did take it to the dry cleaner's."

She went upstairs and when she reappeared she was holding a brown envelope.

"This is what the guards gave me. I haven't been able to look at it." She sat and emptied its contents onto the table. His watch and car keys were in it, his wallet, some papers and crumpled receipts they'd found in the glove compartment.

"They held on to his mobile phone." She caressed the wallet with her fingertips for a moment then flipped it open and checked its compartments.

Out of one, she carefully removed a damp but intact docket for a dry cleaner's. It gave me a jolt to realise why it was wet. It had been in his pocket when he fell into the Blessington Basin.

"I think that's it – I think that's the jacket." She looked at the date, July 18th. She hesitated.

"Would you – could I ask you – would you mind picking it up? I couldn't bring myself to do it. Maybe hand it in to some charity shop afterwards?"

I said I would – glad to have something practical I could do for her. I placed the ticket in my purse and was about to ask about Andrew's job when the doorbell rang. Georgina hesitated before going to answer it.

I could hear a male voice and then heavy footsteps in the hall walking toward the kitchen.

"How'aya."

A short man with a Chihuahua face put his hand out for me to shake.

"Beatrice, this is Lar Sheils. He's an old friend of Andrew's."

"Went to school together, we did. I was just tellin' Georgina I was awful sorry to miss the funeral. I was away for a while."

I didn't ask where, but he told me anyway.

"Workin' in Vancouver, I was. There's a good bit of building goin' on over there." He stood with his hands clasped behind his back and swayed back and forth on the balls of his feet. His shoulder muscles were visible through his pale blue shirt.

"Would you like a coffee, or tea or something?" Georgina signalled for him to sit down.

"No, you're grand. I just wanted to say I was sorry, that's all."

"You're very kind."

There were a few moments of awkward silence.

"Where was it you and Andrew went to school, did you say?" I managed.

"David's, do you know it? On the Malahide Road."

"I do."

"He was some messer back in the day. I was only sayin' the last time we met that we'd have to organise a reunion or something, get all the lads together. He was up for it, too."

"When did you see him last?"

"Week before I left for Vancouver, early July, I think. I was only over there and I heard the news. Couldn't believe it." He paused, judging the atmosphere. "Have they collared anyone for it?"

Georgina, who had been leaning against the worktop, made a small, uncomfortable noise in the base of her throat, as though there was a crumb trapped there.

He seemed to take the hint. "Well, I'll be goin'."

He crossed to the door and into the hall. We both followed him.

"Anyway, I just wanted to say, if there's an'thin' I can do, an'thin' at all."

"Thanks," Georgina said, showing him out.

Back at home, as I pulled the curtains on my living-room window and shut out the glistening lights of Howth Head and Dun Laoghaire across the bay, I wondered what might become of Georgina if Andrew's killer was not found. I'd seen it before, the tearful spouse on the TV, pleading for witnesses to come forward, speaking into a void – the living hell of a life spent searching for answers that would never be found. And even when perpetrators where discovered, it didn't always mean justice. Guilty people walk free from the Criminal Courts of Justice all the time. Inexplicably short sentences are imposed. Even long sentences eventually come to an end and families can only watch when killers walk out into the world again, while their loved ones are gone forever. I admired the families that managed to put some semblance of a life together after such tragedies. At least Georgina had her children. Milly, who was six and James, four, were young enough not to mitigate their demands in deference to her grief and that would be a good thing.

I made myself a cup of camomile tea and considered what sort of a man was capable of hiding a gambling habit from his wife so thoroughly. Had he earned a lot more money than he'd let on, so that Georgina wouldn't notice it disappearing? I had always assumed she was the sort of woman who would notice things, who would have a clear eye on the family finances. But then I'd thought the couple were the type to share everything with each other and I was wrong about that. Still, Georgina and Andrew had seemed close and happy together whenever I saw them and I didn't think that could really be faked. Could it?

For the first time in a long while, I had an urge to lift the phone and call Gabriel so that I could talk over everything with him. I drank my tea almost to the end before picking up my mobile and finding his number. It rang once, twice, three times.

"Hello? Gaybie's phone."

I ended the call immediately. Who was that? A woman? What woman would ever call Gabriel "Gaybie"? What time was it? What woman would answer his phone at home at a quarter past eight in the evening? Perhaps he wasn't at home. Where was he then? Had there been bar noise? I thought not. Just the usual quiet of his little house on Oxmantown Road. It irked me that I was this curious all of a sudden. What did I know anyway, about the months since we'd stopped being . . . I considered the word . . . close?

We had been close. The Stephen O'Farrell case had

brought us a kind of camaraderie, two friends struggling against the world. I'd been glad to be with him and then, suddenly, I'd stopped being glad. Why was that? What was it that had made me turn away from him? Sitting on the couch now, listlessly flicking through the pages of a book I knew I would never read, I could not remember.

When O'Farrell was jailed I had felt an intense kind of relief, as though a burden I'd been carrying around since he caused my brother's death had been lifted from me. It had been a burden I was so accustomed to that I'd hardly noticed it. It brought with it, not only guilt, but a kind of wariness, protection against being hurt again. I had thought that with his jailing I might have been capable of letting that go too. But life isn't like that, and the shield I'd carried for thirty-five years had proved too much a part of me to let drop.

The phone rang then and Gabriel's number appeared on the screen. I took my time answering.

"Were you looking for me?"

"I just, it's not important really . . . there were just some things on my mind."

"About the case, is it?" There was coolness in his tone.

"Yes."

"Can it wait till tomorrow? I'll meet you for lunch."

"Of course, yes, that's fine."

We made an arrangement and I hung up, feeling foolish and cross with myself for having called him.

38

Chapter 5

Monday, October 24th, 2016

In Court 32 the O'Malleys had moved on from money at last to the custody of their children. There were three – a girl of five called Petal, another aged eight called Bluebell and a boy, Robin, aged thirteen and "on the cusp of adolescence". Úna Hollister seemed to enjoy repeating that phrase as though it explained everything about her client's motivation to keep the boy from his father.

Mrs O'Malley was in the box, a neat woman in her late forties, wearing a grey trouser suit. The only unruly thing about her was a cloud of dirty-blonde, shoulder-length curls. She was explaining that her husband was not the man he appeared to be in court and should no longer be given access to his children, much less custody.

"Judge, it's hard to explain . . . there's a cruel streak in him."

"Can you give us an example?" Ms Hollister asked, nodding her head and holding her client's gaze.

"Yes, it's just, you see, with our eldest – that's Robin, judge – it's as though, I mean the way he treats him . . . as though he's an inconvenience." She paused.

"And such an important stage for him, judge, on the cusp of adolescence," Ms Hollister said again.

"Yes, yes." The judge seemed as weary of the term as I was. "Go on, Mrs O'Malley."

"He hit Robin, judge, I saw him." She said the words with her face turned away from the courtroom and from her husband, who got to his feet and shouted, "*Lying bitch!*"

"Your client will have ample time to rebuff these claims, Ms Clements," the judge said.

Ms Clements turned to Mr O'Malley and hissed, "*Be quiet*".

"Mrs O'Malley, you were telling us about your husband's temper." Ms Hollister found it hard to keep the satisfaction from her voice that Mr O'Malley had managed to demonstrate his temper so early in the day.

"Yes, it was when he was in the back room – it looks out on the garden, judge – and Robin was out there kicking football with a few of his friends and the ball hit the window a few times, and I heard Dan shouting at him, telling him to stop. Then he must have done it again, because I heard the back door open and I looked out from the kitchen and Dan was running down the garden, and he was shouting and he grabbed Robin and he shook him and he gave him a slap, right across the face."

"Never happened!" Mr O'Malley was on his feet.

"Now really!" The judge stared down at him until he took his seat, mumbling an apology.

"Do you have other examples?" Ms Hollister asked.

"He's terribly controlling when it comes to money,"

Mrs O'Malley said. "I remember on one occasion he called the local supermarket to find out the cost of their cheapest loaf of bread and insisted I shouldn't pay any more for it. He wanted to see the receipt when I came home."

"Is he controlling with the children?" Ms Hollister prompted.

"He went through a phase last summer when he made them over-exercise. He used to time them running up and down the stairs and insist they continue every evening until they improved their speeds, even little Petal."

"*Rubbish!*" Mr O'Malley shouted.

"Has your husband ever raised a hand to you, Mrs O'Malley?" Ms Hollister said quietly.

"No." She spoke quietly too, and then put her hand over her mouth.

"Judge, it's almost one." Ms Hollister gestured toward the clock at the back of the room.

"Yes. Two o'clock then."

At lunch, despite my usual discretion, I found myself telling Gabriel about the case. We met at Christophe's, one of those cafés close enough to the Four Courts and Phoenix House to attract lots of legal types. But the food was reliable and I liked to see Gabriel eating hearty meals. He hadn't hesitated once he'd seen the stout-and-beef pie and looked happy as we sat with our trays at a little wooden table looking out on Duck Lane.

Without naming them I described the O'Malleys, their torrid relationship. It helped to talk about the case. It meant I could resist the temptation to ask about the woman who had answered his phone the night before.

He hadn't mentioned her and I was determined not to.

Gabriel listened to me while mixing mashed potato into his stew and scooping forkfuls into his mouth.

"A bad marriage is a terrible thing," I said.

"There must've been some good in it sometime, Bea. They had three children."

I thought he sounded preachy and stopped talking and ate my roast-in-a-wrap.

Gabriel softened his tone. "You were going to tell me about Georgina."

A childish instinct made me want to refuse, but I quashed it. I described all that had happened on my visit to her home on Sunday, about the woman in the crèche and how I'd promised to collect Andrew's jacket and dispose of it.

"And did you get it?"

"The jacket? No, I'll do it when I have a chance. Might not still be there – three months is a long time to leave dry cleaning."

Gabriel finished his plate and looked as though he might lick it clean, before deciding he'd better not.

"What was it she said about this young woman in the crèche?"

"It wasn't really about the woman, it was about the way Andrew looked at her – 'with a kind of hunger,' she said."

"Right." Gabriel's eyebrows were arched almost to his hairline. "I wouldn't be making too much out of a look."

"You'd be surprised. Women pick up on these things." I poured myself tea from a small, white pot.

"Or maybe they just let their imaginations get the

better of them. Would you say she's the jealous type?"

I thought that branding a woman jealous because she was uneasy about another woman was unfair. But how could I tell?

"I doubt if jealousy is Georgina's thing. She's too self-assured."

He nodded. "What time do you think you might finish court today?"

"Four o'clock normally."

"I'll call in to Matt and let him know what Georgina said while I'm waiting for you, so." He said it as though it was a given that he would wait for me. He was, it seemed, invested now in finding out what happened to Andrew Dalton.

I tried not to show the pleasure that bubbled up unexpectedly at his words. He was willing to wait for me. There wasn't some woman back in Oxmantown Road expecting him home.

We walked together over to Phoenix Street where Gabriel got on a tram and I went back into court.

When I arrived, the registrar was dismissing the barristers.

"He extends his deep apologies, but he has been called away," she told them. And in a lower voice, she said, "Family emergency, that's all I know."

Once I'd packed up my equipment, I asked Ms Hollister to let me know as soon as she heard when the case would be back. She said she would.

Outside court, I texted **"Case adjourned"** to Gabriel.

"Meet you in an hour," was the response.

I didn't feel like waiting around for an hour. I went

briefly back to my office to upload my work from a memory key onto my laptop, checked I had the dry-cleaning docket Georgina had given me, then took a tram to Mayor Street and found Executive Express.

The dry cleaner's was across the River Liffey from Techworld where Andrew worked and probably the nearest he could find. When I pushed open the glass door a wave of steam and detergent wafted toward me, transporting me for a moment to my mother's Monday kitchen with its steamed-up windows and Omo air and twin-tub gurgling in the corner. I felt a strange connection to her just then that made me marvel at the memory of scent.

"Yes?" A young man stood behind the counter, an impatient expression at what he no doubt thought was a dawdling, middle-aged woman.

I produced Andrew's docket and handed it to him. The man sighed.

"This is months old. I'll have to check our archive."

I was tempted to point out he was talking pretentious nonsense, but stood silently instead while he went out a door at the back to what looked like a storeroom. He returned in ten minutes with a plastic-swathed garment over his arm.

"Now, including storage fee, that's €75."

I coughed.

"This is suede, you know – specialist cleaning – and you can't expect a place like ours just to hold on to clothes for months at no extra cost."

Tempted though I was to tell him what I thought of his storage fee, I said nothing, took my debit card from my purse and handed it to him. When the transaction was complete, he gave me the garment.

"Have a nice day," he smiled as I made for the door.

I gave him, over my shoulder, the most withering look I could muster.

By the time I got back to Phoenix Street, Gabriel was waiting. I spotted him before I got off the Luas, leaning against the stone wall next to the tram shelter. It didn't seem to matter to him that he could have sat down on the steel bench within the shelter and been protected from the cold breeze cutting its way up the street. The up-turned collar on his donkey jacket was the only sign that he could feel the chill.

"Waiting long?"

"You got it, I see." He nodded at the garment, folded back on itself and taped in place, which I was carrying by the hook of its hanger.

"We should go back to mine, take a good look at it." Gabriel nodded his head in the direction of Stoneybatter and his home, a twenty-minute walk away.

We skirted Smithfield Square and walked briskly up North King Street, both with our heads down, saving our conversation for the warmth of Number 9, Oxmantown Road.

When we got there, Gabriel led the way into the little sitting room where a small fire was burning in the grate. We took off our coats and Gabriel threw a couple of logs on the fire and went to the kitchen to make tea.

I sat in an armchair close to the fire and unwrapped the jacket. He came back with a tray and put it down on a low coffee table.

"Looks expensive."

He took the jacket from me by its shoulders and turned it around. Then he sat down on the couch, spread it out and began to feel all over it from its hem up.

"Something here."

He reached into a zipped inside pocket and pulled out a small, resealable plastic bag.

I leaned forward. He held it in his palm, and what looked like a white powder was visible inside it.

"What's that?"

He opened it carefully, took out a little of the powder and sniffed it.

"No idea, but I think I've some pH paper upstairs that might help. Back in a minute."

He went upstairs and sounds of dragging and pulling came through the ceiling. He'd be a while, I decided, and began looking at the bookshelf beside me. Gabriel's collection was dominated by sports biographies and history, mostly Irish and about the War of Independence. There was one about Eamon de Valera from the 1970s, its dust cover tatty-edged but still intact. I reached out and eased it from its spot. The man himself, a veteran and leader, was on the front, all presidential for his official biography and not looking out but off to his right through those round spectacles, at something more important. I leafed through its yellowed pages. It was a heavy tome, and much too worthy and important for my appetite at that moment. I was putting it back in its place when I noticed something tucked in at the back of the shelf. I put my hand in and pulled it out. It was a small, brown diary. I had no idea Gabriel kept such a thing and thought it strange that he would hide it in his own home. I opened the first page and realised it was not his. Inside the cover, in neat, plump writing, was a heart with "*I love Noel Gallagher*" written in the centre. There were doodles of flowers and other hearts, filled in with red pen. The first page was dated July 15th, 2005, and said "*cont'd*" in the corner.

I wondered what Gabriel was doing with it and why he might hide it. I thought of all the cases he'd been involved in through the years. Could this be stray evidence from some old case that he'd taken home and held on to for some reason? Had he worked on a missing child case? When I tried hard, I thought I remembered something about a girl who was never found, a case that was never resolved. When was that? About ten years ago? I was about to begin reading when there was a noise from the hall of a key turning in the front-door lock. Instinctively, I threw the diary into my handbag and stood up.

At the same time Gabriel came down the stairs.

"No luck with that," he said, then "Hello!"

A familiar young woman walked into the living room.

"You're back already," she said to Gabriel.

His smile was wide. "Bea, you remember Billie from Hanlon's? She's lodging with me for a while, till she can find a new flat."

I sat down again. Realisation dawned and, surprisingly, relief.

"So it was you who answered the phone last night?" I said, too late remembering that I had put down the phone without saying a word.

"That was me, yeah." She had a slightly amused smile on her face.

I reached over and poured myself some tea.

"Get yourself a mug, Billie," Gabriel said.

"You're all right, I've got stuff to do." She walked out the door and we could hear the sound of her footsteps on the stairs.

"What's the problem?" Gabriel sounded almost as though he was challenging me.

"I don't have a problem."

"Good, cos she's old enough to be my daughter."

"Granddaughter, I'd say."

"Ah, here!" He laughed and switched his attention back to the jacket.

He turned it over in his hands and checked it again. There was nothing else to find.

"Okay, I should give Matt a ring, let him know about this stuff. And he'll want the jacket."

I had supposed he would and had already decided there'd be no need to tell Georgina I'd given it to him, or to mention what we found in it. There was nothing to be gained by upsetting her. The powder might just have been something left in there from the dry-cleaning process, some sort of stain remover they'd forgotten about. McCann would have it tested.

I drank my tea.

"I think I should get home," I said, gathering up my things.

In the hall Gabriel paused. "She'd nowhere else to go."

"I know. You're very kind." I only just stopped myself from adding 'Gaybie'.

Chapter 6

It wasn't until I got home and was looking for my phone that I saw the diary in my bag. I hadn't meant to take it with me. What should I do? How could I explain it to Gabriel? I didn't want him to think I'd deliberately taken something from his home. Perhaps he wouldn't realise it was missing. I would just have to hold on to it until I could put it back in place.

I had something to eat and then took the diary into the living room to examine it. Now that I had it, though I knew I was snooping, I couldn't resist looking at it. I opened it at the first page. The plump lettering was embellished in places with extravagant, childish curls and was difficult to decipher in places. I began to read.

July 15th, 2005

So excited – last night was brilliant. The Roundabout pub was packed. 25 people were in the competition. The 5th Annual Coolock Artane Star Voice Contest. And hundreds listening, hundreds!! Some of it was crap. Mrs Nugent sang 'Wind Beneath My Wings'. I was mortified for her. Liam's da sang 'New York, New York' in his best

Frank Sinatra voice. Julie sang 'Angels' – she wasn't bad, but not as good as me. I had butterflies going up – I was wearing my best bootleg jeans, my red spaghetti-strap top, and my shiny, silver dolly shoes – but then once I started, it was great. I did 'Porgy' and I swear, the whole place went quiet. It was brilliant when they were all listening to me, even Ollie, the barman, and he's a grumpy sod.

The judge was this fella over from England. Ollie said he used to live in Artane, but he works for some record company now. He was listening too, I could see him, and he liked it. Mam said I was fantastic, the best there, she said. But the judge didn't think so. He gave first place to Glen, the little snot. He sang 'Nessun Dorma', for fuck sake, and waved his arms around and his face got all red and sweaty.

Still, though, when he called out my name for second and the crowd started cheering I thought I'd burst I was so thrilled. I hugged the judge – it was brilliant! €200!! A cheque. I gave it to Mam so she could change it for me.

She wasn't happy though. And it didn't help that she'd had a few. When it was over, we went outside and the judge was standing against the wall in his shirt and jeans, having a smoke, real cool-looking, and she went up to him.

"You're after robbin' me daughter," she said.

I was MORTIFIED!! And he asked her who she was.

"Joan Richmond, Jess's mother. The singer you robbed."

Then he looked over at me. I was with Leanne and Roggie, and I was trying not to listen but I couldn't help it.

Mam said, "She has the best voice of the ⊖
and you know it."

He shook his head. "Look, Mrs Richmond, is it?" He
sounded so, like, full of himself. "Jess has a sweet little
voice, but she has a lot to learn. For starters, the choice
of song – hardly appropriate for a seventeen-year-old."

He thought I was 17!! Mam told him I was 15 and I
could sing whatever I liked. It was getting really
embarrassing so I went over and said me and Leanne
were going to the chipper.

And the judge looked at me then and it made me feel
funny. "I was just about to tell your mother that I think
you have potential," he said. "With a little help you
could make something of that voice."

Then – unbelievable! – he says to Mam that he's due
back in London on Monday, but he'll call by our house –
our house! – for a chat about _my future_!!! – on Sunday.

"Do you know where Castletimon Lawn is?" Mam
said it as though it was perfectly normal for a record
producer to call by.

He said he did.

"It's Number 51. We'll be in around seven."

We got chips after. They tasted better than any chips I
ever had. And Leanne kept hugging me. She says the
judge looks like Kevin Richardson from Backstreet Boys
– he does a bit. "He's Kevie Baby," she says.

So excited about tomorrow!!!

Jess Richmond, Jess Richmond – could she have been
the missing girl I was thinking of? Or had she been
younger? Memories could play such tricks. I googled her
name with _missing_ in front of it, but all I could find was

…embers and none of them were in

…5

…y!! Kevie Baby showed up. He really
… I thought he mightn't when I woke up this
… I thought he might have been one of those
peop… who promise you things and then doesn't do it
and acts like they never said anything. But he did.

So, in the morning, I got ready for town with Leanne
– floral hot pants, blue kitten-bow blouse, black pumps –
but I wasn't feeling great. When I looked in the
bathroom mirror, I could see every little tiny bump on
my face, and my eyebrows looked wrong, and my chin
was too jutty. Mam keeps saying I'm gorgeous, but if I
had the money I'd get myself fixed. I did my eyeliner,
right eye then left. Why is it, no matter how hard I try, I
can never get both eyes the same? I think it's a problem
with my face – it's not symmetrical. This magazine I read
said beauty is symmetry, so that's me fucked. I did my
mascara and then a practice wink. I'm getting better at it
and it gets around the symmetry problem when
someone's taking a photo.

Anyway, I texted Leanne "CU 12 at the Spike".

Mam nearly freaked. She was in her pyjamas,
hanging, puffing one of her Marlboros and reading Celeb
magazine. I told her I'd be back in plenty of time and she
showed me a photo in the magazine of Imelda May.
"That could be you," she said. Right.

In town, me and Leanne spent the whole time talking
about what I'd wear for Kevie Baby's visit and what I'd
sing. She said he would definitely give me a record deal. I

pictured myself at a microphone in a recording studio, and producers standing at a mixing desk, smiling at me. Then they'd call in a higher-up producer and he'd listen too and then he'd give me a pen to sign a contract. I said to Leanne that once I'm successful I'll go to New York and she can come with me and I'll be like Regina Spektor and I'll play a piano on a city corner. I don't know how to play piano, but I'd say once they sign you up they teach you all that sort of thing. "I'm going to see all over America, and all over the world," I said to Leanne and she said she was too.

We went into HMV on Henry Street and I had a look at the jazz section and Leanne said jazz was crap and I was a fogey. So I told her Peggy Lee is Adele's favourite singer and that shut her up. Then we were walking on past Peter Mark and this young fella stopped us. "Hey, girls, yis are both gorgeous. How would you like a new hairstyle for free?" He points over at the hairdresser's. "We're looking for models. Just show up at six and we'll give yis the most fabulous haircuts." Then he said to me – "God, you have fantastic bone structure. We'd do a great job on you."

Me and Leanne burst out laughing and she said we'd think about it. But she whispered to me they just use you to train the apprentices and you could end up like a dog's dinner.

Then we went to Chocolate Heaven, which is Leanne's new favourite place ever. We split a fondue – delicious!! – with strawberries and pieces of biscuit. We talked about stuff – Star Factor isn't coming to Ireland this year and we thought that was crap.

"It's because Irish people are too good," Leanne said. Then she went on about her holidays in Majorca.

Sick of listening to it, I said America is better and Leanne said a girl who lives near her got a J1 visa and works as a chambermaid in this big, fancy hotel. She saw Robert Pattinson in the lobby, and she nearly fainted. Leanne said "God, imagine making his bed!"

Then we went through the options of what I was going to wear when Kevie Baby came and we chose a cream, cap-sleeved dress, sprinkled with green berries, tight at the waist and matched with green high-top runners. Leanne told me to curl my hair and I said I would, but I didn't bother.

When I got home the house smelled of air freshener and furniture polish and Mam was fidgety. She said she was after ironing my green dress and I had to wear it.

There was another page for the same date, but I set the diary aside. My eyes were tired from deciphering the handwriting. I would read it to the end, I knew, before finding a way to return it to Gabriel's bookcase.

I got ready for bed, and tried to sleep, but could not. I went downstairs again, picked up the diary and took it back to bed.

July 16th, 2005 cont'd

Kevie Baby came an hour late and Mam made me go upstairs. She said I had to make an entrance so when the doorbell went I bolted and she let him in. I could hear her saying "Call me Joan" to him. Then she yells "Darling, come down!" Darling? I nearly wet myself! As I walked down the stairs, I could hear them talking about me. Mam asked what he was going to do for me and he said I had promise but I mustn't expect too much.

"She is only, what did you say, fifteen? She needs to do a lot of work. And the music business is tough."

I stood in the hall as he went on talking. He said there was a time he would have offered to help me make a demo tape.

"But it doesn't work like that any more, Joan."

"So how does it work?" Mam sounded like a dealer on Moore Street and I was the fish.

"It's all about exposure. You find a platform first, then the record companies chase you. Exposure first, then deals. I need to hear her sing now, then we'll talk some more."

So I walked in then and he nodded at me. Mam went to put on my music but he said I had to sing unaccompanied and I started into 'God Bless the Child'. When I finished he said I had an 'interesting repertoire'. I told him I could sing anything. Mam, no patience, says "Well?". Then he says – I still can't believe it – he says did I ever hear of Star Factor!!! Friends of his are involved in producing it, he says, and he could get me an audition!!! ME!!!

"But listen to me now, you have a lot of work to do before that. Your mother is right, you have a great voice, Jess, but it's undisciplined."

I was too excited to ask him what he meant. I couldn't stop smiling. While Mam talked to him I texted Leanne and she was thrilled for me.

He said I'd have to improve my breathing and diction.

"And we can't have her singing your songs," he said to Mam and she went a bit red, but she didn't argue.

Then she asked him what it was going to cost her.
And he said it would be nothing!!

"I'm thinking of Jess as an investment. If and when
she begins to make money, I'll make money too. And so
will you, Joan."

He said the magic word there – MONEY. Then he
said he had to stay in Dublin for a bit longer and he
could give me singing lessons!!! He's coming back
tomorrow to start!! I didn't even mind when he'd gone
and Mam started into her wine. Normally, she doesn't
have an excuse. I can't believe it. I never thought a girl
like me could be this lucky!!

There was a drawing below the text, of a girl with a
microphone singing on a stage.

July 19th, 2005

It's not what I thought it would be. Kevie Baby's
mean. He makes me feel as if everything I do is wrong.
He's like the crossest, most grumpiest fecker I ever met.
He hardly even looks at me. I don't think he likes me at
all. "Lift your chin! Open your eyes! That word has a T
at the end!" Prick! I've been trying my best.

"For God's sake! How many times?"

He shouted that at me this morning and that was it.

I just sat down and shut my mouth.

"You just don't get it, do you? This isn't some little
school concert or a stupid competition in the local pub.
This is your chance, Jess, so at least act like you want it."

Stupid competition?? I started to cry and Mam came
in and asked if we wanted tea and he had a go at her in
his snooty voice. "No, Joan, we don't want tea or any
other distractions. I'm trying to get through to your

daughter here . . . she needs to wake up."

"Come 'ere a minute," Mam said to me and I followed her out to the kitchen.

"I thought this was going to be fun. I hate him!" I said.

She hugged me and told me to pretend I was on reality TV and this shite was a test. I said I'd try. And she said if he gets too loud she'll accidentally pour a cup of tea on him. When I went back in to him though, he was a bit nicer. He said I should close my eyes and picture myself on the stage of the Grand Canal theatre with Ronan, Shaun and Cherry waiting for me to sing. He said I was just to visualise it. He said "Visualisation is an essential tool of success".

"From now on I want you to picture yourself on that stage, singing out, winning over the crowd, the judges smiling up at you. Every night before you fall asleep picture it. Understand?"

I said I did, only it wouldn't be that stage, cos Star Factor wasn't coming to Dublin this year. Then he said he'd forgotten, that Shaun had told him there'd been some cutbacks. So I said, "Shaun, do you mean Shaun Bowles? Do you know him?" And he said we had to get back to work. So we did, and I tried to do everything he said and I think it was better – at least he didn't give out anymore.

This evening Leanne knocked for me and asked was I comin' out. I pulled her into the house and told her about Shaun Bowles.

"Jesus! How?" she said.

I said Kevie Baby didn't say how, he just mentioned

him by accident. "He just said Shaun, but I knew who he meant."

She had that face on her like she didn't believe me, but I don't care. She's only jealous.

My eyes drooped then and I could read no more. When I fell asleep I dreamed of a girl in a red hooded coat, standing on a stage, singing her heart out.

Chapter 7

Tuesday, October 25th, 2016

The first thing I thought of when I woke up was the diary. Outside my bedroom window, grey sky merged with grey sea and half the city was already hidden in a cloak of rain. It would not be long before it reached Clontarf. I had no work to go to.

I went down to the kitchen, made tea and toast and took it back to bed. I ate while I read.

July 22nd, 2005

Oh my God!! I'm going to London! I had a lesson again today and at the end Kevie Baby called Mam in, all serious like. He said the auditions for Star Factor were less than a month away so he was going to stay in Dublin and give me lessons four times a week and then he'd take me over to London for the audition!!! Mam was a bit quiet, then he said she wouldn't have to pay anything. "I'll chalk it down to expenses," he said. And Mam said to me, "Is this what you want?" And I said, "You know it is." And she said, "I only wish I could afford to come with you." And she waited for him to offer to pay, but he didn't. He said expenses wouldn't stretch to it "at this point", which I think meant they might later, as in when I'm famous!!!

Mam looked real hard at him for a few minutes, but then said okay. I called Leanne to tell her and he heard me saying "Kevie Baby" and he asked who that was and did I have a boyfriend. I had to tell him that's what me and Leanne call him and he laughed and said it was cool. Leanne started crying when I told her he was taking me to audition for Star Factor. She said she hoped I'd still be her friend after I was on TV. I told her of course I would. Me and Leanne will always be friends.

I got out of bed and stretched and put some clothes on. Then I went downstairs, made more tea and settled down with the diary again. There were almost daily entries, describing Jess's singing lessons in detail and her preparations for London. Each one was filled with excitement and hope. There were no more complaints about how she was being taught. I took a moment to google *Star Factor* singers on my phone, but I could find none called Jess Richmond.

August 16th, 2005

We made it! The plane to Gatwick took an hour and a half and I thought my stomach would flip when we took off, but it didn't. We were ages getting to King's Cross. London is huge and not as fancy as I thought. Still, I've only really seen one street, so it's too early to judge.

We're in the hotel now. It's a bit whiffy and old. Kevie Baby says it's Georgian. Anyway the lift is broken and it's a bit dark but I don't mind. Our rooms are on the second floor – 105 and 109 – and mine looks out onto the train station. It's narrow with a window not far from

*the end of my bed and the curtains are red and a bit tatty.
But the most important thing is, we can walk to Bromley
Hall from here. That's where the auditions are. We're
getting up extra early tomorrow before the queues get
too long. Kevie Baby says they're expecting thousands
and the producer doesn't want to show favouritism by
letting me in ahead, so we'll just have to be patient like
everyone else. I don't mind.*

*I rang Mam and told her we got here safe, then we
went to McDonald's. It's only ten o'clock but I'm going
to go to bed – don't want to be tired tomorrow. The
sheets smell clean so that's good.*

August 17th, 2005
  Yes! Yes! Yes!
*The first thing I learnt was you don't get to sing in
front of the TV judges straight away. That surprised me,
cos then how do all those crap singers get through to the
TV auditions? Anyway, I got up at a quarter past five!!!
and was showered and ready to go by six. I wore my
electric-blue disco pants and a white chiffon blouse over
a cotton T-shirt. I put on my red sequinned six-inch
heels. I wore my hair straight and down over my right
shoulder. Kevie Baby made me change into flat shoes and
I put the high heels in a bag. He asked me had I a belt
and when I said no he promised to buy me one. "It will
accentuate your figure," he said. We ate as much
breakfast as we could before leaving, even though it was
hard because my stomach felt like I was on a roller
coaster. I was glad I was in flats when I saw the queue at
Bromley Hall. There must have been at least 200 people*

there already. Some people had sleeping bags. I texted Leanne to tell her. "Hope I woke you up! Keep your fingers crossed." Everyone was standing and some people were making yodelling noises. At about half eight a woman with a clipboard and one of those headset things arrived. When she got to us, she took my name and address and gave me a form to fill in. "Who's with you?" she asked me. Before I could answer Kevie Baby said, "I'm her uncle". She said I was Number 252 and left before I could ask how long we'd be waiting. I asked him why he said the uncle thing and he explained it wouldn't be good to let them know I'd had professional help. He said it didn't matter that the producer knew cos they were friends.

After ages, the doors at the front of the hall opened and people started to move inside. As soon as we got in, I started my warm-ups. Kevie Baby said he'd nip out and look for a belt for me. He winked at me when he was leaving and said he wouldn't be long, and he asked a woman behind us to keep an eye on me. "I just need to get some smokes," he said. It was embarrassing, like I couldn't look after myself. But the woman was nice. She was with her son Todd, who looked like a lollipop with curly hair. I did my warm-ups and along the queue other people were doing the same. Then Todd started. He had this big booming voice and when he saw me looking he stopped and blushed. I closed my eyes then and listened to all the voices and they were all so good.

Then Kevie Baby came back. He had a paper bag and he took out a wide red belt with a gold buckle. I put it on and it was perfect.

62

After an hour, there was a big cheer and I could see Dave Elby!!! with a microphone and a cameraman beside him. "Hello, London!" he shouted and people shouted hello back. "Can't hear you." They shouted louder. Kevie Baby told me not to shout, that I'd hurt my voice. "If the camera comes down, pretend you're cheering but don't make any noise." He's so clever. The filming and cheering went on FOREVER. I got fed up waving my arms in the air every time they said to. Then it was nearly lunchtime and Todd's mam opened a parcel of sandwiches. She gave me one, which was very nice of her. "Never mind, eh, we'll be getting into the main hall soon," she said to me.

It was one o'clock when the doors of the main hall finally opened and when we reached the door a woman gave me a card with my number on it, and a sticker to wear that I had to write my name on. We all sat down and then Elby came on stage with the cameras. We had to stand up and wave our arms, dance on the spot, sit down and do the Mexican wave. Sooooo tiring. Finally, Elby told us the auditions were starting and he left. Four tables were set up at the back of the stage, with two people sitting at each one. I put on my high heels and we joined the queue. First of all, you could hear everyone's audition, but then people got bored listening and went back to chatting. When I was near the top Kevie Baby said I should go to the fourth table and if it looked like I wasn't going to get it, I should bend down and pretend to fix my shoe. Anyway, I didn't need to do that, cos when we got to the top of the queue I was sent to the fourth table by a woman in a fleece that said "Star Factor" on it. Kevie Baby followed me but stood to one side so he wouldn't put me off. My heart was thumping when I walked over and a man in a pink shirt said, "When you're ready" and I started into "Chasing Pavements". I got as far as the end of the first chorus before he stopped me. "Thanks, you're through." And he gave me a ticket and pointed over to a door. Just like that!! Kevie Baby gave me a hug and I showed the ticket to a security man and we walked through to a smaller room and sat down. I texted Leanne and Mam and said I'd call them later. Kevie Baby gave me a bottle of water and a banana. "Don't get giddy," he said. We sat there for about two more hours until all the seats were filled.

Then Dave Elby appeared again. "Congrats, people. We've separated the wheat from the chaff so give yourselves a round of applause." And everybody clapped. Then he said we were so good the producers were going to audition us. And if we got through, we'd meet the judges tomorrow. We got into two lines and producers took their seats at two tables and the auditions started again. Kevie Baby said to me that I shouldn't let them rush me, so when it was my turn I took a deep breath and relaxed before I started. And the woman producer said, "Jess, is it? Let's hear you." And they let me sing the whole song this time! And I swear, everyone else stopped and listened to me. And the woman producer said, "We'll see you tomorrow"!!! Kevie Baby said I blew them away. He said I was brilliant. "You're gonna go all the way, I can feel it." That's what he said. To me!! I phoned Mam and she was thrilled and Leanne nearly exploded when I told her.

It's like a dream. I'm just getting ready now because

Kevie Baby said I deserved a treat and we're going to a proper restaurant. I'm wearing my high heels, and my white dress with the red cherries on it and I'm putting my hair up.

I had a vision of her suddenly, as though she was standing in front of me in my own living room in her high heels, radiating youth and talent and excitement. I read on.

August 18th, 2005

I don't know what happened really. All I know is I was crap. My voice didn't sound right, I couldn't control it. When we arrived this morning, they told us there was one more audition before we'd go before the TV judges. So we stood in line like before, but I didn't feel right. I told Kevie Baby and he said I should buck up – I was an adult now, he said, and I should start behaving like one.

The restaurant was lovely last night, very fancy. Kevie Baby said I looked beautiful. I liked my food, chicken something, but I hated his garlicky mussels. We had pancakes after, with strawberries. And I had white wine – he let me have a couple of glasses to celebrate, he said. It tasted nice sort of, and it made me feel happy and a bit tired. I think I might have got a bit woozy on the way home. Kevie Baby had to put me to bed. I remember him taking off my shoes and my feet hurt and he rubbed them. And then, I don't really know. I must have fallen asleep.

When I woke this morning my mouth was very dry and my head hurt. I felt achy all over. I drank lots of water and took a Solpadeine. It helped a little bit.

When we queued up I thought I might faint. I didn't

feel like me. And when it came to my turn, I tried, I really tried my best to sing like I did yesterday, but I couldn't do it.

"Thanks, love. Sorry, not this time," a woman producer said.

Kevie Baby put his arm around me and said it would be okay, that there'd be other auditions. We went back to the hotel and packed our bags. He said he'd take me to see Buckingham Palace but I didn't want to. I just wanted to go home. I think I hate London now.

When I got to the airport, he left me at the gate. He said he'd wasted too much time in Ireland, and he had work to go back to. "Wasted", he said.

I'm on the plane now and I don't feel well. I wonder if the chicken was off or maybe the wine was very strong. When I close my eyes, it's the strangest thing, I can smell garlic and feel . . . I don't know, something. Something happened last night, only I can't remember, I can't be sure. Did we do it? Did he do it to me???

Is that what it was all about? All the singing lessons, all the preparation, was it all just meant to lead up to last night? I can't remember now why I thought I could go over to London and get on Star Factor. How could I? I'm just an ordinary girl, there's nothing special about me.

I closed the diary and I thought my heart would break for her, this girl I'd never met. I wasn't surprised that Gabriel had kept it. I supposed he must have investigated what happened to her. Had there been a conviction? If there had, her name wouldn't have come out because of her age and the nature of the crime. Or perhaps the investigation had failed and he'd held on to the diary in the hope he could help her someday. I felt like calling and asking him, but how could I explain having the diary and reading it and not telling him?

I looked over the remaining pages. She had written little else. There were dates and some doodles, but no entries except under August 30th. And that only said: "TOLD LEANNE." I searched the internet again to see if I could find her. On Facebook, there was a Jess Richmond in Brisbane, Australia, and others in Pennsylvania, Manhattan and in Liverpool. There was only one I could find in Ireland, a teenager too young to fit.

I put the diary aside. I would return it and say nothing.

Chapter 8

Wednesday, October 26th, 2016

Georgina made no mention of Andrew's jacket when she phoned me, but she did say she had another favour to ask. And, though I was reluctant, I allowed myself to be persuaded into going along with what she said would be a harmless subterfuge.

"I just want to see the place for myself, see what it was that attracted him," she had pleaded. But she didn't want them on their guard. She didn't want to be the grieving widow. And I had agreed I wouldn't mention Andrew.

That was why I found myself standing outside Spin in Phibsboro waiting in the cold and dark at 8pm. I had parked off Whitworth Road and walked from there, though I wasn't quite sure why I had done that. I should have brazened it out and parked in a VIP space just as, I could see, Georgina was doing now. She pulled up in her jeep and got out of the car as though she was stepping onto a red carpet. She'd had her hair done. It was pinned dramatically on top of her head, and she was wearing a ruby-coloured silk blouse and black palazzo pants, no coat. I, in my usual off-work jeans, white blouse and winter coat felt underdressed.

Georgina linked me.

"I'm Holly here," she said.

Her tone and the glow of excitement about her made me catch my breath. I couldn't have imagined the woman crying in the kitchen a few days earlier could be the same woman standing beside me now. Before I could express any misgivings, she had pressed the buzzer on the door and was chatting with the doorman about having an appointment.

We stood in a reception area with a black marble-topped desk and a gold telephone, while the manager was fetched. The walls, cream with gold coving, were adorned with gilt-framed paintings of dead American performers who had all probably played Vegas. I was sure it was one of the Rat Pack I could hear from the speaker on the wall, singing about some doll. The overall effect made it hard for me to take the place seriously.

Dressed in a black, three-piece suit, the manager, who approached us through wooden, panelled swing doors, was tall and thin with slicked-back hair and a mouth full of crowns that I was sure his unfortunate customers had paid for. He extended his hand to each of us in turn, but focused his conversation on Georgina.

"First off, I'm Ralph Dowling. Thank you for considering Spin, Ms Davenport. We would be delighted to have your custom."

"Please – call me Holly."

His accent, I noticed, was mid-Atlantic with occasional Cork undertones that he worked hard to conceal. And Georgina was putting on her wealthiest voice.

"Membership has a lot of advantages," Mr Dowling said. "Not least an opportunity to meet all manner of people. Though I can't be specific, you'd be surprised at the household names we have on our members' list."

He pushed open the swing doors then and ushered us through into the gaming area. The lighting was so low that it took me a while before I could make out anything. Beneath my feet, the carpet felt thick and expensive, but the air was stale, as though second-hand smoke left over from pre-smoking-ban days still lingered in the fixtures and fittings.

We were led to a roulette wheel nearest us. It was populated with half a dozen players, men and women who had an air of money about them. A croupier in a dinner jacket was calling for bets in a singsong rhythm.

At another table, three suited men sat on high stools playing blackjack against the house.

Mr Dowling gestured toward the back of the room.

"We have other card games if you like them: Texas Hold'em, Baccarat, 7s, and plenty of 'slots' if that's what you're into."

He said *slots* as though he had a low opinion of the machines. I could hear the digital tunes they were playing and could make out a few lone figures feeding them. I was brought back briefly to a summer's day in my childhood on the seafront at Bray. I remembered dropping coppers into slots and, once in a while, hearing the satisfying *ching-ching* of coins in the tray.

The manager waved his arm then in the direction of a wide staircase.

"Upstairs there are private poker games, invitation

only, and the bar and so on." He explained that different members had different expectations of the casino: some came for light entertainment, some for a social life, and others, the serious gamblers, came for the money.

"At weekends, we have our own resident singer." He pointed at a poster on one wall of a man in a tuxedo, almost a doppelganger of Dean Martin. "Top notch."

"Nice," Georgina said, smiling at him almost flirtatiously.

He smiled back, his crowns glinting in the half-light. "We're open until 5.30am so there's never any pressure. Our time is your time." His expression changed then, making his face look almost sad. "Unfortunately, since you're not members, and due to the strict regulations under which we operate, I'm not in a position to let you try a hand, but you could see a demonstration if you'd like."

He walked us toward another blackjack table, which had not yet attracted any players. The croupier was a young woman in a fitted, black dress, bare at the shoulders. Her long, dark hair reached almost to her waist and glossy red lipstick emphasised her soft wide mouth. I imagined she could have just stepped off the set of a Bond movie.

"Good evening, ladies," she said. "Time to play?"

I was about to respond but Georgina had already turned away.

"It's time we were leaving." She walked swiftly toward the wooden doors.

I followed and the manager scurried after us.

"Ms Davenport, is everything all right? Has Claire upset you?"

71

"It's fine, really," Georgina said, pushing open the doors into the lobby.

I thought she looked pale under her make-up.

"Thank you, Ms Davenport. Perhaps you might have a drink at the bar before you leave – on us, of course?"

"Not tonight."

He walked quickly behind the reception desk and took out some papers.

"May I give you these? Membership forms for our records. We'll need bank details and some identification. It's a requirement of the anti-money-laundering legislation. You could fill them in now if you wish." He took a pen from his inside pocket and offered it to Georgina.

She took the forms from his hand. "I'll be in touch."

"Very well." He looked a little defeated and I wondered what would happen to Claire when he returned to her table.

Outside, we sat into the car and Georgina pulled away.

"I'm parked on David Road," I said. "Who was she?"

"I told you about her – the woman in the school club, remember? The one Andrew was staring at." All of her earlier good humour, the facade she had created for herself, had disappeared and she sounded shocked, frightened even.

"Well, that explains it – he was probably afraid she'd recognise him from that place and tell you."

Georgina took a deep breath and let the air out in a slow exhale.

"So then, he wasn't hiding anything else, just the gambling." She said it more to herself than to me. "That makes sense, doesn't it?"

"It certainly seems to."

We had reached the traffic lights on the corner of Whitworth Road. Georgina put on her indicator.

"It does make sense," she said again.

"Yes, I think so."

"You think?" She looked at me quickly and looked away.

"Yes, I'm sure."

Georgina pulled the wheel around and the car turned.

"Just along here on the left." I pointed at the turn-off. "She's working at the school club in the daytime and at the casino at night. Hard work. You have to hand it to her."

"Really?" She glanced at me sharply, as though she thought I was taking sides against her, before looking back at the road again. "Okay, I suppose it wasn't her fault if a casino client happened to be a dad too." She held the steering wheel in a tight grip. "You don't think there was anything else going on in there, do you?" she asked. "Upstairs, I mean?"

"What, like a brothel or something? No, no. You heard what he said – those places are strictly regulated."

"Okay." She seemed reassured. "Thanks, Bea, you were good to come with me. I think it helped seeing the place." She indicated left into David Road. "I didn't like it, though. And I find it hard to imagine Andrew in there. It makes no sense to me."

"I know. It's hard. You should try to forget about it if you can." I knew that was ludicrous – as though a woman whose husband had been murdered could forget about it, as though she could put it in a box in her head

73

and close the lid. Of all people, I should have known better.

"I'll try." Georgina gave me what passed for a smile.

We had pulled up beside my car and I got out.

"Call me if you need anything, anything at all." I closed the passenger door and watched as she turned the jeep and pulled out into the traffic.

Driving home, I thought about the young croupier. She must have been in her mid-twenties, very pretty. Alone, I was not quite so certain of my assurances to Georgina that Andrew's discomfort had been all about hiding his gambling. The look Andrew had given the young woman did not sound like a look of fear. I wondered if the girl had recognised him too when she saw him. It was possible there had been something between them, some sort of affair. Even the best of men were capable of a slip into infidelity under the right circumstances. I was sure of that.

As I drove up Clonliffe Road, through Fairview Strand and onto the coast road, I knew I'd have to tell Gabriel about where I'd been with Georgina and I knew that he'd tell McCann. I could imagine the detective's irritation at me for having gone along with Georgina's ruse, and the lecture he would deliver if he got the chance. But, also, I knew he would not be unhappy at the connection between the casino and the children's afterschool club. He wasn't the sort of person who believed in coincidences. He would ask the right questions.

I realised then that I'd forgotten to ask Georgina about the young woman's name. She was called Claire at the casino, but Claire what? And it was possible she could be called something else at the children's club. I considered if I should text Georgina when I got home, find out Claire's full name, but decided against it. I would be better off leaving all that to the guards. That is what I told myself as I locked the hall door behind me for the night.

In bed, I checked work emails on my laptop. There was an email from Úna Hollister telling me there had been a bereavement in Judge Peter Hadley-O'Toole's family and that he was unlikely to sit again until next week. There were no other requests for stenography services for the rest of the week. I wasn't surprised. I had turned down work to cover the O'Malley case.

Logging out, I wondered if I might offer Georgina some help. Perhaps I could collect the children from afterschool club tomorrow and take the pressure off her a little.

Chapter 9

Thursday, October 27th, 2016

Georgina had been surprised but grateful when I called her first thing on Thursday morning and said I'd be happy to collect the children from afterschool club to give her a break.

"Thanks, Bea, I'll be able to catch up a bit at work. It's been piling up."

"I'm sure it has."

She had told me how it had been at TechWorld, going back to work in the office where she had first met Andrew. Daunting, she'd said. Like most workplaces, the company had been supportive when he was killed, especially since he was an employee. There had been no pressure on her to return for weeks and when she did her boss had agreed she could work a shorter day. But once she was back in the office and the initial days of accepting condolences from colleagues were over, she felt she was expected to just get back to normal, whatever that was.

"I'll leave sandwiches in the fridge for them to eat when you bring them home. I'll make dinner as soon as

I'm back. Are you sure you'll manage?"

"Of course, see you later."

I promised to pick them up at five o'clock, drop by a local playground and bring them home by six. I'd felt guilty saying goodbye without telling her that I'd intended finding out some more about Claire, the childminder who worked at the casino. But I reasoned that if it turned out there was nothing to tell, I would just have upset her unnecessarily.

As I walked into the front garden of St Louisa's afterschool club, next to the primary school of the same name, parents brushed past me, coming and going. The club was a private house that a clever person had converted to accommodate children whose parents worked longer hours than the school day. A prominent sign on the wall beside the hall door read: *St Louisa's Afterschool Club has no connection with or affiliation to St Louisa's National School*. I imagined a letter from the board of management of the school to the owners of the club, insisting on it.

I didn't hurry to ring the bell. Having little experience of looking after children, I was in no great rush to collect them. I had parked at Georgina's earlier and walked to the club in 20 minutes. I had reasoned that we could walk to the playground which was on the route home and ten minutes away. I could sit on a bench and mind their schoolbags while they did what children do in playgrounds. At ten minutes to six we could leave and be back in Belford Avenue on time for Georgina.

Before I got around to ringing St Louisa's bell, the hall door opened and a man emerged with a child by the hand. He brushed by me, making my bag slip from my shoulder.

"*Oops!*" he said.

I thought he sounded slightly drunk or overexcited when he said that. He turned then and waved his thanks to the woman standing in the hall and I realised why. I immediately recognised Claire, looking lovely though she was not dressed up like the night before. Her long hair was in a high ponytail and she was wearing dark jeans and a T-shirt, and no make-up, but she was unmistakable.

"I'm here to collect Milly and James," I said.

"Beatrice, is it? I'm Claire Davis."

"Hello."

There was no sign of recognition from her. I reminded myself that the casino had been dimly lit and, while I was always interested in people I met and readily remembered faces, others were less attentive.

"I'll fetch the children."

"Can I just ask you something first?" I stepped into the hall and closed the door behind me. Low chatter emanated from rooms to the left and right, like the sound of a million worker bees and there was an odour of cooked chips and air freshener.

Claire was looking at me, waiting for the question.

"Privately?" I said.

She beckoned me down a corridor into a small office at the back of the house. There was a desk and chair close to a wall, a bookcase with ring-binders and, near the window, a low round table with two chairs either side.

"I'm just a little worried about Georgina," I began.

"Okay." Claire indicated the chairs.

We both sat.

"Well, as you can imagine, things haven't been easy for her." I was uncomfortable about the conversation.

"I'm sure." She looked steadily at me.

"Andrew was such a great support for her. She misses him terribly." I thought I noticed a momentary flinch.

"The children miss him," Claire said. "Milly likes to draw pictures of him. We encourage it."

"Well, that's good. I'm sure he was in and out of here lots." I tried to get the tone right, interested but not inquisitive.

"Not really, no. I don't think he was that kind of dad." She gripped the end of her ponytail, pulled it over her right shoulder and stroked it as though it was a small animal.

"What sort of dad was he?"

"Oh, I don't know. The busy sort, I suppose." She shook her head then and the ponytail flicked back. "So what was it you wanted to ask?"

"About Georgina – if there's anything you notice, if she looks like she's struggling to you, or anything, would you give me a call?" I took a business card from my purse and passed it to Claire who studied it.

"You're a stenographer. I've never met one of those before."

"There aren't too many of us around. I suppose you've had the guards by?"

"No, why would we?" Her tone was suddenly defensive. "I hardly knew him – we hardly knew him here at all."

She stood up, made for the door and opened it.

"Did you know him from Spin?" I asked.

She closed the door again and turned back to me.

"What did you say?"

I could see the first signs of panic in her eyes.

"I wondered if you'd met him at work in the casino."

"*Shhh, please* – they don't know I work there." She sat down again. "They'd probably sack me if they did." She stared at me. "What is it you really want?"

"I'm not going to tell them. I'm just wondering if you came across Andrew while you were at work?"

"I only work part-time. No, no, I didn't."

I raised myself out of my seat.

She opened the door and I stepped out into the hall.

"Just wait here. I'll get Milly and James."

When the children arrived they were already in their coats.

"Hello," I said. "Ready?"

They looked up at me shyly, Milly from under a brown fringe. Curly-blond James blinked at her a few times before deciding he would cooperate. Neither of them said anything.

"Off you go!" Claire gave them a little push in the direction of the door.

"Bye."

Outside, they turned and waved at her and I thought they might try to go back inside, but she shut the door.

"Right so." I led them up the drive and out the gate onto the street.

"Where's your car?" Milly asked.

"At your house. Keep together now."

"We're walking?" James stood still in the centre of the

path, looking as though he'd been asked to do something barbaric.

His older sister took on a sensible tone. "It's okay, it's not raining."

He still didn't move.

"I thought maybe we could visit the playground on the way?" I put my hand out to him and he took it. "This side," I said to Milly and she moved to my right side and took my hand.

We weaved along the footpath to avoid the SUVs that were two wheels up on the kerb. I wondered what it was people said to small children. I was conscious of the warmth of their hands in mine. James' was very small and slightly sticky.

"How was school?" I tried.

"*Bor-ing*," James sang, dragging his feet and scuffing the tips of his shoes.

"Fine," was Milly's reply. "Lift your feet, James."

I was surprised at how she spoke to him, as though she was used to playing the mother.

"Who are you, anyway?" James said after a few minutes of walking and kicking small stones on the footpath as he went.

"I'm Beatrice, your mother's friend."

He made a kind of growling noise, like a suspicious animal.

"Stop being silly, James – she's been to our house. Look!"

They could see the park.

They pulled away from me and broke into a run, dashing down the footpath, through the gate and on to the playground. I was sure they had been there many times before and didn't mind them running ahead. When I caught up they had already dumped their bags on the ground and were queuing up for a slide.

I sat on a nearby bench and marvelled at their energy and their uninhibited play. And I thought of how Georgina and Andrew must have sat here too and how miserable it must be for Georgina to be here alone now and see them like that, playing without sadness. She must know that with time, though their father loved them very much, they would forget the reality of him.

There was a cry then. Milly had fallen and scraped her knee. She came limping over to me and sat down, her eyes shiny with tears. I examined the graze and said we could wash it out when she got home.

"You'll be better before you're twice married," came out of my mouth unbidden. It was something I had heard my mother say a hundred times, but hadn't realised it was still buried in me, an antidote to every injury.

"Are you married?" She looked up at me.

"I'm not."

"Do you like wine, then?" Her nose crinkled as though she was thinking deeply about the connection between the two.

"Not really, no. Why do you ask?"

"Because when Mammy was married she didn't like wine and now she's not married anymore and she loves wine."

I thought of another saying of my mother's then — "out of the mouth of babes". I couldn't think of any response, so I changed the subject.

"It's time we were going – will you be all right to walk?"

She stretched out her injured leg, stood up and tested it. "Yes." She nodded solemnly.

When we got to Belford Avenue, as instructed, I searched behind a potted bay tree, in need of a prune, found a key and opened the door.

The children burst into the house, dropped their coats and bags in the hall and made for the kitchen. I followed them.

"Up you get," I told James, before lifting him onto a stool at the kitchen island.

I poured two glasses of milk, took the prepared sandwiches out of the fridge, unwrapped the cling film and put them before the children.

"Okay. Eat up, your mother will be home soon. Oh! Your knee, Milly – first let me have a look at it."

I moistened a kitchen towel under the tap. Milly reluctantly held her knee out and I dabbed it gently to remove the worst of the dirt.

"There now – we'll let your mother put a plaster on it."

She nodded and turned back to her sandwich.

I put the kettle on for myself, and while the children ate I wandered into the study. The small room, which looked out on the street, was dominated by bookshelves. A large leather armchair with a reading lamp next to it was in one corner, and behind the door an opened roll-top writing desk was filled with papers. I began leafing through them. They seemed to be mostly bank statements – a mortgage account, some joint accounts. Some of the papers were a few years old. At the bottom of the pile there were two documents showing accounts in Andrew's name with dates in January, 2016. One had an overdraft of €35,000, the other a credit card debt of €62,000. I didn't see the car pulling into the drive or hear Georgina turn the key in the front door. I did hear the children though, running down the hall calling for their mother. I moved quickly from the writing desk to the bookshelf and pulled out a book at random – *Love your Garden: The Herbs That Help*. I could see it was one part of a series of books.

"Bea? There you are." Georgina was at my shoulder. "You can borrow that if you like."

"Great, thanks." My front and back gardens on Clontarf Road got little of my attention, but a man came in during the summer to keep the grass clipped and the few shrubs neatly trimmed. I wouldn't be reading the book or planting herbs, but I put it, all the same, into my bag.

"Tea?"

"No thanks, I think I'll leave you to it."

"Right then." She seemed relieved that I wouldn't be staying. She looked exhausted. "You're very good for collecting them – thanks, Bea."

We walked to the door and, as I closed it behind me, I could hear Georgina telling the children to pick up their bags and put away their coats. I supposed it was a daily ritual between parents and children, a desire to impose order on youngsters who might otherwise be feral. I could see it, particularly in James as he careered down the slide, his eyes shining and his cheeks pink – that potential to go wild. I was glad there had been no children for me to domesticate. That opportunity had passed me by.

I drove without thinking of my destination and found myself in Stoneybatter instead of in Clontarf. It was six forty-five and the traffic on Manor Street trailed past the shops, pubs, and people, who were scarfed and gloved and bending into a cold wind that had only begun to blow. I noticed Gabriel then, his straight walk not yielding to the weather, and beeped my horn. He spotted me immediately and, when I pulled up, he hopped into the passenger seat beside me.

"On your way home?" I pulled back out into the traffic.

"I am. And what has you in this neck of the woods?"

As if he didn't know.

"I wanted to talk to you."

I edged the car toward the left turn for Manor Place. I indicated and inched into the turn.

"Rotten traffic. I'd have been quicker walking," Gabriel said grumpily.

The remark irritated me and I was tempted to pull over and throw him out.

"You're coming from Ryan's, are you?" I said, a little too smartly.

"No, actually, I'm coming from Store Street." He sounded indignant now.

It would be better to say no more for the moment, I decided. I was too familiar with how, if we were both in the wrong form, conversations could escalate into arguments.

When we pulled up outside Number 9, Gabriel jumped out of the car, opened his front door and walked inside, leaving it ajar behind him. I thought it showed poor manners but when I stepped inside I realised there had been method to his actions. He had begun tidying around the living room, which was strewn with clothes and towels. There were empty food cartons on the coffee table, and cups on the bookshelf. Gabriel stopped tidying, dropped onto the couch and put his head in his hands.

"No good deed goes unpunished."

I was surprised at how pleased I was to discover the source of his poor form.

"For the first day or two she was falling over herself cleaning. But now it's like this. Stuff everywhere." He picked up a blue towel from the floor which was pockmarked with white patches. "Look at this." He held it out for me to examine. "Do you know what that is? Hair dye. And when I complained she said she'd spread the towels on the floor so she wouldn't get dye on the tiles. Like I was supposed to be grateful."

His exasperated tone made me want to laugh.

"She's young," I said instead. "Put the kettle on."

While he was in the kitchen, I collected the damp towels and clothes, the empty food cartons, plates and mugs, bundled them in one large towel and carried them all upstairs to Billie's room. She was occupying the small front bedroom looking out onto the street. The curtains were closed and I elbowed on the light switch. The room was almost filled with cardboard boxes and black sacks, with only a narrow passage through them to the bed. I dropped my burden onto the bed, plates and all, intending to leave them there. Then I looked around and felt sorry for Billie, with her life crammed in around her like that.

"*Tea!*" Gabriel called from below.

I put the towels in the laundry basket on the landing, picked up the plates and cups again, brought them back downstairs with me and put them in the sink. Gabriel had taken a tray into the living room.

"So what did McCann have to say for himself?" I asked as I put milk in my tea and then sat into the armchair next to the fireplace.

"He said it'll take a while to identify what's in that bag we found – he has to send it off to a lab in the UK."

I told him about the bank statements I'd seen and how uneasy I thought Claire Davis was when I'd asked about Andrew.

"The guards haven't even called in there yet."

"They'll get round to it."

I knew they would – the question was, how long would it take them?

Chapter 10

Friday, October 28th, 2016

I'd been searching the Courts Service website after lunch, for potential civil cases I could pitch to work on until the O'Malley case resumed, when my phone rang. It was Gabriel.

"Are you at work?" he asked as soon as I answered.

"No, is everything okay?"

"It's Billie."

"Billie?"

"She's dead, Bea." His voice was tight with shock.

"How? What happened, was she ill?" How could she be?

"Barney found her."

"Who?"

"Barney, in Hanlon's – she didn't come out of the cellar and he went down and she was lying there."

I wondered if she'd collapsed. Did young people have heart attacks?

"He said the back of her head was caved in."

"No! Had she fallen?"

He began gulping in air, as though he was drowning, unable to speak.

"Are you at home?" I asked.

"Yes." He was barely audible.

"I'm coming over."

I grabbed my coat and bag, closed the hall door behind me and got into the car. How could such a thing happen? I imagined the cellar. Could she have tripped on the stairs and hit something as she fell? Was there anything overhead – pipes or something – that could have fallen down and hit her? Or had someone hurt her deliberately?

I switched on the radio just in time for the two o'clock news headlines.

"*Gardaí are investigating the death of a woman in a pub in North Dublin. The woman died in Hanlon's pub, North Circular Road, earlier today under suspicious circumstances. Our reporter, James Knutall, is at the scene. James, what can you tell us?*" There was a brief pause and then the reporter began to speak, the sound of traffic behind him. "*The alarm was raised by a customer who found the victim in the cellar of the pub shortly before midday. The pub's in a busy spot, on the junction of North Circular Road and the Old Cabra Road, not far from the Phoenix Park. I understand the victim was a member of staff and had sustained head injuries. Sources tell me there may have been a robbery under way at the pub, but at this stage it is unclear exactly what happened. The victim has yet to be named.*"

A robbery? So it was not an accident. An image of Billie the last time I saw her came into my head. So full of vitality. And I imagined the cellar below ground – probably cold and damp and dim. What a horrible place to die.

By the time I got to Oxmantown Road, there were two Garda cars parked outside and the front door was open. In the sitting room, Gabriel was on the sofa, talking quietly with a uniformed officer. He seemed to have regained his composure, but he looked dreadful, as though half the blood had been drained from his body. When he saw me he stood up and offered to make some tea.

"I'll do that – and a cup for you, officer?"

The young woman shook her head and got to her feet.

"I'll let Detective McCann know," she said to Gabriel, before picking up the laptop from the coffee table and walking out of the room with it.

While I made tea, I could hear what I presumed were gardaí moving around upstairs, looking, I supposed, for anything that could tell them about Billie Nichols.

I found a bottle of whiskey in the kitchen cupboard, poured some into a glass, and gave it to Gabriel. Then I poured myself tea and sat beside him on the couch. His hand was shaking as he lifted the glass to his lips.

"I'm so sorry, Gabriel."

He took another drink. "What the fuck is wrong with the world, Bea?" He spoke quietly but with a kind of desperate anger in his voice.

"I don't know. I can't believe anyone could have done such a thing to Billie, and for what? A few euro?" I told him I'd heard it was a robbery on radio news on the drive over from my house. "How much would have been in that till?"

He shrugged. "Very little, €200 or so, I'd say. But I don't believe it was robbery, it doesn't make sense." He took another drink, just a sip this time. "Imagine you're

90

a thief, Bea – you walk into the pub, no one behind the bar, you open the till, you take the money, then what do you do?"

I nodded. "Run."

"You leg it. You don't go down into the cellar and crack the barwoman's head open."

"Did you see – were you down there?"

"No. They wouldn't let me."

"Just as well." I drank some tea. "Did you speak to Barney?"

"Yes, he was outside the pub when I arrived. Couldn't believe it when I saw the Garda tape everywhere." He rubbed his eyes.

"What did he say?"

"Who?"

"Barney."

"He was in a bit of a trance – kept saying if he'd only noticed the open till in the first place, he wouldn't have waited so long to go down and look for her. Don't think it would have made any difference though."

"No?"

"Matt told me – he said it looked like two sharp blows. They would've killed her instantly."

"Poor Billie." I winced, a picture in my mind of Billie's blonde hair matted with red, and bits of eggshell bone.

"Barney said he told her he was just going to nip out to the bookies and to keep his stool at the bar for him – though he was the only customer in there. When he came back she was gone. He figured she'd gone down to change a keg, so he waited. Then he thought she might be having trouble so he went behind the bar and called down to her.

91

When she didn't answer he went down and found her." He took a gulp of air. "She was slumped over a keg."

"God, that's awful, Gabriel." Awful and impossible to imagine. How could that young woman be gone forever?

"I asked him if he saw anything on his way back from the bookies. He said he saw someone walking away, wearing one of those navy padded jackets and jeans, heading toward Annamoe Road. Had his hood up, Barney said." He was shaking his head as though he could shake loose the images now lodged there.

After a while, he spoke again.

"I'd been down to Ryan's for my lunch and decided to walk back up and ask Billie if she needed anything at the shop. The ambulance was pulling away when I got there. The lads were cordoning off all around with tape. Barney was just standing there, staring." His eyes were wide with disbelief as he recalled the spectacle that had confronted him.

"Anyone else there?"

"I saw the owner going in – Derek Johnston – and the manager, Piotr Gromczewski. I don't think you met him, only back today from a visit home."

I hadn't met either of them. I'd only been to the pub in the mornings when Billie had manned it alone.

"Then Matt McCann arrives, while I'm standing there. Says it's a terrible business and wants to know if I knew her." He smiled to himself. "You should have seen his face when I said she was lodging with me. Had to explain she was stuck for somewhere to stay. He went puce, then he said to me 'Anything between ye?'. I told him she was only a kid."

"McCann's not stupid, he was probably just embarrassed to have to ask." I knew the detective could be awkward, but he had more sense than to think Gabriel could have any involvement in Billie's death.

"I know, but it makes it a bit messy for him, if you see what I mean."

I knew exactly what he meant. I could already see the headlines: "Tragic Victim Billie lived with OAP Garda."

"He asked me to go in to the station later, make a statement."

"That would be normal, wouldn't it?" Gabriel would have more information about Billie than most. "Did McCann say why he was involved in this case? Hanlon's is a long way from Store Street."

"No – resource issue, I'd imagine. He asked me where I was when it happened."

"Did he?" I tried not to sound indignant on his behalf.

"Just doing his job – I told him I had a pint in Hanlon's, walked through the park, sandwich in Ryan's. Then back."

Gabriel was sitting forward in his seat now, an elbow on each knee, looking into the fire.

"Will I top you up?" I took the empty glass from his hand but he shook his head.

"I don't want to go to Store Street with the smell of whiskey off me." He sighed and the air that came out of his lungs seemed to vibrate with shock.

"Why do you think someone would do such a thing to her?" I asked.

He leaned back into the couch again. He looked worn out from thinking about it.

"I don't know. They've been asking me all about her

93

and I didn't know what to tell them, Bea. I hardly knew her at all."

"Did she say anything about family or friends?"

"I heard her on the phone a few times, but she never said who she was talking to and I never asked. The only thing was, when she found out I was from Donegal, she said she was third generation Dublin."

"Not much to go on there." I asked him why the garda had taken his laptop.

"Billie borrowed it a few times – when I checked it I could see she'd been searching for a hostel. She must have been organising to move out. There was other stuff too, but password-locked. The lads in HQ should be able to get it though."

Gabriel checked his watch and signalled toward the ceiling.

"They'd want to hurry up there, or I'll be late for meeting Matt."

"I'll stay till they're gone if you like."

"Would you? Thanks. I'll just make sure they don't need me."

He left the room and I could hear his heavy-footed stride across the landing to Billie's room and then his voice like a muted bassoon before he came down again.

"Right, thanks, Bea. Here." He threw me a key ring with two keys attached. "The back door is locked, but that key will open it in case they need to go out to the yard." He indicated a key with a yellow piece of plastic on the top. "When they go, will you pull the front door, lock it and put the keys back through the letter box? I have my own set with me."

"I will."

I stood by the sitting- room window and watched him drive away. I felt so sorry for him. He'd been kind to Billie and fond of her. She had been like a bright spark around his house. I knew he'd seen death many times in the past, before he retired from the force, but it was one thing to investigate the death of a stranger and another to face the death of a friend. I'd give him as much support as I could. It was the least I owed him.

Chapter 11

I carried the tea things into Gabriel's kitchen and set about washing them, then went back into the sitting room. I picked up a newspaper left on the nearby bookshelf and sat down in a corner of the couch. It was folded onto the crossword page and half the puzzle was filled in. I took a pen from my handbag. I didn't think Gabriel would mind if I completed it. I looked at the clues. "*Four down, a rare character in code, five letters.*" Blank, blank R, blank, blank. Of course. I was about to fill it in, but then I looked at the unfamiliar writing already on the grid, probably Billie's. It seemed like desecration to add to it. I put the paper aside just as the thumps of eight strong boots came down the stairs.

The gardaí were making their way down, carrying boxes. I could hear them going outside to their cars.

A woman guard came back into the house.

"Did you know Billie?"

"Not know her, no. I met her a couple of times, in the pub and once here."

"What did you make of her?"

She said it in a friendly, casual way, but I could see there was a reason behind her question.

I thought for a moment. "Bright, kind, a bit troubled maybe, mostly just young. Anything upstairs of use?"

"I couldn't say. No drugs though."

"Good. Are you finished? Would it be okay for me to tidy up her things?"

"Work away."

I closed the door and watched from the window while the gardaí drove away. Then I found a roll of black sacks in the kitchen and went upstairs. Gabriel would find it too hard to tackle the room – best if I just bagged up everything. Billie's stuff could be stored then to be given to relatives once they were found. There had to be relatives somewhere.

The room was in chaos. All of her cardboard boxes had been opened. It looked as though their contents – books, old records, toiletries, shoes, a lamp, a picture frame – had been spilled out, gone through and then half-heartedly stuffed back in again. Her black sacks had been ripped open and their contents strewn around. The bed had been stripped of its covers and the mattress was turned over on its wooden frame, the drawers of the bedside locker were open and books were scattered. The doors of the wardrobe, an old-fashioned, dark, freestanding kind that almost touched the ceiling, were open wide. It felt strange to be there, picking over what was left of Billie, to know that she would never again put on those clothes or lie on that bed, or tie the laces on her runners.

I gathered up the bed sheets and stuffed them into the laundry basket on the landing. Then I began picking up

Billie's clothes, folding them and putting them into black sacks. I tipped the various jars and creams that were sitting on her bedside locker into a small bag. There was only a little make-up – she hadn't really needed any.

I pulled out the clothes that had remained on hangers in the wardrobe. They looked like they came from second-hand shops – high-waisted jeans, men's shirts, oversized jumpers. Collected together, they took up only two sacks and a half. I tidied the contents of the boxes as best I could, putting books into one of them. They made for an odd collection – some science fiction, biographies of various singers, books on psychology. One tome, called *Cognitive Behavioural Therapy: How to Retrain Your Brain,* looked well-thumbed. I picked it up and opened it. On the inside cover someone had written: "*Let the past go – make the future your own.*" I wondered what it was that had prompted that sentiment.

The gardaí had taken Billie's phone, but left chargers and an old MP3 player. I put these into a small plastic bag. I got a sweeping brush and swept under the bed. A few items of dusty underwear and socks came out with the brush, as though from under a child's bed. I picked them up to deposit in a black sack. One sock was heavier than the others. I felt it – there was something solid inside.

I sat on the bare mattress and emptied out the contents. There were three small aerosols with Chinese print on them and two words in English: "**Pepper spray.**" Only frightened people carry pepper spray. Billie must have been frightened of something. I set the canisters aside. Gabriel could pass them on to the guards if he thought it was worthwhile. When I'd finished cleaning, I

piled the bags and boxes in one corner of the bedroom –
six black sacks, five boxes, all that remained of Billie.
How sad that a life could come down to that, a small pile
of belongings.

I lifted out the small bag of rubbish I'd collected –
takeaway cartons and boxes, empty tampon packs, a
hair-dye box, a can of Coke. I took it down to the
kitchen, unlocked the back door, and left it outside in the
yard. Then I locked the door again, collected my own
things and, as Gabriel had asked, locked the front door
and put the keys back in through the letterbox.

I had only let myself into my own house when the phone
went off in my handbag. It took a minute to locate it and,
as I did, Gabriel's number flashed and then disappeared. I
took off my coat and hung it up, and then called Gabriel
back.

"How did it go?"

"Okay, fine. I told them everything I could, which
wasn't much. Matt said they're having trouble getting
background on her. They can't seem to find out much
about her at all."

"That's strange, isn't it? I mean in this day and age,
with mobile phones and ID needed every time you turn
around."

"I know. Matt said she was paid into the hand in
Hanlon's, so no PPS number. Derek Johnson, Hanlon's
owner, knew her, but they've nothing from before he met
her, nothing at all."

"No family?"

"Not that they can find – not yet anyway."

He said if something didn't turn up soon the guards would put out an appeal to try to find someone who knew her. I remembered then about the pepper spray and told him.

"Yeah, Matt mentioned they found some on her – she was carrying it on a thing around her neck, for all the good that did."

I thought of the young woman, down in the pub cellar, wary of the world, yet not wary enough.

"Will you be all right?" I asked. I could hear his breathing.

"I'd like to help them catch whoever did that to her." He almost whispered it, as though it was only occurring to him how much he hated that person.

"I know you would, and you will." I hoped I was telling him the truth. I knew there would be nothing more cruel to Gabriel now than not finding Billie's killer.

Chapter 12

Saturday, October 29th, 2016

I was disturbed during the night by one of those intense, unsettling dreams that insert themselves into the first wakeful moments, so that I was sure I heard a girl's voice in my bedroom calling out to me. It took me more than an hour to settle back to sleep, which caused me to sleep in. As a consequence, though I got a taxi in to the city-centre hairdresser's to have my colour topped up, I was fifteen minutes late and lucky to be seen at all and I was late for meeting Gabriel in Hanlon's at lunchtime.

The pub had reopened once forensics had finished in the cellar. And Gabriel had suggested we talk to the pub's manager, Derek Johnson. I was happy to agree, glad to be of use.

Gabriel was in his usual spot and I said I was sorry for my lateness, but he didn't seem to have noticed the time. He looked preoccupied and tired and didn't even smile when a barman put a pint on the table for him.

"Who's that?" I asked.

"Piotr Gromczewski, the manager I was telling you about, just back from his holidays."

"Some timing. How are you feeling, Gabriel?"

He shrugged. "It just doesn't seem real, does it?"

"No." The shock was still there, I could see it, a kind of deadness in his eyes. "All we can do for her now is find her killer. Will we see about Johnston?"

Gabriel had said the best chance of catching him was when he helped serve food at the pub's carvery.

"Will we get some food, so?" Gabriel said.

We both queued with brown plastic trays, shuffling behind local pensioners until we reached the bain-marie, which was covered with an arched glass shield. There were the usual choices, turkey and ham, roast beef, chicken in a sauce of some sort and salmon. Gabriel asked for turkey and ham – I went for the salmon.

"All the veg with that?" the man behind the counter asked, ladling on cabbage and turnips before I could protest. He was in his early thirties and short, with flat, brown hair in a side parting, sinewy arms and the eyes of a blackbird. He was wearing a white T-shirt stained yellow under the armpits, jeans and a white apron tied around a generous stomach. I thought he had the look of a fruit-market worker, as tough as the boots I couldn't see but felt sure he was wearing.

"Derek, is it?" Gabriel asked.

"Yeah, mash and roasters?" He spoke without looking up.

"Both. Would you have a few minutes to talk to us when you're done?"

He looked up at us then with a puzzled expression, his ladle frozen in position for a second in mid-air.

"About what?"

"We're friends of Billie," I said.

"Give me a few minutes."

We carried our trays back to our table in the corner, and unloaded plates, cutlery and paper napkins. I had a glass of iced water and Gabriel had a pint of stout.

I ate the fish, having dug it out from under a cabbage mountain.

"If you're not eating the cabbage, I'll have it." Gabriel reached across and forked the limp leaves onto his plate. Shock had not diminished his appetite. "You know you could have got a half-dinner?"

I knew that. But most of the other customers were eating half-dinners and their age profile had made me shy away from a reduced portion.

I pushed the plate to one side, brought my cup and saucer nearer and began to drink the tea. It tasted limy today and was not as hot as I liked, but I said nothing.

"That was grand." Gabriel finally put down his knife and fork. He looked content for a moment and then pained, as though Billie's death had been forgotten and then swiftly remembered.

The queue at the carvery had petered out and Derek came over to our table. We introduced ourselves and he wiped his hand on his apron and shook both of ours, pulled a stool from a nearby table and sat down.

"What can I do for you?"

"As I said, we're friends of Billie," Gabriel began.

"Yes."

"We're just trying to understand . . ."

"Okay."

"Did you know her well?"

He shrugged. "Did anyone know Billie, really? Lovely girl, but."

Gabriel leaned toward him.

"I heard ye had a thing for a while."

He didn't seem to mind being asked.

"Not for long and before she started working for me. That's how I gave her the job – after like, she needed something after."

"Were you close?" I asked.

Derek smiled. "We had a bit of fun. She lived in my place for a few months. Great for a while. She was working in a café in the city centre – she lost that job, found it hard to get another one – hanging around the flat all day, then she shut down on me."

"Why?"

"I don't know. Billie was . . . you know the sort of woman . . . you can only get so close, then the wall goes up."

"Sure," Gabriel said.

"It used to cause rows – too much at the end, so I told her she'd have to leave, but I offered her a job here to keep her going."

"What about her background? Was she from around here?" I looked directly at him.

"I don't know, she never said. But I think she had a shitty time when she was younger and never really got over it. She used to give out about her mother."

"Ever meet the mother?"

"God no. Piotr said she came into the pub once and Billie wouldn't even talk to her."

Derek pushed his stool away from the table, about to get to his feet.

"Where were you when it happened?" Gabriel used his garda tone, firm and direct.

"Ah here . . ." Derek looked from him to me and back again. "Who the fuck do you think yiz are?" He stood. "We had our rows, but I'd never hurt Billie. I can't imagine why anyone would."

"Me neither," Gabriel said.

Derek went back to the carvery and began cleaning up, putting lids on the stainless-steel bain-marie that held the last of the vegetables and gravy. As he worked, a man approached him, a tray in his hands.

"Too late, I'm afraid," Derek said, looking up only briefly from his cleaning.

"Could I not have a bit of that turkey? I can see it there."

"You're too fucking late, I said, we're closed." Derek spoke so loudly and with such aggression that everyone in the pub stopped talking.

He looked up then, realising that he could be heard.

"For fuck sake!"

He threw the metal lids to one side with a clatter, slopped out the last of the potatoes and vegetables onto a plate, put the stub end of a turkey joint beside them, then picked up one of the metal containers and emptied the remains of the gravy all over the meal. He dropped the plate onto the man's tray.

"There now, are you happy?" He threw the metal container back into its slot with a noisy clang, turned around and went into the back office.

The bar manager, Piotr Gromczewski, went over to the customer and apologised. I could hear him explaining that Derek had not been himself and that he wouldn't have to pay for the meal.

"Bit of a temper there." Gabriel drained his pint.

"But it wasn't really a temperamental killing, was it?" A man with a temper would kill on the spot, I thought, in the flood of his anger. "Men who kill in anger are messy – this seemed clinical to me."

"Do you know, the guards missed out when they didn't recruit you," Gabriel gently mocked me.

"I'm only thinking out loud. There was something very cold about it."

"I know, and you could be right."

Piotr came over and began picking up our cutlery, slipping Gabriel's wiped-clean plate under mine.

"Have you a sec?" Gabriel asked him.

"Pardon?"

"Will you talk to us for a minute?" I said.

Piotr looked over his shoulder. There was no-one waiting to be served at the bar and his boss was not in sight.

"Derek said Billie's mother was in. Do you remember when?" Gabriel asked.

"About three weeks ago, I think. But Billie wouldn't talk to her."

"Why not? Did Billie say?"

"No, and I told her 'This is your mother', but she just said I should mind my own business." He put the plates back down on the table and reached into his back pocket, taking out his wallet.

"She gave me her number, to give to Billie if she changed her mind – it's here somewhere. You want it?"

He searched and found a slip of paper with a number on it.

"Please." I found my phone in my handbag and Piotr read out the digits. While I keyed them into my phone, Gabriel did the same with his.

"Her name?" he asked.

"She didn't tell me. I gave this number to the police too – they'll find her."

"Thanks."

He picked up the plates again, manoeuvred the cutlery and glasses, and balancing everything walked back to the bar.

As we organised ourselves to leave, Gabriel took out his wallet and left a fiver on the table.

Outside he asked, "Will I try it or will you?"

"Best you – we don't want to frighten her."

We stood outside the pub, me with my scarf wrapped twice around my neck against the cold wind, and I took out my phone. I began to dial but, with the traffic rumbling around us, thought better of it. We walked down the road to the park gates and once inside I tried again. The phone rang ten times before going to voicemail.

"Can't talk now – God knows what I'm up to. Leave a message and I'll ring you back."

I hung up.

"Would you not leave a message?"

"I hate those things." But I tried again and this time said I was a friend of Billie's, and left my number.

Chapter 13

Monday, October 31st, 2016

I was making breakfast and had put a slice of wholemeal bread in the toaster when Gabriel rang.

"Are you sitting or standing?" he asked.

"What? Sitting down now."

"Good, I thought you'd want to know – the pathology results point to one weapon for both deaths – Andrew's and Billy's."

"I don't understand." It didn't make sense. "Is your friend, what's-his-name, sure?" Gabriel had friends everywhere and I knew the man he'd been talking to worked as an assistant to the state pathologist, but I just couldn't remember his name.

"Bob. Yes, he said the pathologist told the guards it was the same cause of death, same force to the head, even the indent shape the same – very distinct, he said."

The toast popped and I brought it to the kitchen table and sat down again.

"Does that mean he used the same weapon?"

"Looks like it."

I thought about what sort of person would kill

someone and then hold on to whatever it was to use again later. "God, he must have kept it somewhere, hidden it away. That's ... it's sick."

"Exactly. And no weapon found in Hanlon's."

"What does that mean? Do they think it could happen again?" I thought of Georgina and felt a knot in my stomach. Could she be next?

"They haven't ruled it out . . . but it's much too early to start thinking like that."

I trapped the phone between my ear and my shoulder and began to butter my toast.

"Do they know the sort of weapon they're looking for?"

"Something heavy with a rounded end, Bob says. Maybe like a baseball bat, or a cosh or something. They'll know when they find it, anyway."

"If they find it, you mean." It could be anywhere. "Don't guards carry those kinds of things?"

"What, baseball bats?"

"No, coshes, truncheons."

"They do – they're called batons now. So like that, with a bit of weight in it."

I moved the phone a little away from my mouth and bit into the toast – I couldn't bear to wait until after the call when it would be too cold.

"You're eating? Sorry, I'll call later."

"No, it's fine." I chewed and swallowed and took a gulp of tea. "I'm just thinking about Georgina – this is going to be hard for her. I mean, what possible connection could there be between the two of them? Did Billie ever mention Andrew's murder to you?"

I could hear Gabriel sigh and realised I had forced him back from thinking of the deaths in the abstract, to thinking in the particular about a woman he had known and liked.

"I don't remember her saying anything about it, no."

I had an image then, for just a second, of a cosh coming down on the back of Billie's head.

"I think I should let Georgina know. The papers are bound to get the post-mortem results." I waited for him to dissuade me, but he didn't.

"Would you . . . do you want me to come over with you?"

He was asking cautiously, I knew, because he wasn't sure how I'd respond. I didn't hesitate.

"Would you? Thanks."

It was close to four o'clock when we rang Georgina's doorbell. The door was flung open and we were greeted by Emma who had a bowl of sweets in her hand.

"Oh!" she said, withdrawing the bowl.

"Hello." I was surprised to see the teenager and simultaneously surprised to remember that it was Halloween.

"Who is it so early?" Georgina came into the hall then, looking flustered.

"Sorry, I forgot it was Halloween . . . We can call back another day."

"No, no, don't be silly. Emma's just getting organised to take the other two trick or treating. Come in."

We stepped into the hall, which was decorated with pumpkin lights and candles. On a side table, a witch with a broom looked menacingly at us.

"Go on into the living room and I'll be with you in a minute."

We went in.

Gabriel took off his jacket and sat on the couch. I took an armchair.

"This is bad timing," I whispered. "Will we just say we were in the area and thought we'd drop by? Leave the other thing for another time?"

"But what about the papers?"

"What about the papers?" Georgina came back in and closed the living-room door behind her. "Bea?"

"Sorry, I should have phoned first."

"You'd better tell me." She sat on the edge of the couch, her hands clenched in her lap.

"It's about the other murder, the girl, remember? The guards think it might be the same killer."

"But . . . why?"

Gabriel was about to launch into a detailed explanation about the killer's modus operandi but took his cue from a barely perceptible shake of my head and said nothing.

"They both died from blows to the head and they think the weapon might have been the same."

"Ah no." She didn't seem inclined to believe us.

"Did Andrew ever have any business out Parkgate Street way?" Gabriel asked. "Did he ever drink in Hanlon's pub, or mention it even?"

She shook her head. "Never heard of it. And no, he never mentioned that area of the city. Was that where she was from?"

There was a noise then at the door and Milly and

James ran in, dressed in costume. They both bounced onto the couch beside Georgina who put her arms around them.

"You probably don't recognise these little people," she said. "This is Elsa and this is Olaf."

The children giggled and we both smiled.

"Off you go now," Georgina said when Emma came into the room.

Georgina stood and waved from the window as the three walked down the drive and out onto the avenue, then she sat down again.

"Good of Emma to take them around at her age," I said.

"She's very patient with them."

"She must be on her mid-term?" An image of St Columba's flashed into my brain from brochures I'd feigned interest in when Georgina was deciding where to send her daughter. It was an ancient building, with gothic, granite-framed windows and doors, red-bricked chimneys and a fine, wide driveway.

"Yes, mid-term or maybe – maybe longer." The frown line between her eyebrows deepened.

"Longer?"

"When I picked her up from school her principal called me to his office. Oscar Mulcahy, not a man I could easily warm to. You know the kind, a long face like a miserable spaniel."

She paused, adjusted herself in the seat and spoke directly to me as though she had forgotten Gabriel was present. He did nothing to draw attention to himself.

"He told me there'd been incidents at night. Emma had been disturbed, he said, crying out, but when her dorm mother tried to comfort her, she couldn't wake her up. She just kept shouting and screaming."

"Poor thing. Did he say what she was shouting about?"

"I asked, but he didn't know, didn't seem to care about that. It was the fact of the shouting – 'disruptive for the other children' he said. They called the doctor for her, according to Mulcahy."

I couldn't tell whether that was what distressed her, that the school had got medical advice without informing her first or whether she didn't believe him.

"And?"

"The doctor said it was night terrors. He said it might be best if she stays home for a while, to help her settle down. I was getting that second-hand, of course, no note from the doctor or anything."

"And how had she been otherwise?"

"In the daytime, fine, he said. And the strange thing is she doesn't remember the nights at all." She looked weary with the worry of it. "He was all sympathy, but you know yourself, he didn't want the trouble."

"Maybe she just needs some time at home with you. It can't have been easy going away after."

Georgina rubbed her right temple. "That's what our GP said when I took her to him. He said you never know at her age how Andrew's death might have affected her. She might be burying her feelings about it and then they're coming out at night in her sleep. It could be a bit like post-traumatic stress disorder, he said."

I got the distinct impression the diagnosis had been no comfort.

"How has she been since she got home?"

"Sharing my bed, still having night terrors. I'm not sure she'll be going back to St Columba's for a while – I mean, I'm not sure they'll have her back."

"If there's anything I can do . . ."

"Thanks." She turned abruptly to Gabriel then and straightened up in her seat as though preparing herself. "Now tell me about the dead girl."

He told her about Billie, her work and her housing problems and how she ended up in Oxmantown Road. She kept looking at him as he spoke, nodding and sighing her way through his explanation.

"Such a young woman . . . what an awful thing to happen," she said when he was finished. "But a connection between them? I can't understand how. Did she ever mention Andrew to you at all?"

"No," he said. "And as far as we know the guards haven't found any connection yet."

"No?"

"But if the pathologist is right, there should be one, and if there is the lads will find it eventually."

I admired Gabriel's certainty, his faith that the truth would emerge.

Georgina nodded. "Well, I can't think of a thing. If I do, I'll tell you. And thanks for warning me, both of you. It means a lot to know I have your support."

The bell rang then and she got to her feet. We could hear little voices chanting "trick or treat" when she answered the door.

"We should go." I stood and moved to the door. Gabriel followed, putting on his coat.

Georgina returned. "You're leaving?" She sounded as

though she was sorry to see us go, but at the same time relieved.

"It'll be a busy night for you, I expect. Are you okay?" I put my hand on her arm.

"Yes, and thanks again. I'm glad I won't have to hear that from a stranger."

She waved us off from the door and looked so vulnerable standing there that I was tempted to go back and sit with her for a while. I thought perhaps I might have if I'd visited her alone.

"We should do all we can to help her," I said as I reversed the car out of the drive.

"I'm sure it's very hard for her," Gabriel responded.

I pulled out of Herbert Park into the Merrion Road. The traffic was light and dominated by taxis. And there were groups of men and women in costume making their way into the city centre on foot.

"When did all this start?" Gabriel sounded disgruntled. "It was bad enough the kids doing it, but adults dressing up?"

"What harm are they doing?" I glanced at him briefly then returned my gaze to the traffic lights at the corner of Lansdowne Road.

"That's not the point. It's the Americanisation of everything. What was wrong with bobbing for apples and a few ghost stories by the fire?"

I tried but failed to smother a laugh. "Come on now, Gabriel – you're not that old."

"And 'trick or treat', I hate that."

"You'd better stay away from home a few more hours so – there's plenty of children on your road. Will we get something to eat?"

"All right."

I drove on through the city, past Christchurch Cathedral and the Four Courts. In Stoneybatter I parked in Arbour Place so we could eat in Mulligan's.

"I haven't been here in a long time – it's gone a bit arty," Gabriel said.

We sat on stools as far away from the door and the cool breeze as we could get.

I picked up a menu and read the choices. "Pan-fried Hake, free-range Ham Kassler, Lamb Tomahawk Chops."

"See what I mean?"

"Hipster, I think you mean."

"Whatever you call it, you won't find shepherd's pie."

I thought about the changes in Stoneybatter, how it had gone from working class to gentrified over the years. There were a lot more cool young couples now, and most of them had paid ridiculous prices for their homes or were paying exorbitant rents.

"You could make a fortune if you sold your house now," I said. "You could buy something in Donegal half the price and with twice the space."

"What would I be doing with space? Anyway, I don't think I could leave the city now."

I could hear the fondness in his voice and it warmed me. Despite his love of Glenties in Donegal, he was content in Dublin.

We ordered our food: two fish pies, with a pint of stout and a pot of tea.

"I thought Georgina took it well enough," Gabriel said.

"She did. I expected her to be more upset."

"Why wasn't she, do you think?"

116

I hadn't thought of her reaction as an issue in itself.

"I suppose, with the children there, and with her worried about Emma, maybe it didn't really sink in, or maybe she's just had so many things to deal with since Andrew's death . . ."

"Right."

"Gabriel?" I watched him as he took another mouthful of his pint.

"No, you're right, you know her better than I do and she has a lot on her plate." He rubbed his mouth though there was no beer froth there. "It will probably only hit her tonight – keep her awake probably."

"If that doesn't, Emma will. Night terrors. The poor girl must be tormented." I remembered as a child waking up in the middle of night, screaming from a nightmare, the figure of some ghostly woman who had been pursuing me still in my head. And it had been Laurence, not my parents, who had sought me out in the dark and comforted me, singing until my fear subsided and I could get back to sleep.

"They're not the same as nightmares, are they?" I asked now.

"I think there's more fear in them. When I was training in Templemore I remember a lad would shout and scream and you couldn't wake him. They could get no good out of him. Sent him home in the end."

"What happened to him, do you know?"

"Met him years later working in his father's pub in Ballyporeen. Homesickness was all it was, he told me – never had them once he got home."

His phone rang then. He reached into his pocket,

answered it, then stood up and indicated with his head toward the smoking area at the back of the pub.

"Trouble," he said when he sat back down. "Matt is not happy with either of us."

"What did we do?"

"I said we'd told Georgina about the weapons being the same. He was raging. Said we'd no business telling her things, that was his job and that I ought to know better."

"We were only trying to protect her – he knows the papers will hear about it soon enough."

"He said he wasn't even sure the pathologist was right. 'Too tidy' he said it was."

"God, and I went and made her think it was a certainty. That's awful." I felt a flush of guilt and began searching in my bag for my phone.

"I'd better call her and explain."

"No, you'd better not, Bea."

I stopped what I was doing.

"Matt says if we do anything else he's going to have us both up for interfering in an investigation."

"That's a bit over the top." As though he'd have the time or resources to do such a thing – and hadn't he asked me to help in the first place?

"He doesn't think so. After I told him he said the reason he called in the first place was to give out. Claire Davis said you questioned her about Georgina and Andrew."

"Oh."

"He says we should take it as an official warning to butt out of the Dalton murder. He said to tell you not to have any more contact with Georgina."

That was too much and Gabriel knew it. I was firm.

"Georgina is my friend. I'm not just going to abandon her because McCann tells me to. And he can't make me no matter what he says." I would have been angry if it weren't for the fact I felt guilty now about what we'd told Georgina and a bit sheepish about being caught out asking Claire Davis questions. I drained a last drop of tea from the tiny pot I'd been given and drank it back.

"He didn't say we should butt out of Billie's case, did he?"

"Not explicitly, Bea, no. But . . ."

I ignored the implication and we finished our food.

"Will I drop you up to the house?" I organised myself to leave.

"I'll walk, thanks. I'll just pay for this."

"You can get it next time," I said.

He frowned at me but didn't argue.

Outside on the street, a cool breeze licked at us.

"Not sure if I should even tell you . . . the other thing he said . . ."

He had my full attention.

"The test on the stuff we found in Andrew's jacket. Rohypnol."

"No! Isn't that the date rape drug?"

"'Fraid so, and Bea . . . Matt said if you tell Georgina he'll personally rob the tax disc off your car and then have you charged for not having one."

I drove home, McCann's message still in my ears, and when I parked I checked that my tax disc was still in place.

Chapter 14

I had indigestion going to bed and blamed it on the relish served with the fish pie I'd eaten in Mulligan's. I'd swallowed three antacids and taken a glass of milk with me to bed, but every time I lay down I had a burning sensation in the centre of my chest. I knew it wasn't just the food. It had been a stressful day. I couldn't help thinking of Georgina, at home, worrying about Emma, and worrying afresh about Andrew and whether or not he was connected with Billie.

I was tempted to phone her, not to tell her anything, but just to offer an ear. At half eleven, though, I knew it was too late. She might already be in bed and a call would disturb Emma.

Fresh from McCann's admonishment, I felt wary of contacting her, too. I had to admit to myself that if I did phone I might be tempted to share what I knew about the Rohypnol. I decided it would be best to leave it for a day or two.

Apart from the heartburn, the Rohypnol was also keeping me awake. I had searched the internet when I got home and "date drug" had jumped out from every page. There were photos too of a little white pill that looked no different from an aspirin. There were connections to cases from all over the world in which women had been drugged and then assaulted, and their memories of the events were, at best, sketchy. Some websites offered the drug for sale. Other, more reputable sites, explained the drug's chemical name was flunitrazepam and it could be used to treat severe insomnia. I remembered then Georgina had told me she suffered from insomnia and took a sleeping pill regularly. Perhaps that was what it was – Andrew had borrowed some of his wife's pills to help him sleep. But why carry them around in his jacket pocket? I thought again of the little package and the white powder. Why had it been ground? Or perhaps the dry-cleaning process had broken it up? Or had Georgina done it with the iron? Could that have been the reason for his outburst when he saw her ironing the jacket?

I felt cold in bed all of a sudden. How well did I know Andrew? Could he have been the kind of man who would carry around such a powerful drug in the hope he would find an opportunity to use it? I had seen him with his children, he was loving and attentive. And he'd adored Georgina. He'd seemed to me to be a contented man. Contented men didn't go around looking for opportunities to use a date-rape drug. No, that couldn't be right.

What was it that Gabriel had told me? "The simplest explanation is often the right one." The simple explanation was he couldn't sleep so he borrowed his wife's medication. And who knew how it got crushed? It was in that zipped-up pocket for at least three months. Ideas and notions circulated in my head. I tried to sleep but knew I couldn't until I had voiced them. I realised too that there was really only one person I wanted to talk to. Gabriel.

I told myself I'd let his phone ring three times then hang up.

He answered on the second ring. "Hello."

"Were you asleep?"

"No, sitting up in bed reading *The Donegal Democrat*."

I had forgotten he had the newspaper posted to him every week so he could keep in touch with events back home.

"Anything in it?"

"The usual local stuff, nothing too exciting. Births, deaths, marriages. Photos of a charity do in the Highland Hotel. And someone opened an internet café in the village. Can you believe it? Not the place I left, anyway."

"What's that line – 'the past is another country' or 'a foreign country', something like that, a strange place anyway."

"That's for sure. When I think of my childhood there . . . the innocence of it."

I could hear him put the paper down and imagined him taking off his reading glasses. When he spoke again his voice was lower, softer.

"Haven't really been able to concentrate on the paper, to tell the truth, Bea. Can't stop thinking about Billie."

"I'm sure."

"Can't help thinking of how cross I was with the state

she left the living room in and the wet floor in the bathroom and the bleached towels."

"That was only natural, though." There was a part of me at that moment that would have liked to be in bed beside him so that I could put my arms around him.

"The house is dreary without her, Bea. She was so . . . I don't remember ever being as bright as she was in my twenties. I don't remember even knowing anyone that bright. I was too busy acting the serious policeman and trying to get on in the force. Too busy to even try very hard with women."

His tone was intimate, wistful. I thought it must have been the effect of the time of night and the fact we were both in our beds, at that most personal point in our days.

He went on. "It wasn't that I didn't want to, it was just when I was young I thought women took my focus away and I resented it at the time. Then it was too late to try."

"It's never too late." I said the words without thinking of their impact.

"No?"

"What I mean is, you never know what woman is around the corner for you." I coughed. "I phoned to ask you about the Rohypnol."

"Right." His voice was flat now.

"I couldn't sleep thinking about it. Do you think it could have got crushed in the dry cleaning?"

"Crushed in the dry cleaning? That's what you phoned me to ask? I really don't know, Bea, and right now I'm not sure I give a damn. Do you want to know what's been keeping me awake? Do you?"

123

"Of course, you know I do."

"Every time I close my eyes I can see the shape of Billie's head from the back, her spiky blonde hair, and the red running through it and the caved-in bone."

"Ah no, Gabriel."

"I keep thinking I should have known."

He sounded angry then and I felt he was angry with me as well as with everything else.

"How could you, though?" I wasn't saying the right words, I wasn't soothing him.

"Do you know what it is, Bea? Sometimes you just . . . I'm tired. I'll call you tomorrow." He hung up then, without saying goodnight.

I put my phone down on my locker where the diary I'd found in Oxmantown Road still sat. I'd been tempted to talk to him about it, to find out what happened in the case. I was puzzled about why he kept it. Shouldn't I just have asked him?

I imagined his reaction then – he would be angry that I'd taken it like a sneak thief, that I'd kept it and that I'd read it without telling him. He would be hurt that I'd do such a thing to him. It didn't matter that I'd taken it accidentally. No. I would have to return it without Gabriel finding out. I would have to do my very best to forget about it afterwards, to pretend I hadn't seen it. That way, I wouldn't need to say a word about it to anyone.

Chapter 15

Tuesday, November 1st, 2016

I had checked my email early on Tuesday morning and found a note from Úna Hollister saying the O'Malley case was resuming on Wednesday. So when Georgina called and asked me to meet her for coffee I'd said I could.

"I've left the children with a neighbour. They have half a dozen DVDs and their trick or treats, so they'll be fine for an hour or two," Georgina said when I sat down at her table in the window of Bewley's café on Westmoreland Street.

Despite its takeover by a multinational and the green mermaid sign in its window, I refused to call it anything else. I was sitting at a table on an uncomfortable chair, with Georgina opposite me. She had sounded distraught on the phone, saying she wanted to meet "away from the house". Now she tasted her coffee and picked at a slice of chocolate cake she had ordered but obviously did not want.

"I'm afraid at the house now, sometimes," she said, explaining why she wanted to meet me in town.

"Afraid of what?" She wasn't the easily frightened sort.

"Do you remember Lar?"

It took a minute for me to recall the man. "That friend of Andrew's who called by?"

"That's him. He came by again last Friday. He had a photo of when they were kids together." She stirred her coffee. "I think he wanted to prove their friendship to me, you know?"

"Oh?"

"Then he said Andrew owed him money. Ten thousand. He said Andrew promised in July that he would wire it to him in Canada. Then, of course, he didn't."

"What did you say to him?"

"Nothing. I didn't know what to say. I mean, I haven't got that kind of money."

She put her head down and I thought she might cry. But after a while, she lifted her chin and looked at me, her eyes glistening with anger.

"I didn't know him at all, did I? I didn't know anything about him." She opened her bag, took out a photo and slapped it onto the table.

"*There*."

She pushed it across to me with her fingertips. I picked it up. It was a group of boys. She pointed out Andrew and then Lar Sheils – his hand, I could see, was resting on her husband's shoulder. There was something proprietorial about the gesture. It was uncomfortable to look at.

"I asked him what Andrew was like back then and he said they were the best of mates. 'Gas', he called him.

Said they were 'thick as thieves and always gettin' into scrapes', made it sound like they were in some Enid Blyton story."

I tried to picture Andrew as he was then, sitting behind a school desk, carrying a satchel, walking home with his friends.

"I asked him if he knew Andrew's parents. He said he'd only met his foster family. The Brophys, he said they were called."

I tried to hide my surprise.

"You'd think that would be something I'd know, wouldn't you, that he was fostered for a few years?"

I supposed there were plenty of people who had tough childhoods and just didn't want to talk about them and I said so.

"He might have felt embarrassed."

"Embarrassed, with me? I'm his wife . . . was his wife." She exhaled a short breath. "If he was hiding that, Bea, what else was he hiding? And what about his sister, Tracy? She never said a thing about it."

"You should ask her. Maybe she knows Lar Sheils."

"And do you know what Sheils told me? He said Andrew was very bright in school and that Andrew called the Brophys 'nice but thick'. Doesn't that seem cruel?"

I didn't know how to respond to that. I had found it was never a good idea to either agree or disagree when a friend criticised a member of her own family. I poured myself more tea.

"I got the impression Andrew had been sneering at them, like he thought he was better than them."

127

"He was a child. Children can be very judgmental."

She played with her cake again, dividing it with the edge of her fork as though she might eat it.

"He never told me he was fostered. Then this man shows up and knows more about my husband than I do."

"Hold on, hold on – did you say you feel frightened at home?" Wasn't that what she started out telling me?

"I feel as though, this sounds crazy, Bea, as though someone is watching the house, maybe him." She gave up on the cake then, pushing the plate away from her.

"You're the sanest person I know, Georgina. What happened to make you think that?"

I handed the photograph back to her. She glanced at it once more and put it away.

"I don't know – there was something last night, when I went out to the car to check I'd locked it, I thought I saw someone. Maybe I imagined it."

"What did you see?"

"I thought there was someone stopped at the gate – there was a shadow, then footsteps – but when I walked out onto the avenue, I couldn't see anyone." Her voice shook as she said that.

"Georgina – if you saw someone, you saw someone. And that's not something you can ignore. You should ring Store Street." I was thinking about the weapon that killed Billie and Andrew, still out there somewhere.

"No. I'll feel like a fool telling the guards. Maybe I imagined it, I don't know."

I pitied her. She had been through so much and now another worry.

128

"The thing is I don't have that kind of money to pay Sheils."

"Even if you did, you couldn't give it to him. He could have made the whole thing up, for all you know."

"You think so?"

She didn't look convinced. It puzzled me that she seemed ready to believe this stranger about her husband's debt when she hadn't known anything about it.

"Of course. But you'll have to tell the guards. And if that man comes to the door again, don't answer it. You don't know what he's capable of."

She nodded. "I hate all this. I hate hearing things about Andrew and knowing people are judging him. And judging me."

"No one is judging you, Georgina. You can't be responsible for a life your husband hid from you."

I called Gabriel on my way home and spoke to him tentatively at first, afraid that our conversation from the night before might still be lingering between us. But he seemed brighter and talked to me as though nothing had happened. I told him about meeting Georgina.

"I'm very worried . . . Will you see what you can find out about this Lar Sheils?"

"Do you think she'll call McCann?"

"I hope she does, but it's hard to know, the way she is at the moment."

"Maybe I'll tell him myself anyway." He said it as more of a suggestion than a decision.

I told him I'd prefer if he didn't. I was still smarting from McCann's threat about interfering.

"Would you not see what you can find out yourself?" I said.

He sighed on the other end of the phone. "You're no end of trouble, do you know that?"

"Sorry." I knew I didn't sound sorry and had to admit to myself that I wasn't. I intended to do all I could to help Georgina, even if it meant pestering friends. "I wonder if Andrew's foster parents are still around. Could we find out anything about them?"

"We could try, but the Child and Family Agency is notoriously tight with information – I think McCann would need a court order or something, if he wanted the file."

"Or . . ."

"What?"

"Suppose Andrew got into trouble at some stage when he was a kid. Wouldn't it all be on PULSE?" PULSE, the internal garda database, was used to hold records of all cases, going back years. "Maybe one of the lads would have a look for you, get the name and address?"

"You know that could get someone into a lot of trouble."

"What harm could a quick look do? If there's nothing, there's nothing."

Gabriel sighed again and I knew he would do his best.

"Should you not be back to work?" he asked.

"Tomorrow. The O'Malley case is back."

"Maybe they'll kiss and make up."

I laughed and said goodbye.

While I prepared my evening meal, I thought about Georgina. It seemed only a short time since she was helping me, offering me a break away in Wexford when things got difficult after the O'Farrell trial. How perfect her life had seemed to me then, with her Seafield Cottage in Ballymoney, her lovely husband and sweet children. Now the lovely husband was gone and she seemed always on edge, always worried for herself and her family.

I supposed that no one could really know what other people's lives were like. It would probably be unbearable to know such things, too great a burden for any one person to carry. What was it Mother used to say, trying to console me as a child after some great disappointment? "The Lord only gives you a cross you can bear." I wondered if she had still believed that after my brother Laurence died. That had been too great a cross for anyone and Mother and Father had withered beneath its weight. What nonsense, it seemed to me, that some great omnipotent power had pre-ordained such things. The truth, as I saw it, was that bad things happened to good, bad and middling people, randomly and with no great plan. I didn't think my life, or anyone else's, was a tapestry stitched and predetermined. It was only in the looking back that people can discern the twists and turns that make up their stories. One casual "yes" instead of "no" could change everything and nobody could convince me otherwise. I remembered having that conversation with Gabriel, one evening after we'd had a meal together. He had taken a theological perspective and after I had, as best I could, deconstructed his argument, he had seemed so disenchanted with me that I'd thought he'd never want to speak to me again. But the following day he'd said it had only been pity I'd seen on his face and that he'd light a candle for me at Mass on Sunday.

In the midst of these thoughts and of making a carbonara sauce to put on pasta, my phone rang again.

"I forgot to say," was Gabriel's opening, "they've had the laptop looked at. Matt says I won't be getting it back anytime soon."

"Did he tell you what they'd found?"

"He said he couldn't, said he wants me to come in for a chat."

I thought he sounded not worried, but perplexed.

"What about?"

"General things, he said, about Billie, and a few questions about the laptop. Said I'd drop by tomorrow morning."

"Is there anything . . . Do you want to run over a few things?"

There was silence and I imagined him rubbing his chin.

"Better not. No point – sure, I've told him everything already."

"I'm getting the impression you think there might be more to it."

"Ah no . . . it'll be grand. I'll talk to you after."

He rang off and I mixed a double portion of spaghetti into the sauce. I could eat one and take the second to Phoenix House for lunch tomorrow. I hoped they'd let me use the microwave in the Courts Service canteen. I'd never liked cold pasta.

Chapter 16

Wednesday, November 2nd, 2016

In Court 32, Mrs O'Malley's evidence against her husband had resumed. And he was struggling to control his reactions, shouting occasionally when he didn't agree with his wife, much to the growing annoyance of the judge.

His wife was complaining now that since he moved out, into an apartment at Spencer Dock, near the Irish Financial Services Centre, he had reduced his contribution to the family finances and was not providing enough for their children.

"Do you work outside the home, Mrs O'Malley?" Úna Hollister asked her client.

"Yes, I'm a buyer for Arnotts, but I don't earn enough to manage everything on my own."

"Of course not, and you shouldn't have to. The children are not just your responsibility. Now your outgoings . . ."

Figures are trickier to record than words. I required all of my powers of concentration not to drift. Úna Hollister went through everything – the mortgage, the household bills, the children's clothing, their medical and dental expenses, the private school tuition fees, ballet, piano, clarinet, extra-curricular French, and wall-climbing lessons.

There was some rudimentary maths done then by Ms Hollister, with a lot of adding up and a little division.

"Do you think child maintenance of €150 per week per child would be sufficient, Mrs O'Malley?"

"Yes, provided I have help with the mortgage."

I could hear Mr O'Malley gasping at the back of the room.

"Do I have all that documentation, Ms Hollister, income and expenditure?" the judge asked.

"It's in the affidavit, judge."

"Fine."

"Now the mortgage." Ms Hollister launched into the details, giving the judge the address of the current family home, its cost and the monthly repayments.

"And you wish to remain living there, Mrs O'Malley?"

"Of course! I mean, as long as the children are still in education anyhow."

"And your husband should pay half the mortgage?"

"Yes, I think that's fair."

Again Mr O'Malley was on his feet.

"*You can't have everything!*" he shouted at his wife.

Instead of ignoring him, as she had no doubt been advised, she let herself go.

"You left, you're the one who left!" she spat, as though she had been waiting for the chance to throw blame at him.

The judge raised his hand.

"I'm not having this. I know these things can be –

emotional, but I'm not having shouting matches in my court." He looked from Úna Hollister to Ruby Clements and back again. "I'm going to give you five minutes." He stood up and swept out of the courtroom, an air of indignation cloaked about him.

The two barristers whispered intently to their clients. My mind drifted to Georgina. I had texted to see if she'd had any more night-time visitors. She messaged back: **"No, don't think so, but Emma very upset again last night."** I suggested she take her to the doctor again and she said she would.

When the judge reappeared, Ruby Clements was the first on her feet. "Apologies, judge, it won't happen again."

"Yes, judge, my client also apologises," said Úna Hollister.

"Right then. Where were we?"

Mrs O'Malley took her position in the witness box and the questioning continued.

"Your husband has said he wants joint custody – do you object to that, Mrs O'Malley?" Úna Hollister asked.

"He's not fit. Do you know on one occasion we were at the park and Robin was no more than five and he picked him up and dangled him by his heels over the side of this little bridge going over the river? And Robin was screaming with fear and *he* was laughing like it was great fun. He can't be trusted with them. Robin came back from his place last month with a black eye – I don't know what happened to him."

"What did Robin say happened?" the judge intervened.

"He said it was an accident, that he walked into a door. But he would say that, wouldn't he?"

"What do you mean?" Ms Hollister asked.

"He's afraid, isn't he, of what his father might do?"

An exasperated "*bah*" came from Mr O'Malley but he said nothing.

"And how is your husband with the girls, Mrs O'Malley?" the barrister asked.

"The girls? He treats them like they're invisible most of the time. I let them stay with him for a weekend in September and when they came home they looked completely neglected."

A loud "*Ah!*" came from the back of the court.

"In what way neglected, Mrs O'Malley?"

"They were both dirty and Petal's hair was in knots and Bluebell said she had to help her little sister to get dressed and she had to brush her hair. 'Daddy doesn't care,' she said to me when she got home. I could have cried."

"Anything else?"

Mrs O'Malley looked down at her husband. "Bluebell said he went out in the evening and left them alone for hours."

"*No!*" Mr O'Malley couldn't control himself any longer.

"Are there welfare concerns?" the judge asked Ms Hollister.

"We believe so, judge, yes."

Ruby Clements stood up. "Judge, there are no welfare concerns. Mr O'Malley is a devoted father. He would never neglect the children or use violence or leave them alone. Mrs O'Malley is fabricating."

"*Hmm.* Perhaps in the best interests of everyone,

including the children, we should have a Section 47 report? I would be happier if we did that."

There was a brief conversation between the barristers and then with the O'Malleys. I could hear Ms Hollister explain that a report would be written for the judge by a psychologist after speaking with the children and both parents. And there would recommendations made about the children.

"Anyone in mind, then? Dr Rita McArdle perhaps?" the judge asked.

Ms Clements glanced over her shoulder and nodded at her client who nodded back. "My client has no objection to Dr McArdle."

"And Mrs O'Malley is fine with that," said Ms Hollister.

"Very well, let's proceed with the Section 47. Any thoughts on length of adjournment?"

Ms Clements was back on her feet.

"Judge, my client feels he has not been able to tell you his side . . . he would prefer if there was no adjournment and he could give his evidence before you receive the Section 47 report."

The judge sighed. "Very well, the Section 47 can be put in train and I will hear evidence from Mr O'Malley beginning tomorrow. Any objections to that, Ms Hollister?"

"None, judge. But cross-examination of my client?"

"Yes, tomorrow morning for that I'd imagine at this stage?"

"Yes, judge."

"Let's continue then."

At lunch, I managed to heat up my pasta in the Courts Service canteen microwave without challenge. I took it back to my office and ate while uploading the O'Malley file onto my laptop. Gabriel came into my mind then and the questioning he would face in Store Street. McCann knew him too well to think he was involved in Billie's death, so what was it in Gabriel's voice that had so worried me? What had he not told me?

Back in court, the afternoon sped by, the words of Mrs O'Malley's evidence flowed through my fingers and into the machine, indelible and definitive.

It was not until five when I checked my phone before packing away my equipment that I noticed a missed call from Gabriel and then, a minute later, a text message.

"Any chance of a word this evening? Would you call here?"

I thought about going straight to Gabriel's from Phoenix House but realised this might be a good opportunity to return the diary. It had been on my conscience and I was keen to put it back where I'd found it. I would just say nothing at all about it to Gabriel.

"See you at seven. Please have food."

He responded straight away that he would. I went back to Clontarf, changed, put the diary in my bag and drove to Stoneybatter.

Salty batter crackled in my mouth and made way for the creamy cod inside. The chips were just how I liked them, with too much vinegar. I had to admit there was nothing quite like being hungry to help me appreciate food.

Gabriel had arrived at his front door with the brown-paper bag from the local chip shop just as I'd pulled up in the car.

138

"Perfect timing," I'd said, following him into Number 9.

He'd responded with a bare nod and when he spoke he'd sounded tired.

"Divvy it up, will you? I'll make the tea." He turned on the kettle and buttered rounds of bread while waiting for it to boil.

When all was prepared, we took our food into the living room and sat with the plates on our laps.

"Were you there long?" I opened the conversation after a few mouthfuls.

"Long enough."

I waited. He bit into a sandwich he'd made with his chips.

"Tell you the truth, it was very strange."

"Oh?" I was sure it must have been for a man like him, so used to asking the questions.

"Sitting the other side of the table. Matt there firing the questions. Recorder on."

"Recorder? Why?" That seemed a bit excessive.

He shrugged. "Matt said it's just the way they do things now. Bit of a shock though."

"I can imagine."

He turned his plate anti-clockwise on his lap and attacked the tail end of his fish.

"All about Billie first – when she moved in, where I met her, what hours she kept, had she anyone back to the house with her. I told them everything I could."

"Course."

"Then the laptop – when did I lend it to her, how often did I use it, did anyone else use it. Dates and times . . . hard to remember." He stopped to eat again.

"Did they say what they found on it?"

"After, when the interview – Jesus, me being interviewed – when I was outside the station, Matt told me."

Gabriel described standing shoulder to shoulder with the detective just outside the door of Store Street watching a silver tram go by, packed with people. McCann had remarked on the willingness of people to put up with uncomfortable conditions "like sardines in a can". Then he'd said it was the searches they were interested in.

I noticed Gabriel's discomfort then, and thought I saw a few beads of sweat on his upper lip.

"She was looking up sex stuff, searching for porn films."

It seemed to me that he was embarrassed on her behalf.

"They think she might have got mixed up with some nasty types. Needed to make sure it wasn't me searching." He drained his mug and suggested he'd make more tea. "Wash the grease down." When he came back, his colour had returned to normal.

"Had he anything else to say?"

"Talked about the weapon – remember I told you what Bob said?"

"I do."

"The lads agree now with the state pathologist, they think Billie and Andrew could have been killed with the same weapon, a bat or something like that."

"Okay . . ." I thought I saw, for just a moment, a kind of confusion in his eyes. "Go on."

"Thing is, Bea, I can't find my old cosh." He stood and picked up his plate, placed it on mine and collected the knives and forks.

"Hold on, sit down for a second." I remembered seeing him with it once or twice, a kind of baton with a heavy, metal weight at the business end.

He put the cutlery down and sat.

"I haven't told Matt mine's missing. Strictly speaking, I should have handed it in at the station on the day I retired, but I never got round to it."

"Okay. I'm sure we can figure this out. Start with when you had it last."

He scratched his head. "I had it in the drawer by my bed for a long time. Then one night a few months ago I heard noises out the back and I took it out and went downstairs. I put the light on in the kitchen and I caught a glimpse of a young lad through the window, scrambling over the wall of the yard, black tracksuit bottoms, T-shirt, skinny bit of a thing. He'd been trying to jimmy open the back door into the kitchen." He took a breath and pushed his lips together. "I definitely had it then, but I don't remember bringing it back upstairs and I can't find it."

"Will I help you look?"

He nodded. We cleared away the dishes and started the search. After a few minutes of rummaging around, I stopped.

"Wait a minute, wait. We need to be systematic about this. I'll take the kitchen, you take the living room, the backyard and under the stairs."

"Living room?"

"You never know."

I searched as thoroughly as I could, pulling out the contents of each press and, despite the desire to dispose of his out-of-date tins, I returned them carefully to where I'd found them. I could hear Gabriel briefly in the living room, then the yard and then knocking around in the cupboard under the stairs. When I'd finished in the kitchen and came out to the hall, I found him half in and half out of the cupboard, throwing items behind him as he searched. When he emerged, there were cobwebs in his hair.

"No." He straightened up and stretched his arms above his head.

I began passing the objects strewn around the hall back to him: old boots, fishing gear, a bag of empty bottles, rusted tools, a heavy coat rolled in a ball. He bent down again to replace them in the cupboard.

While he tidied, I went into the living room, took the diary from my bag and quickly put it back where I'd first found it, behind De Valera. Then I returned to the hall.

"Upstairs?" I said, already starting up. "I'll do Billie's room." I knew I wouldn't find his cosh there. The guards had already been through it and I had cleaned up after them, but I hadn't wanted to suggest I help search Gabriel's room. Too many ghosts.

The black sacks I had packed the last time were still resting inside the door of what had reverted to being the spare room. I opened the empty wardrobe and checked it. Still empty. I got down on my hands and knees to look under the bed. Nothing. Then I stood up on the bed to look at the top of the wardrobe. There was only a small space between it and the ceiling. I put my hand in and felt around. There was something just out of reach at my fingertips, something solid, wedged in place. I went downstairs, found a sweeping brush and took it back to the room. Standing on the bed again, I inserted the brush handle behind the object and pushed forward, managing to manoeuvre it gradually until it was sticking out and I could grasp it. A shallow biscuit tin, with a red bus embossed on the lid.

"Gabriel!"

"No luck." He spoke as he came into the room. "What's that?"

I handed it to him. "Is it yours?"

"No."

He turned it over a couple of times and then eased the lid open. There was a faint smell of shortbread. Inside were photos mixed with hair pins and bobbins.

"Let's go down."

In the kitchen, he spread the contents of the box on the table, separating the photos from the hair accessories. I picked up one of the photos. A teenage Billie looked out at me, dark-haired, with a wide smile and eyes filled with merriment.

"Just look at her." I passed the photo to Gabriel.

He examined it and turned it over in his hand. On the reverse, someone had written "*Dream big*".

"She looks so . . ." I couldn't find the words for her loveliness.

"I know."

There was nothing written on the backs of any of the other photos. They were all of Billie at various ages, I guessed between ten and seventeen years old. In some she was alone, in others in a group. In one she was with a woman who looked like she could be her mother.

"I suppose you'd better give all of this to McCann."

He put them back in the box then.

"I'll call Matt and let him know." He hesitated. "Maybe I'll just tell him I was going to paint and I moved the wardrobe?"

I nodded agreement.

When the phone call was over, Gabriel asked whether I might be able to stay a while longer. "Matt said he'd call over himself for this – and I'd be happier with a bit of company."

"Did he say how long he'd be?"

"He's knocking off now, so he said he'd come straight here."

"Have you any paint?"

"Why?"

"Wouldn't you want evidence that you were painting?"

He left the room and came back with an old can of white and two old, poorly cleaned brushes, their bristles congealed with paint remnants.

"I'll just leave these up in the room and he'll see them if he asks to go up."

I didn't laugh, though it was hard not to. He had always been a terrible liar.

But when McCann called fifteen minutes later, he didn't ask about the painting at all.

He sat on an armchair in the living room and scanned the photos without comment, then laid the box on the coffee table.

He accepted a small whiskey from Gabriel – "just a drop – I have the car," he said, and sat back, his legs stretched out in front of him like a man in his own home. "I needn't tell you – we're struggling with this one." He lifted the amber liquid to his lips and put it down again without drinking. "If the weapon is the same, then there has to be a connection between Billie and Dalton, but I just can't see it." He lifted the glass again and this time sipped. "Apart from you two of course."

"Pardon?" I hadn't expected him to say that.

"I mean in the sense ye knew both of them – not well, I'm not suggesting well." He took a second sip of whiskey and sighed. "It's all very messy."

I had promised myself before he'd arrived that I'd keep my mouth shut, but I found that impossible now.

"What about the childcare woman in the casino – Claire Davis?" I asked. "Have you nothing to go on with her?"

"Yes, well, she has nothing in her background we know of. She did have a bit of a . . . something with Dalton, briefly she says, and we've nothing to show otherwise. And no connection with Billie."

"So Georgina was right then, she didn't imagine it." I blurted out the words without thinking.

"What's that?" He turned his head as though he hadn't quite heard me, though I knew he had.

I found myself then telling McCann about Georgina's suspicions that Andrew might have been having an affair because of the look that Andrew had given Claire Davis.

"A look?" He glanced at Gabriel, who nodded at him as though they were both in agreement that nothing could be ascertained from a look. "And is she the jealous type, do you think?"

"Ah no, she's too sensible," I said quickly, regretting that I had mentioned it at all.

"Not sensible enough to be telling us everything, though, is she?" He scratched his head, the fingers of his left hand digging through his black curls. "What else are you not telling me, Bea?" His tone was headmasterly.

I looked away from him and glanced at Gabriel, who was scrutinising the back of his own hand.

"Lar Sheils."

"Who?"

"A friend of Andrew's. He's been calling by and asking Georgina for money. Says he's owed it."

"For feck sake!" He drained his glass. "Who is this fella? When did he call?" He took a notebook from the outside pocket of his jacket and a pen from the inside. He sat forward and clicked on the top of the pen.

I hesitated.

"Well?" he said, turning the pages of the notebook to find an empty space.

"A couple of days ago. He says they were in school together, and Andrew borrowed ten thousand from him and never paid it back. Says he was in Canada when he died and was waiting on the money."

He continued writing. "And?"

"That's it."

"Did you meet him yourself?"

"He called in once when I was over there, but only to sympathise."

"So that's not all then, is it? Tell me what he looked like."

I closed my eyes and did my best to describe Sheils in as much detail as possible. I couldn't get beyond "Chihuahua" for his face.

"Right then." McCann snapped his notebook shut and replaced it in his pocket. "This case is hard enough without you working against me."

"I'm not."

"Do you want me to catch this killer or what?" He looked at me and then Gabriel, and I thought I could see in him a level of desperation.

"Of course we do. And from now on, anything I hear, or see, I'll tell you." I felt guilty for not having kept him informed, and at the same time protective of Georgina.

"Okay then."

"Should be getting home."

Gabriel walked him to the door and then I noticed Billie's biscuit tin still on the table. I ran out as he was pulling away and stopped him. He rolled down the window.

"What?"

"You forgot this." I handed him the tin.

"That's a man under pressure," I remarked to Gabriel as the detective's car rounded the corner at the end of the road.

Chapter 17

Saturday, November 5th, 2016

It was Gabriel who was late arriving at Hanlon's this time – half an hour late. We'd arranged to meet at noon, hoping we might be able to talk again to Derek Johnston and glean more information about Billie's past. I had driven to Clontarf, taken the DART to town and walked out to the pub.

Gabriel hadn't even messaged me to let me know he was delayed and I was all set to complain, but the sight of him made me change my mind. There were dark shadows under his eyes and his grey hair, normally so neat, was standing on end at the crown of his head. He sat down on the chair opposite me as though he had dragged himself to the pub like a sack of potatoes.

"Bad night?"

He lifted his shoulders and dropped them again, filling his cheeks with air as he exhaled.

"Every time I closed my eyes I could see Billie smiling at me, standing there at the bar, smiling."

"Oh Gabriel."

"I keep replaying things in my head."

"Would you go to the doctor? Get something to help you sleep?"

He looked at me as though I'd suggested he go to the moon.

"Will I get you a pint then?" I signalled to Piotr the barman without waiting for an answer.

"I used to go down to breakfast and in she'd come to the kitchen, like, I don't know, a firefly or something, all energy."

"I know." I could see Piotr filling a glass out of the corner of my eye.

"I keep thinking of the last morning – it goes round and round. Did I tell you she slept late?"

"No, you didn't."

"I had to wake her for work. She went out the door still chewing that muesli she liked. I said to her that if she didn't hurry up I'd be at the pub before she was. And she said 'That's no great boast on your part' and wouldn't I be better off getting an allotment and growing a few veggies." He half smiled at the memory.

The pint came and Piotr put it on the table. Gabriel didn't seem to notice.

"And I said 'You're in sharp form this morning' and she came back with 'Wouldn't I have to be around you, old man?'."

He paused, picked up his pint then and took a long sup out of it.

"She was just the sort of girl, if you had a daughter, that you'd want her to be. Do you know what I mean?"

"I do."

He was not looking at me but was focusing on his

half-empty glass and I could see he was struggling to hold on to his emotions.

"I keep thinking what if I hadn't knocked on her door to get her out of bed? She might have been so late she'd have lost her job, and she wouldn't have been down in that cellar. Or what if I'd hung around that day in Hanlon's instead of going off for my walk?"

"Don't, Gabriel."

"When I had my two pints, she said to me I could always have another. Couldn't I have my lunch with her, she said, instead of going out in the cold. But of course I said no, I needed the exercise. Didn't want to change my routine."

He finished his pint with one gulp and I signalled for another. A part of me wanted him to stop talking, to tell him there was no reason for him to feel that way, but I knew he needed to keep going.

"I didn't even thank her for the offer. It never occurred to me that she wasn't just being kind, that maybe she was afraid of something and wanted me to stay. If I'd only listened properly, if I'd looked at her properly even, I might have realised that." His words oozed regret.

"You were kindness itself to Billie, you have nothing to feel guilty about, Gabriel."

He picked up his second pint and took a mouthful and, though he didn't say anything, I knew he had dismissed my attempt at consolation as only flannel talk.

He rubbed his eyes and then waved at Piotr. The barman came straight over.

"Your boss around?"

"I'm expecting him in twenty minutes."

"Tell him we want a word, will you?"

He had regained his composure and I chided myself for feeling happier with him like that. What was it that made me uncomfortable about seeing him vulnerable? Wasn't it laudable for him to show his emotions and hadn't he every right to be upset? What was wrong with me that I found that hard to take?

When Derek Johnston arrived, Piotr directed him to our table.

"What's up?" He stood with his arms folded.

"Have yeh a minute?" Gabriel asked. "We won't keep you. We're just trying to figure out a few things about Billie, why she was killed."

He reluctantly sat down beside us.

"The till, wasn't it?" He waved vaguely in the direction of the bar.

"You don't believe that, do you? It makes no sense," Gabriel said.

Derek ran his hand over the top of his flat hair. "I don't know what you want me to say – what information are you looking for?"

"Tell us what she was like, what she did the last few days before she moved out of your place. Was there anything bothering her?"

Gabriel's tone was cool now and steady. I admired him for it.

"Apart from the usual? We were always rowing about the state of the place. Believe it or not, I'm a bit of a neat freak, but she was so disorganised, so messy."

Gabriel nodded in sympathy. I had a flashback to his living room, strewn with wet towels and dirty dishes.

"How did you finish up with her?" I asked.

"Okay, so we had this big row, bigger than usual, and I said I just couldn't take it anymore and she'd have to go. I gave her a couple of days to get organised. There was one thing – a bit odd now that I think of it." He paused and bit his lower lip. "The day before she moved out, she was getting her stuff together, but she had it everywhere. And I was growling about it and she said she'd clean it up. Then she said she had to go out. And the place was a tip." His voice lifted an octave as though he still couldn't believe she could walk out and leave such a mess behind her. "I couldn't sit there just looking at it while she was gone, so I started clearing it all, just shoving it into black sacks. Then she came back. I remember she looked excited or something. So I asked her why."

"And?" We both leaned toward him.

"At first she wouldn't tell me. But then I said 'Ah, come on – I can see you're on a buzz' and she said she'd made a promise to herself and now she'd kept it and it didn't matter anymore." He paused, breathing hard, like a man beginning to realise that someone he had loved was really gone.

"What time of the day was it, do you know?" Gabriel asked.

"God, now . . ." He bit his lip again. "I think she went about four and was back a couple of hours later, maybe at six or seven."

"And when was that, do you remember? The date?" I pressed him.

"Ah Jaysus, June sometime, maybe toward the end of June, or else early July."

"Where did she live, do you know, before she came to my house?" Gabriel asked then.

"Just up the road. She got a room in a basement on the North Circular. She said the landlord threw her out. He wanted to sell the whole place. Bullshit. He probably just wanted to put her rent up."

"What makes you say that?" I asked.

"I've seen some of them, some of the other tenants that were there when Billie was. They're still there – they must've agreed to pay extra."

Gabriel had mentioned that Billie was vague about the details when she'd told him she'd nowhere to go. I wondered if there was something about her old digs that she hadn't wanted him to know.

"What number?" Gabriel asked.

"Can't remember. Could point it out for you though. Will you be here much longer?"

"We can wait," I said.

"Right so. Give me half an hour." He stood up and moved away from the table, calling to the barman at the same time. "Piotr, pint here please like a good man."

Gabriel didn't decline, though it would be his third of the day. I wondered what had changed Derek's attitude. The defensiveness seemed to have gone and he seemed to want to help. I supposed grief affected people in different ways and his prickliness the last time was driven by shock. And guilt too maybe. Perhaps he, like Gabriel, felt a sense of responsibility for what had happened to Billie in his pub.

The third pint was well finished by the time Derek was ready. It was after two o'clock.

"Are you right?" he said, waiting by the door for us to put our coats on. He gestured in the direction of the park and we followed him, none of us speaking as we walked down the North Circular Road.

"This one." He stopped at Number 30, resting his hand briefly on the silver-coloured railing before turning back in the direction of the pub.

"Thank you!" I called after him.

The three-storey was part of a red-bricked terrace, the height of elegance 100 years before. There were bay windows and more than a dozen granite steps leading up to the front door at first-floor level. The wrought-iron railing that ran at the front of the property and between it and its neighbour was a simple design, well maintained. The door to the basement flat was tucked in behind the flight of steps, like an understairs cupboard. Its windows were curtained with heavy netting, the yellowing of which, in contrast to the railing, seemed to signal neglect.

"We need to find tenants who were around when Billie was here," Gabriel said.

He walked up the steps to the black front door, which was set back from an arch of red bricks that constituted an open porch. I followed. He pushed the doorbell in the centre of an ornate brass disk, its crevices dulled with grime. Neither of us could hear it ring inside the house, so he pressed again, this time harder. After a few minutes, he resorted to a large brass knocker, tinged green, in the centre of the door. Two firm knocks brought the sound of feet in the hall.

A brown-limbed young man in vest and shorts opened the door and squinted out at us.

"What you want?" He looked as though he'd been woken from a deep sleep.

"I'm looking for . . . Do you know Billie Nichols?" Gabriel stepped into the hall without pausing and I followed behind him and closed the door.

The young man didn't try to stop us.

"Who?"

"Billie Nichols, she used to live downstairs."

"Oh. No, I'm only here a month. Dewain might know though, he's here longer. *Dewain! Dewain!*" He called over his shoulder and another man appeared from down the hall.

He was black, muscular, as tall as Gabriel and also wearing vest and shorts.

"Keep it down, man," he said.

"These people want to talk about some Billie woman."

"Billie?" Dewain looked at Gabriel and then at me.

"Yes."

"Go back to bed, Royston, I'll handle it."

I got a glimpse of a room filled with bunk beds, some of them occupied, as Royston disappeared.

"Come on."

We followed Dewain down the hall to a small kitchen that reminded me of a 1980s flat, with its chipped Formica worktop, stained metal sink and faded yellow cupboards. We sat at a small round table.

"We were hoping to speak to someone who knew Billie Nichols when she lived here. She was in the basement," Gabriel said.

"I know. Killed, wasn't she?"

"Yes."

155

"I saw it on the TV. Who are you, police?"

"No, well, I was once, not now. We were friends of hers. Do you remember her at all?"

"Course I do. I was living here when she moved in. Met her coming in the drive, I remember, gave her a hand with her stuff. Nice girl." He picked up a bowl of what looked like soggy cornflakes and took a spoonful.

"Do you know, had she any visitors, any trouble or anything?" I asked.

"A man called by a few times, seemed to be a friend of hers. Short, stocky guy. She didn't seem to mind him, though I heard them rowing once or twice."

"Sounds like her boss. Do you know what they were rowing about?"

"Couldn't make out the words – just the volume I noticed, and the door banging. There was a woman, too. Knocked on the door here one day, said she was Billie's mother. I told her Billie lived in the basement, but she was at work. I told her where to find her."

I remembered what Piotr had said about Billie refusing to speak to her mother.

"Did she say what she wanted?" I asked.

"She said she was her mother – what do all mothers want?" He laughed at his own joke and ate some more breakfast.

"Why did the landlord throw her out, do you know?"

"Landlord? He didn't throw her out. She went cos her mother kept calling by. I heard her banging on the door a few times. I ask Billie why does she never let her in. She says to me 'My life was poisoned and she did nothing to stop it' – sounded real bitter."

156

"Poisoned? What could that mean?" I asked.

He shook his head. "That was all she said. I didn't ask again." He yawned and stood up. "I have to get to work."

"Shift, is it?" Gabriel asked.

"We're all on shifts here, for the work and for the beds."

I was shocked. I had heard about houses that were crammed with beds but never knew the beds might be shared.

We found ourselves back in the hall.

"And the landlord?"

"Jason, his name is. Hang on, I'll find you his number." He went back into the kitchen and returned with his phone, scrolling down through his contacts.

"Here it is." He read out a mobile phone number and I keyed it into my phone.

"Thanks. Do you have a surname?"

"Armitage. Jason Armitage." He opened the door for us. "And sorry about Billie. If there's anything I can do to help – why don't you take my number?"

He called out his number and Gabriel put it into his phone.

We both shook hands with him.

"Dewain what?" Gabriel asked.

"Babangida." He spelt it out so that Gabriel could store it with the number.

Walking up toward the park gates, Gabriel wondered aloud why Billie had told him she was thrown out by her landlord instead of saying she was trying to hide from her mother.

"Maybe she just didn't want to have to deal with the questions you'd probably ask her." It was easy to imagine him trying to cajole her into calling the woman.

"Maybe."

I walked with him to eat a late lunch in Ryan's. His step, I thought, was slower than normal and I put it down to the grief he was carrying with him. He surprised me by not ordering a pint with his stew and having a glass of water instead.

"Had my quota," he said when he saw my face.

"I didn't say anything."

We started to eat and he said he'd give Matt a call. "It might help if he spoke to Dewain."

Halfway through eating his stew, he stopped to talk about the value of legwork in policing.

"Sometimes I think the lads were better off without computers. You made the phone calls, you went and knocked on the doors until you found out what you needed to know. I can't understand why it's taking them so long to find her mother, when she only came looking for Billie a while ago. The woman can't have just vanished."

"It's very odd."

"You know what gets me, Bea? Billie's still up there in the morgue, in storage till they can find some next of kin."

I shivered at the thought of her, lying there cold and alone, waiting to be dealt with. It wasn't decent.

"It's not really Billie," I said. "Only the shell of her."

Chapter 18

Sunday, November 6th, 2016

Jason Armitage had proved easier to find than expected. Gabriel had phoned his number after we'd finished our meal in Ryan's and the call had gone straight to voicemail and a recorded message.

"If you're ringing about Belton Park Gardens, it's on view Sunday afternoon, three o'clock. I'll need two references and a bank statement."

Gabriel and I stood outside the house, in Donnycarney not far from Clontarf, at the appointed time, queuing with half a dozen others, waiting for the door to open in the cool, crisp air. It was a three-bedroom terraced with the pebble-dashed exterior of a former council house. A sign outside said "Armitage Properties" and "For Rent". The number Dewain had given us was also on the sign. There was no landline which we both agreed was not a good thing. It meant there was no office and therefore nowhere a person could go to complain.

At ten past three the door opened and we followed the queue into the hall. It was obvious, once inside, that the house had been Ikea'd. There were new laminate floors and Scandinavian furniture all over the place. When we'd finished our required exploration, we went out to the small back garden. An egg-shaped, check-suited man, with thin, brown hair in a kind of fuzz on his head and a dubious-looking moustache, was balancing on a kitchen stool and having a smoke. Beside him, a pretty young woman, in a close-fitted black skirt, white blouse, black jacket and red patent-leather high heels, stood holding a clipboard.

"Jason Armitage?" Gabriel asked.

Armitage looked us up and down and said, "Twelve hundred a month".

That seemed exorbitant to me for such a tight little house, and I wondered if he'd set the rent based on what he thought we could afford, but I said nothing.

"We're hoping you might be able to help us, Mr Armitage," Gabriel said.

The man got off the stool, dropped his cigarette and ground it under the heel of a shiny black brogue. He was as tall as Gabriel and he moved his feet hip-width apart, as though he might be bracing himself for a complaint.

"We just wanted to ask you about a friend of ours, if you remember her – Billie Nichols."

Armitage glanced at the woman he was with as though deciding whether or not to admit knowing Billie.

"Name's familiar," he said then, tapping his temple with his left index finger. "Billie Nichols, Billie Nichols. Was she a tenant?"

"We believe so, on the North Circular Road," Gabriel said.

"Ring any bells, Felicity?" He turned to the young woman. "This is Felicity Scott, my assistant."

The young woman put out her hand for us to shake in a formal kind of way and spoke as though she was watching her words. "I'm the deputy manager of Armitage Properties. Isn't that the woman who was killed?"

"Oh yes," Armitage nodded, "we heard about that, terrible business. Yes, she was a tenant briefly."

"Why did she leave, do you know?" I asked.

He shrugged. "No idea, I called round for the rent one day and she was gone, never heard from her again."

Gabriel caught my eye. "There wasn't any difficulty with money or anything – I mean, she paid?"

Armitage looked to the woman again who shook her head.

"I don't recall any difficulty," he said.

"And a man like you has the time to collect the rent himself?" I asked, wondering why he wouldn't have staff for that.

He smirked. "Not all the time, of course, but it's good business to check up on tenants now and then."

The woman looked away. I couldn't help feeling there was something she'd have liked to add.

"Who are you, if you don't mind my asking?" Armitage said then.

"Apologies, we're both friends of Billie, just trying to understand what happened to her," I said.

"Yes, but who are you?" he repeated a little more sharply.

"Gabriel Ingram is my name – this is Beatrice Barrington." Gabriel's voice came out in a growl.

"Well, I don't think I have anything else to tell you.

161

She rented for, what was it, only a few months?" He nodded toward the woman. "Then she left. There was no outstanding rent, I don't think."

"No, she was fully paid up." Again, the woman looked away from her boss and I was sure there was more she could have told us.

"If anything strikes you, that you think would help, you might give us a ring," I said. I took two of my business cards from my handbag and gave one to each of them.

"What are you? PIs or something?" Armitage asked.

"I'm a retired guard," Gabriel said, giving the man a very direct stare, "but no, we're just friends who want to know what happened to Billie."

"You'll have to excuse me, I have work to do." Armitage brushed by us then and approached a young couple who were standing at the back door. "What d'ya think?" he boomed, like a ringmaster at a circus.

"Thanks," Felicity Scott said, and carefully put the business card away in her bag.

Outside, we stood beside my car.

"Will you come back to the house?" I asked.

Gabriel agreed and followed me in his car, down Collins Avenue and St Lawrence Road to the coast. Driving with the heating on, alongside the calm sea, a mirror for the winter-blue sky, it was possible to pretend that it was a summer's day. The illusion of summer ended quickly though once I opened the car door outside my home and felt the tingle of frosty air on my cheeks.

"Have you eaten?" I asked Gabriel when I'd let us into the house.

"I had my usual in Ryan's, no pints though." He

wanted to ensure I knew he hadn't been drink-driving.

"You're hardly hungry now then?"

"Well . . ."

I thought what a stupid question that was to ask of Gabriel, a man for whom one of the great pleasures in life was eating. He was not and never would be a gourmet, his tastes were far too simple for that, but he enjoyed good, plain food in the same way that some people enjoyed watching sport.

He sat in the kitchen and texted on his phone while I grilled a few rashers of bacon and made sandwiches with them, along with a pot of tea. I set them down on the table and we tucked in.

"Perfect," he said, the butter melting on the bread and dripping between his fingers.

"Mind your phone." I passed him a napkin when it buzzed.

He wiped his hands. "Interesting."

"What?"

"I asked Matt about Armitage and he said the lads have been looking into him. Been in property since the crash in 2008, but it's not his only game – likes to make porn films apparently."

"Here in Ireland?" I couldn't hide my surprise and Gabriel laughed at me.

"Sure it's everywhere, Bea."

"I didn't think it was home grown."

"Matt says Armitage has been at it about ten years – not what you'd call high production-value stuff, he says, cheap set-ups and straight onto the internet. Makes his money out of the advertisers."

163

"It's not illegal, though."

"No. Consenting adults and all that."

I put the kettle back on to make more tea.

"Did Matt say any more about your laptop?" It occurred to me then that there might have been a connection between Armitage and what Billie had been looking at online.

Gabriel nodded. "Those searches were for Tasteful Productions Ireland Ltd – that's one of Armitage's companies."

"Specifically? Why?" I'd had to admit I'd been surprised when Gabriel first told me that Billie had been searching for porn. I'd had that struggle in my own mind about free will, and consenting adults and sexual liberation, but I couldn't shake off the conviction that porn was essentially exploitative and demeaning.

"That's the question, isn't it?" Gabriel said. "That's what the lads are trying to find out. They'll be talking to Armitage in the next few days."

My phone rang then with a number I didn't recognise. I hesitated before answering it.

"Hello."

"Is that Beatrice Barrington?" It was a woman's voice.

"Yes, can I help you?"

"It's Felicity, Felicity Scott. I need to talk to you." She sounded nervous. "Can I meet you?"

"Where?"

"You live in Clontarf, don't you? There's a shelter not far from the Bull Wall."

"That's fine."

"This evening at six," she said, before ringing off.

Gabriel thought it was a strange place to meet when I told him.

"She must be frightened of something," he said. "Will I come with you?"

"No need, I can just walk over from here." If she was frightened, I didn't want to scare her off.

He stood up. "I suppose I should go home, then. I'll let you know if I hear any more from Matt." He picked up his coat from the hall.

"Thanks, Gabriel. I'll call you later."

I stood and watched him as he got into his car and pulled slowly out into the traffic. We both knew he wouldn't be going home. He'd be parking outside his house on Oxmantown Road and walking to Walsh's or Hanlon's. He hadn't had a drink all day. I wondered whether he wanted it or needed it. I supposed it was easy to fall into his kind of routine, with the pints a part of it. The pub was company for him, better than sitting at home drinking anyway.

When the time came to meet Felicity Scott, I wrapped up in my camel coat, twisted a lamb's wool scarf around my neck and put on my blue leather gloves.

The evening sky was dark and clear, there was no wind and the linear park that ran alongside the coast as far as the Bull Wall was almost deserted. I walked from the roadside across the grass, which crackled with the beginnings of frost beneath my feet. The shelter, painted a chalky lime-green, had its back to the road, and was essentially a single curve of concrete with a concrete seat inside. It was empty and I sat down and contemplated the red-and-white chimneys of the defunct Poolbeg Power Station, the dim stars, and the orange city lights. My feet had begun to get cold and I was stamping them, left then right, when Felicity Scott arrived.

"Sorry, I got delayed." She sat beside me, a black padded coat like a lagging jacket around her.

"That's okay." I waited for her breath fog to slow down. "You wanted to tell me something?"

"Billie and me used to be friends."

"Used to?"

"Years ago – we both worked for Jason then." Her hands were deep in her pockets.

"For the property business?" I asked though I had a feeling that would not be the answer.

"No. Jason makes . . . he makes these films, porno stuff . . . not the fake kind, you know what I mean?"

I said I did.

She took one hand out of a pocket and dabbed her nose with a tissue. "He offered good money and we needed it at the time."

"I'm sure."

She gave me a quick, hard look. "People like you haven't a clue," she said. "Billie left home at sixteen, did you know that?"

"I didn't, no."

"Well, I met her for the first time at one of Jason's films, this grotty house in Ringsend he was after renting, had it all set up, he had. And she came in looking a bit lost. Anyway, she got used to it. We all did. She stuck it out for about a year."

"Can you remember when she stopped working for him?"

166

"Ages ago. We lost touch. Then last month she turned up looking for Jason, making all kinds of threats."

We heard footsteps then and she pulled up her hood and hunched down, as though trying to make herself invisible. A man walked by us, with a dog on a lead. He kept walking.

"I shouldn't be here," she said.

"Why did she come looking for Jason?"

"She showed up at a property viewing and, when everyone else was gone, she came over to us. She asked him to erase all the films he'd made with her in them. She wanted them all down off the internet. He told her to fuck off, said even if he wanted to it would be impossible. He'd never be able to find all the sites they were on now, he said. And she said if he didn't she'd go to the guards."

I remembered what Gabriel had said about the law – it wasn't illegal.

"But what would she have said to them?"

"Were you not listening to me?" She sounded impatient. "She was only sixteen. The age of consent is seventeen. He may as well have been making child porn as far as the law's concerned."

"Of course, and what did he say? When she said she'd go to the guards?"

"He said if she didn't keep her mouth shut, he'd shut it for her." She shivered then, despite her heavy coat. "That's why I'm here. I thought someone should know that."

"Do you think he could have . . . do you think he's capable of it?"

"I don't know. He has friends who might."

"Okay, thanks for telling me. Will you be okay? Are you still . . .?"

"Ah no. I just do his admin now, keeps me on cos I know all his secrets." She got to her feet. "Don't be calling me now, sure you won't?"

"I won't. Mind yourself."

She walked away.

I waited a while before leaving. I felt sad for Billie, for what she had been through, and I worried about telling Gabriel.

I called him as soon as I got home.

"It makes sense now, doesn't it, the searching?" he said. "I only wish she'd told me – I could have helped her."

"Do you think Armitage would have killed her because of it?"

"It's possible. Wouldn't be too difficult to convict him if Billie gave evidence. The age thing makes it legally cut and dry."

I knew what he was going to say next.

"I'll have to let Matt know."

Of course he would but it felt shabby. Felicity had trusted me and now I could be putting her in danger.

"Will you ask him to make sure Armitage doesn't find out where the information came from?"

"I won't tell him where it came from. And if they find the footage Billie was looking for on my laptop they won't need another source."

I hoped that would be enough to protect Felicity.

Chapter 19

Monday, November 7th, 2016

I'd been thinking about Billie on the way to Phoenix House. If Jason Armitage had a role in her murder and the weapon used to kill her was the same weapon used on Andrew Dalton, then there had to be a connection between Dalton and Armitage. Could Dalton have had some interest in Armitage's business? Or did he owe Armitage money? If that was the case there didn't have to be a direct connection between Dalton and Billie. That was why we hadn't been able to see it. It wasn't there. Would Georgina have heard of Armitage? I texted her to ask if I could call by later but got no response.

I put the matter out of my mind once I reached Court 32. The cross-examination of Mrs O'Malley had been due to start the previous Thursday, but evidence from a witness, a specialist in taxation, who had only been available then, had taken her place. Now she was back in the stand and being questioned thoroughly.

She was asked about her "nights out with the girls" and whether resulting hangovers had meant she was incapable of looking after the children.

"Of course not. I look after my children well."

"Have you ever taken your children to the pub, Mrs O'Malley?"

"No, well, only on family occasions."

The judge frowned.

"When their cousin made his Holy Communion there was a lunch in the pub and after Jamie's christening and their granny's 80th birthday."

"And would you drink alcohol at these events, Mrs O'Malley?" Ms Clements looked like a scientist watching a bug through a microscope.

Mrs O'Malley's face contorted. "I–I . . ."

"You are under oath now, Mrs O'Malley."

"Well, I would have one or two, but doesn't everyone?"

"You were solely in charge of three children, Mrs O'Malley." Ms Clements was at her most sanctimonious. "And is it true you gave Robin money on more than one occasion to take his little sisters to a nearby shop for sweets to keep them amused while you drank?"

"Socialised, I socialised with my family. And the children were with their cousins, isn't that normal?" She looked baffled and exposed.

"You're not denying it then?" Ms Clements asked, looking at the judge.

Mrs O'Malley shook her head.

"So you drink while in charge of the children?"

"You've made your point, move on, please, Ms Clements," the judge said.

By four o'clock Mrs O'Malley looked beaten down and exhausted.

"Are you done, Ms Clements?" The judge raised an

eyebrow at her.

"Yes, judge."

"All right. Now I know evidence in chief from Mr O'Malley was due to begin tomorrow. Unfortunately, I am unavailable. If you recall, this case was scheduled to run for two weeks. I know I've been partly responsible for the overrun, nevertheless . . ."

The barristers looked at each other, aware now of what was coming.

"I have two important judgments to deliver and some short matters I must dispose of. I will be available again on November 14th."

There was a groan from Mr O'Malley. And I couldn't help thinking that I might have difficulty finding work until then.

"Very well," the judge said, leaving the courtroom before the barristers could complain.

I packed away my equipment and went briefly back to the office. When my phone began to ring I didn't hear it, but felt it vibrating at the bottom of my handbag. By the time I found it, it had stopped. The screen said, "Unknown Number". I hated that. I was not one of those people who screened incoming calls, but I still preferred callers to identify themselves with their number. Otherwise, I felt there was some power imbalance since they quite obviously knew mine. The phone rang a second time then, but on this occasion with a number displayed. It was not one I recognised, but at least it was there. I answered as I made my way to the lobby.

"Is that Beatrice Barrington?"

"Speaking."

"It's Claire, Claire Davis. Remember me?"

"Yes, of course."

"You said I should call you if . . . Are you free for a coffee?"

I said I was and we arranged to meet in a city-centre bar at five. I wondered if I should let Georgina know I was meeting Claire. But what would she say? Don't do that, probably. How would I explain I was only trying to help? No, it would be best to say nothing until afterwards.

Still, as I stepped off the tram in Abbey Street, I couldn't help feeling that I was, yet again, betraying Georgina while trying to help her.

It was five when I crossed the packed city quays. I turned right and walked as quickly as I could, threading through the people walking toward me and the queues of shivering commuters at the bus stops.

In Sweetman's, I recognised Claire Davis by her long, glossy, brown hair. She was sitting on a stool at the bar with her back to the door.

"Will we . . . ?" I indicated a table against the back wall.

"Yes." Claire got down from her stool.

"Will I get you another one of those?" I pointed to her half-empty glass.

"It's Brother Bowen." She took her glass and bag and moved to the empty table.

"A pint of that," I gestured toward one of the craft-beer taps, "and a pot of tea, please."

The barman nodded. "I'll bring them over."

I paid him and joined Claire.

"Nice place." I smiled in an attempt to encourage conversation.

Claire looked agitated. Her coat was laid across her lap as though she was preparing for a quick exit.

"Sorry I'm late, took longer to get in than I thought."

"It's okay."

The barman arrived and unloaded the beer, tea and its paraphernalia from a tray.

"Thanks." I opened the lid of the little tin pot he'd put before me and stirred it. Pouring the amber liquid into the off-white, bowl-shaped cup, I added a splash of milk. A brown, plastic-covered biscuit the size of a matchbox was perched on the edge of my saucer. I snapped it in two before opening the wrapper and offering it across the table.

Claire waved it away with a small laugh. I put half the biscuit in my mouth and swallowed some tea.

"Well now, what was on your mind?"

"You asked me to call you." There was an edge of defensiveness in her voice.

"I did, if you had any concerns."

She opened her handbag and took out a piece a paper.

"I wasn't sure whether to show you this or not but you're her friend and . . . Milly drew it." She passed it to me. It was a crayon picture with two stick figures – one big, holding something in its hand, and one small with what appeared to be teardrops on its face.

"She said it was her and her mummy. And when I asked her why she was crying she said it was because Mummy was having her wine and that made her sad."

"That's terrible." I gave her back the picture and she put it away.

"And the thing is, Georgina didn't bring the kids to school today."

"Oh?"

"They were due back from mid-term this morning, right? No sign of them, so the boss sends a text. No answer. She asked me to go round to the house. No one there."

I picked up my handbag, took out my phone and sent a message to Georgina: "**Everything all right?**" I remembered that she hadn't answered my earlier text. I waited, watching the screen. There was no reply.

"See?"

"Thanks for letting me know." I would try again in a few minutes – there could be lots of reasons why Georgina wasn't answering. "How have you been, Claire? I mean, is work going well for you?"

She looked worried. "You haven't told, have you?"

"You mean told St Louisa's about the casino. Of course not."

"They wouldn't be impressed, even apart from it being a casino, if they found out I was only getting six hours sleep a night. I'd be getting the 'childcare demands 100-per-cent engagement' lecture." She thought for a minute. "No, actually, they'd probably just sack me."

I felt tired just thinking about getting only six hours sleep a night.

"How do you manage it?" I knew I couldn't, not even in my twenties.

"I have rent to pay and I'm saving to go back to college. If I want that, I have to work."

It was hard not to be impressed by her determination.

"What is it you want to study?"

"Music. I got lessons for a while when I was younger, but . . . it didn't work out. I'd do anything to get back to it now."

"Can I ask you something?"

She looked doubtfully at me. "What?"

"Are you sure you didn't come across Andrew Dalton at the casino? Did he know you worked at St Louisa's?" I knew what McCann had told me, but I wanted to hear it from her myself.

She was quiet, weighing up whether to tell me the truth or not.

"It only happened the once. I wasn't long working at Spin at the time – March it was. He was handsome, but he had something else, charisma maybe."

While she spoke I was thinking of Georgina and the children.

"Whatever it was, I fancied him, and it was clear he fancied me. Then, one night, he was still there at the end of my shift so we went along to a hotel not too far away. The Maples. Just the once. He didn't know I was working at St Louisa's." She looked down at her glass, picked it up, drank from it.

"But then he recognised you when he picked up Milly and James?"

"Yes – that was early June. He just said, 'I'll see you again', like any other dad, but I knew what he meant." She drank more beer. "A week or so later he turned up at Spin and waited for me to finish my shift. He said he just wanted to talk so I walked with him. He went on about how much I must love my work at St Louisa's and how well-respected I was there. We went into the park at Blessington Street and once we were out of sight he started mauling me." She shivered. "Anyway, we heard a noise and I gave him a good shove and ran as fast as I could back out onto the road."

"That must have been terrible." I drank some of my tea, which was almost cold. "Can you remember when?"

"I think maybe about a week before he died. Anyway, he didn't try it again. I suppose he was just having a laugh or something."

"Not very nice," I said. I was having trouble reconciling this version of Andrew with the man I thought I had known.

"Have the guards been around yet?"

Claire didn't have time to reply.

A man approached the table, bent down and kissed her lightly on the lips.

"This is my – my Nikolai." She smiled at the words.

"Pleased to meet you." I shook his hand and he pulled over a stool and sat down, the expanse of his muscular body making him look like an adult sitting on a child's seat.

"Should I get you another drink?" His eyes searched Claire's face intently, as though her response was the most important thing in the world, and I felt a pang at the intensity of new love.

Claire patted the big hand he had rested on her knee. "I'm okay. I'm just going to the loo."

He stood up to make room for her to leave and watched until she disappeared from view. Then he turned back toward me.

I smiled at him and he looked bashful.

"Are you together long?"

"A few weeks. I met her at work."

"The casino?"

"Yes. I'm security, I keep them all safe."

I was going to ask him what they needed prot
from, but the answer seemed obvious. "I'd say you ge
few rough types."

"It's not the rough types. They are okay. They lose
their money, they take it. It's the ones who think, you
know, they are special. When they lose, they are trouble."

"The man who was murdered, Andrew Dalton, was
he trouble?" I spoke quickly, aware that Claire would be
back at any minute.

"Him? He was *slime*." When he said the word he
made a face as though he'd smelled something rotten.

His forcefulness surprised me. "What do you mean?"

He looked over his shoulder.

"He couldn't keep his hands off of her."

"She wasn't interested?"

"I heard her say no to him, but he tried to force himself
on her –"

"Nikolai?" Claire had come from the opposite
direction and was standing now with her hand on his
back. "What are you saying?" She sat down.

"I'm telling her the truth, I'm telling her I saw him all
over you."

"You saw him?" Shock registered on her face.

Nikolai looked like a dog kicked by its master.

"I'm sorry, I followed you one night, when he took
you to the park."

"We weren't even together then, Nikolai." She

177

..ed bewildered and I felt I was sitting in on a private conversation.

"I was afraid for you, I wanted to be sure he didn't harm you." He looked desperate to defend himself and seemed to brace himself for an onslaught.

But she leaned in and kissed him on the cheek.

"Oh Nikolai – isn't he lovely?" Her question was directed at me. "So kind. You know he sends most of his money home to his mother and sister in Omsk?"

"A good son," I said. I took my phone out and checked for a response from Georgina. There was none.

"Anything?" Claire saw me checking.

"No."

"She didn't look right the last time I saw her."

"What do you mean?"

"I don't know. She looked a bit out of it."

I tried to think how she'd been when we spoke last. Had she been "a bit out of it"?

"I think I'd better go." I put my coat on. "If you hear anything, if she turns up or rings St Louisa's or anything, will you let me know?"

"Okay," she said, already turning back to Nikolai.

Chapter 20

On the quays I put my hand out for a taxi. I didn't have the patience to stand on a cold platform, even for a few minutes, to catch the DART to Clontarf. I texted Georgina and then phoned.

"The person you are dialling is not reachable."

I texted again and again and began to really worry. Should I call the guards? But what would I say to them? I phoned Gabriel instead and told him about meeting Claire and what she'd said about Georgina. He said he'd meet me at home.

Rain had begun to fall and it seemed to me that everyone who lived on the north side of Dublin was trying to get home at the same time. In the winter dark, headlights blurred with rain stretched on ahead up through Amien Street and the North Strand. The taxi spent a full five minutes on Newcomen Bridge, long enough for me to ponder on the tile mosaic of a train decorating the nearby block of flats which seemed to be mocking my choice of transport.

I got out of the taxi at Clontarf train station and

picked up my car. When I finally got home, Gabriel was already there, sitting outside in his car, waiting. I dashed to my front door through the downpour and he followed me inside. I took off my coat and shoes and padded into the kitchen to put the kettle on, leaving damp footprints behind me on the tiles.

"I'm just not sure what to do," I said, continuing the conversation we had begun on the phone. "Claire said she wasn't at home."

"That was earlier. Maybe she's at home now. Maybe something happened to her phone. Has she a landline?"

I struggled to recollect whether I had seen a home phone in the house. Even if there was one I was sure I didn't have the number.

"Let's eat first." I couldn't think straight on an empty stomach. I began searching in the fridge. "Will you have some soup?"

"What kind?"

"Vegetable? Or chicken and veg?"

"I'll have the chicken."

Of course he would. I shook each carton, poured them into bowls and put them into the microwave.

"I think I still have some turnover – will you cut it?"

He looked relieved that I wasn't offering him wholegrain or some of that spelt bread I sometimes bought. I left him with the breadboard and a sharp knife and went upstairs.

My feet were uncomfortably wet in my nylons. I peeled them off, took off my work suit and put on jeans and a green polo-neck jumper. I found a pair of thick socks and put trainers on over them. Heat began to return to my toes.

180

I could hear the microwave ping as I came downstairs. Gabriel had set the table.

"You're very domesticated," I couldn't resist remarking.

"I had a good teacher." He caught my eye and smiled.

I turned away and found a tea towel to lift the bowls out with. Both soups looked the same. I said nothing and put them down.

After a few spoonfuls and two chunks of bread, he asked if I wanted him to call Matt.

"I don't want to overreact."

"You mean you don't want him finding out something before you do."

I looked at him. Was that true? Did I feel like I was in some competition with McCann, as though we were on two different teams? No. Of course not.

"I just don't want to make a fool of myself, that's all."

"Right so, finish up there and we'll drive over. If the house is empty, we'll think again." He dropped the remaining chunks of bread into his soup and ate them with his spoon. When we'd finished, I hastily put the bowls in the dishwasher and followed him out to his car. I knew he was more comfortable as a driver than a passenger and I didn't mind.

The rain had stopped and the traffic was considerably lighter. All the same, he took the East-Link Toll Bridge from Clontarf to Ringsend to avoid the city centre. The CD player was turned low, but I could still hear his favourite, Johnny Cash, singing "Port of Lonely Hearts".

"Miserable stuff," I said.

"There's no educating some people."

I went through my meeting with Claire again and what she'd said about Georgina. And I told him about Nikolai Strofsky and his obvious animosity toward Andrew. We talked about Billie and Jason Armitage, too. I mentioned my latest theory, that there might be no connection between Billie and Andrew, but they both could be connected to Armitage.

"I'll have to ask Georgina if she's heard of him. It's a delicate one, though." I didn't relish having to mention how Armitage made his money.

"You don't have to go into details. Even if she just knows the name, that would help."

I knew he was right, but I also knew that if I got into a conversation about it, I might end up telling Georgina everything.

"Maybe I'll leave it for the moment."

When we pulled up outside Georgina's house, her car wasn't there. The curtains were open and there was darkness beyond them. We got out and walked to the front door.

"There's no-one here," I said.

"Try the bell anyway."

I pressed on the buzzer and the ring echoed through the empty rooms. I pressed my face to the front window and could just make out the shape of the furniture. I rang the buzzer again to be sure, then remembered something – the plant pot in the garden. I found the right one and lifted it, but there was no key.

Gabriel made his way to the side of the house and put his hand on the wooden door that divided the side passage and back garden from the front. He turned the handle and it opened inward with a small squeak.

"Let's have a look around the back." He disappeared and I followed him.

"It's not like Georgina to leave a door unlocked."

I was whispering now but he shushed me anyway. He pointed to the bolt on the inside of the door. The screws that had held it were hanging loose. It had been burst open. He put his index finger to his lips and stood still. I concentrated. What was that? Breathing? As we stood, I thought I could catch a faint odour of cigarette smoke in the air. Gabriel began to move again, this time making as little noise as possible. I followed, my heart playing double-time in my chest. We rounded the corner of the house and I saw Lar Sheils then, sitting on a chair at the patio table, a cigarette held between his thumb and index finger.

"You all right?" he asked without moving position.

I whispered his name to Gabriel.

"What do you think you're doing?" Gabriel growled.

Lar took a last draw on his cigarette and dropped it on the ground. He looked at me.

"Where's your friend?"

"I said, what do you think you're doing?" Gabriel stepped closer to him.

Lar stood up and took a step forward. His head was at the level of Gabriel's nose, but he seemed undeterred by that.

"Mind your own fucking business."

He made to walk around us and toward the side passage, but Gabriel planted one hand flat against his chest and pushed until he was pinned against the wall of the house.

"I'm not asking you again."

I thought Gabriel might punch him in the face, and Lar looked as though he thought so too. He put both hands up, palms out.

"Take it easy."

Gabriel relaxed his grip slightly.

"I'm owed money and I'm here to collect. She said she'd be back, she isn't back and I need that money."

I asked him when he'd seen her last.

"This morning – she said she was going shopping. Drove off with the kids, never came back."

"You better not have hurt her." Gabriel pushed into his chest again.

"Do you think I'm stupid? Would I hang around here if I had?"

"Have you been in the house?"

"No."

I supposed he was telling the truth. Why would he wait in the garden if he could wait inside?

"Alarm's on," he said, by way of further proof.

"*Hey! What are you doing?*" A head appeared round the side of the house then the body of a uniformed garda. When he saw us he let out a roar over his shoulder. "*Pádraig!*"

"Shite! Let go of me, will yeh?" Lar pushed Gabriel's shoulder, but there was no movement. "I don't need this."

"Tough." Gabriel stayed where he was.

"Let him go," the officer said, his colleague now standing beside him.

Gabriel released his grip then but stood close enough

to grab Lar again if he decided to run. The young gardaí, standing side by side, were wide enough to block the side passage. The first took out his notebook.

"Names?"

"Beatrice Barrington and this is Gabriel Ingram," I said. "We're friends of Georgina O'Donnell who owns this house. We called by to visit her and we found him in the back garden."

"That's not true. I'm a friend of Georgina's and she asked me to keep an eye on the place for her, so I dropped by this evening and found these two snooping around."

"And your name?" The guard looked as though he didn't believe either of us.

"Laurence O'Toole."

"He's lying, his name is Sheils." I said.

Gabriel put out his hand to the officers. "I'm a retired garda – Gabriel Ingram. What Beatrice said is true. This man is Lar Sheils."

"Wait a minute – if you just found him here, how do you know his name?"

"I met him before, in the house – he called in to see Georgina," I said.

"So he is her friend?"

"Yes," Sheils said.

"No," I contradicted.

The two gardaí looked at each other.

The officer called Pádraig spoke for the first time. "None of you own this house?"

We all shook our heads.

"You're trespassing so. We'll sort this out down the

185

station. Call it in there, will you," he nodded to his partner, "and ask for another car?"

His colleague got on the radio.

"There's no need for that – sure, I'll drive down," Gabriel said.

"Eh, no, you won't. Right – addresses."

We gave our addresses in turn and I repeated Lar's address in my head to memorise it – 22 Maryfield Crescent, Artane. We waited half an hour for the second Garda car to arrive, then we were loaded into the vehicles and driven away, Lar in one car, Gabriel and me in the other.

"This is ridiculous." I rubbed my eyes as though I might wake myself up from some bizarre dream.

"Don't worry about it," said Gabriel. "These lads are only doing their job."

Donnybrook Garda station looked more like a stately home from the outside with its grey granite and its arched glass window above the main door. But we weren't brought in that way. The cars pulled round the side, through pillared gates into the back yard. We were led in through a low door.

Gabriel strode in as though he knew where he was going and was entirely at home.

"Was three months in here when I started out, hasn't changed a bit," he told me.

I was less impressed.

We stood in a queue, waiting for the grey-haired desk sergeant to process us.

When Gabriel got to the counter the sergeant smiled.

"Greg, you fecker, you're still here!"

"Well now, look what the cat dragged in."

The men shook hands and the two young gardaí exchanged glances.

"What's this all about?" The sergeant spoke as though he'd just stepped between a group of children brawling in the playground.

"Give Matt McCann a ring, will you, Greg?" Gabriel said. "He knows."

We were shown into one waiting room, and Lar was brought to another. The sergeant offered us tea and we both accepted.

"It's important that Matt talks to him." Gabriel pointed his thumb in the direction of where Lar had gone. "Might know something about a murder case the lads in Store Street are working on."

"Right so, I'll call him now."

The tea came in white styrofoam cups and tasted as though someone had waved a teabag vaguely in its direction.

"Hasn't changed much." Gabriel drank it anyway, but I put mine down on a nearby table.

"I'm worried about Georgina."

"We'll speak to Matt about it when he comes."

We didn't have to wait too long, and we heard him before we saw him, greeting officers in his Cavan accent, louder than usual, almost boisterous.

"Well, what ails you two at all?" was his greeting to us.

He sat down across the table from us. We told him what had happened, how we were worried about Georgina and had decided to call over to her. I expected him to understand and I thought he might show a little gratitude for the information Gabriel had given him about Jason Armitage.

"I hadn't heard from her in a few days and when I rang the phone wasn't connected." I'd decided it would be simpler not to say that I'd met Claire Davis.

"So you both just decided to drop over to the house."

We nodded.

"And this Lar Sheils was in the back garden?"

We nodded again.

"And you couldn't have just phoned for help, instead of confronting him?" This time, he was looking directly at Gabriel. "You know this looks bad, don't you, considering everything?"

"Ah, come on . . ."

"Don't give me that, Gabriel. I'm answerable, you know that. This will be going down in the records here and there's feck all I can do about it."

I began to feel the colour rising in my cheeks. "We did nothing wrong. Georgina is my friend and we can't find her. Her husband was murdered, now she's missing and her children are missing and you're sitting here quibbling about why we were at her house. You know why."

McCann drummed the table with the fingers of his left hand as though he was counting in order to keep his temper under control.

"You don't know she's missing. She's allowed to take a break for a few days and, contrary to what you might think, she doesn't have to tell you everything. As it happens, she phoned me today and told me about Lar Sheils and where to find her if I need her. She's taking a break in Wexford for a few days. So panic over."

I was taken aback. I hadn't expected McCann to be better informed than I was about Georgina's whereabouts. Why had she not let me know she was going away?

"Now, I'm going to talk to the two lads who picked ye up and I'm going to persuade them there's nothing to worry about and then I'm going to have a word with your Mr Sheils. I'm advising you two to go home and close your front doors and mind your own business."

Gabriel looked chastened when we left the station. One of the officers had offered to run him back to Georgina's house to collect his car but he said he'd rather walk.

He waited with me until a taxi came by. Then he stood on the street and watched as it drove away.

On the way home I thought about Georgina. She would be down in Seafield Cottage with the children. Why hadn't I considered that instead of panicking? The phone signal could be hit and miss down there, I knew from experience, and that would explain why I couldn't get through to her. And why would I think she needed to tell me? I wasn't entitled to know everything. Still, I wondered why she hadn't at least told St Louisa's she wouldn't be bringing the children in. That would have been the conscientious thing to do – that was the Georgina I knew. I supposed the pressure had got too much for her. She had struggled on since Andrew died and had tried to keep everything going for herself but mostly for the children. Perhaps Lar Sheils hanging around had pushed her to a point where she couldn't keep on doing that.

I imagined her at the house, hurrying the children into the car, packing a few things, and Sheils lurking around, demanding money. Who wouldn't run? I took out my phone and composed a careful text message.

"Hi Georgina, hope everything is okay with you. I hear you've taken the children away for a few days. Let me know if you need me to do anything – post or anything like that. Give me a call if you need to chat."

It was only after I'd pressed send that I realised it was much too late to be texting anyone. I wished there was some magic code I could type that would intercept the message and allow me to snatch the words back in mid-air.

As the taxi approached Clontarf Road my phone began to ring. I answered it immediately.

"Georgina?"

"Beatrice, Beatrice, can you hear me?"

Chapter 21

"I can hear you."

"Can you talk to me, just for a while?" Her voice sounded slurred.

"Of course, are you all right? Where are you?"

"I'm on the beach."

"What? Where?"

"Just near the cottage, you know, Seafield Cottage."

"Where are the children?" I was aware of a slight, anxious sensation in my stomach. What was she doing there? What was she about to do?

"In the house, Emma's there."

"Okay, and you're on the beach. Is it raining?"

"A bit."

I thought I could hear waves crashing now against rocks. I wondered how close Georgina was to the water's edge.

"Would you not go inside? It must be very cold."

There was no response.

"Georgina?"

We'd arrived at my house. I handed over the fare,

fished my car key out of my bag and stepped out of the taxi.

"Thanks."

"What?"

"Not you, the driver. Never mind. You said you wanted to talk to me."

"No one understands."

"What? What don't they understand?"

"It was all a mess anyway."

"What was?" I got into my car and threw my bag into the passenger footwell.

"Before, it was a mess before he got himself dead, Beatrice." She began to sob. "He – we – it wasn't right anymore. I couldn't trust him."

"What do you mean, Georgina?" I started the engine, put the phone on speaker and turned the car toward the city.

"Did you ever see an apple? And it's all red and shiny and you bite in and it tastes great. Did you?"

"An apple? Yes." I signalled right to head for the East-Link Bridge. "Go on, I'm listening."

"And then you take another bite and there's a little brown maggot in there. That's what it was like. There was rot hidden in it."

It seemed to me that the sound of the waves on the phone had got closer.

"Where are you now, Georgina?"

"The sea is lovely, isn't it? Have you ever seen it at night? It goes on forever."

"It's very cold, though." There was silence for a few moments. "Georgina?"

"They say you don't notice the cold after a while."

I was on Strand Road. The traffic was light and the rain had stopped. To my left, I could see the tide was in and the waves were white-topped. Killiney Hill was spotted with lights and beyond that I could see the shape of Bray Head. It would take at least an hour to get to Ballymoney.

"I'd love a cup of tea, Georgina."

"What?"

"I'm cold. I'd love a cup of tea. Do you mind if I call in?"

"But you're in Dublin."

"No, no, I'm not far from you now, I'm on my way. Would you put the kettle on?" I could hear breathing on the other end of the line.

"I don't want to go back inside."

I tried to picture the little beach in my head, the curve of rocks around it, the path leading back to the road and Georgina's house. Wasn't there a bench somewhere, set back a little from the beach?

"Don't so, don't go back. I'll meet you on the bench – you know, the green bench. Turn around – can you see it there?"

"Yes."

"Sit up there then, will you, out of the wind a bit? Then we can talk properly."

There was no response, but I thought I could hear the crunch of sand beneath feet and the waves quieting a little.

"Georgina?"

"I'm here."

"Okay, good." I heard sloshing then and swallowing. "What's that you have?"

"A very nice red. Never knew it tasted good straight

from the bottle. No middleman – no middle-glass, I mean." She began to laugh and it sounded to me as though her whole body was convulsing, as though she might laugh herself sick.

"Did you take anything else, Georgina? Any pills?"

"No, forgot about those." She sounded regretful. "If I did that, I could just be gone. Do you know how much I wish I was gone?"

"No."

"If it wasn't for Milly and James . . ."

"And Emma, what about Emma?"

"We had a row – I think she hates me."

"Of course she doesn't – she's just being a teenager."

"You didn't hear her – Lar Sheils called by again and Emma made me tell her what he wanted. And she said, she wanted to know why I didn't believe him about the money – she said it would be 'typical of Andrew'." There was a teenage petulant tone in her voice, imitating her daughter.

"But why would she say that?"

"I don't know . . . She spewed out all this stuff about things that had happened – only ordinary family things, Bea." She paused as though considering whether those things were ordinary. "She said, 'Do you think just cos he's dead that I only remember good Andrew?' That's what she said." Georgina began to cry a bit. "Then she said 'What about the time he just disappeared when we were out in that pub for lunch and we had to get a taxi home?' and I told her, Bea, that he'd had a work emergency and she said, 'Yeah, right – I heard you screaming at him that night'. I hadn't thought she'd heard, I'd thought they were all asleep."

I wasn't equipped to say the right things to calm her. "Try not to dwell on it," was all I could manage.

"Don't you see, Bea? If I walked into the sea right now, I'd be doing it for her."

I didn't see and I didn't know what to do except keep driving. I heard her take another slug from the bottle.

"I don't know what you mean," I said.

"Course you don't. You don't know about marriage, do you? You're innocent of it."

I had never thought of it quite in that way before. I had only met one man I considered marrying and my judgment on that occasion had been deeply flawed. I never trusted myself to choose someone after that.

The leafless trees of the Glen of the Downs swayed and bent either side of the road as I sped past. I remembered the young men and women who had lived in them for a while, trying to fight for their retention. Had they won or lost? I couldn't remember.

"Do you remember the eco-warriors, Georgina?"

"Hm?"

"Up in the trees on the N11, remember, with their dreadlocks? Did they win or lose?"

"Why are you asking me that?"

"Sorry. Don't know. It just came into my head. How is Emma now?"

"She's angry, that's how she is."

I heard her drink again, this time, making a sucking noise as though she had reached the end of the bottle.

"Do you know what she called me tonight? 'A hypocritical bitch'."

"Aw, I'm sorry."

195

"What have you got to be sorry for? For God's sake!"

I was afraid she might hang up the phone.

"Georgina?"

Silence.

"*Georgina?*"

"Leave me alone!"

I thought I could hear another voice, a man's, but I couldn't make out what he was saying.

"I said, leave me alone." There was a sound of smashing glass. "Do you want this, do you?"

I could hear the man cursing and then nothing.

"Georgina?"

"What?"

"What was that?"

"He's gone. People interfere too much, do you know that?"

"Who was he?"

"Some old man. Wanted to help me get home."

I imagined some poor man, out for a walk perhaps, coming across Georgina in a state and getting threatened with a broken bottle for his trouble. I was passing the Bee Hive pub now, half an hour to go.

"I really want a cup of tea – would you not put the kettle on?"

"I'm too tired."

"You're not. Get up, Georgina, get up!"

Silence.

"Georgina?"

I knew I had been over the speed limit for miles now, but I put my foot to the floor when I got no answer after several shouts. I turned on the radio, volume up, found some rock – Whitesnake's "Here I Go Again" – and held the phone next to it.

Georgina cursed. I turned the radio down.

"What was that for?" she asked.

"Go on, will you? Go and put the kettle on."

I could hear her getting up then.

"*Ow!*"

"What?"

She didn't reply but I could still hear her, breathing as though it was taking tremendous effort, as though she was having to drag herself away from the beach.

"I'll be with you shortly," I said and hoped I would be.

The sound of waves faded and I could hear a door being opened.

"I'm putting you down for a sec," Georgina said.

There was a sound of running water, a switch being flicked.

"Now, it's on, happy?"

"You must be cold. Get yourself a blanket."

"You're very bossy."

More footsteps and I could picture exactly where Georgina would find a spare blanket in the airing cupboard. I remembered not so long ago going there for fresh sheets to make up the spare bed in the cottage.

"Where are you now, Georgina?"

"I'm too tired to talk now, Beatrice."

The phone cut off and its silence echoed around the inside of the car. I had reached the turnoff for Ballymoney and was driving now on narrow country roads, edged with hedgerows that moved only slightly in a weakened breeze. A watery half-moon was visible between thinning cloud over Tara Hill. It seemed to me that the whole of the countryside was now asleep. I noticed for the first time that it was almost two thirty. The panic that had gripped me on the drive down and forced my foot to the throttle had receded now. I thought it was just as well – I could not have kept on speeding on these dark, winding lanes. I would be glad to reach the cottage and see beyond the stretch of my headlamps. At night, the unknown countryside didn't feel like unknown city streets – the depth of its darkness made me uneasy.

When I got to Seafield Cottage the downstairs lights were on and the hall door was ajar. I parked outside and, without knocking, walked in, closing the door behind me. I went through to the back of the house and into the kitchen. Georgina was on the couch, sitting upright, a pink blanket around her, eyes closed, mouth open, snoring gently. I wanted to laugh with relief. I wondered about guiding her to bed, but couldn't bring myself to waken her. I stretched and yawned, conscious now of the tension of the drive carried in my shoulders and neck. I walked to the cupboard, took out a cup, found a teabag and brought the warm kettle back to boil. I rinsed two wine bottles under the tap and put them in the bin. Then I sat in an armchair, drank the soothing tea and observed my friend. How thin she had become, gaunt even. She looked older than the last time we'd met. Her hand was resting on something – a photo album. I moved quietly, lifted her hand up, slid out the album, and tucked the blanket around her a little better.

They were family photos, mostly of the children, first

as new babies, then toddlers, first days at school, in a playground, on the swings. Typical family snaps taken by adoring parents. There were a few of Georgina with the children, sitting on a picnic rug, pushing a pram, happy. Andrew didn't feature in any and I supposed it was he who must have been behind the lens. Toward the back though, I found a couple of Andrew with the family, or at least I supposed it was Andrew. Though his trunk and limbs were there, his face was no longer visible. It looked as though someone had taken a sharp blade and cut his head out, neatly, so that in each photo there was a square of emptiness.

"What are you doing here?" Emma was standing in the doorway.

I closed the album and put it down.

"Your mother phoned. I think she wanted company."

The girl looked around. "Bottles?"

"In the bin. Did I wake you?"

"No. I got up to check on her. I was going to put her to bed." She slumped onto the couch at the opposite end from her mother, pulled her knees up to her chest and dragged on her nightdress until it covered her bare feet.

So she was used to this.

"I didn't know this was going on," I said.

"She's getting worse. I don't know what to do."

The girl began to cry, low sobs, as though trying not to wake her mother, her shoulders shaking. "It's his fault."

"Who? Your dad?"

"He *wasn't* my dad." Her childish, tearful expression transformed, twisting itself with temper.

"No, of course not. Andrew, I mean. How is it his fault?"

Emma shook her head. "Nobody knows about him. They all think he was great. Did you hear them at the funeral? Well, he wasn't great – he was a pig."

She seemed utterly tormented and I didn't know what to say to her. "I'd like to help," was all I could manage.

"What? What did you say?" Georgina woke, looked first at Emma and then at me, rubbed her eyes and looked again. "You're here."

"Yes, I said, remember?"

The whites of her eyes were streaked red with blood vessels. She opened and closed her mouth, trying to create moisture.

Emma got up, poured her a glass of water and gave it to her.

"I'm going back to bed." Emma nodded a goodnight at me.

"I'm sorry," Georgina said. "I don't remember you saying you'd call by."

"It's late, why don't we talk about it in the morning?"

Georgina stood and looked down at her sandy feet, flip-flops still attached. I noticed that there were speckles of blood on her toes.

"Oh!" she said.

"Hang on." I found a tea towel and ran it under the tap. I made her sit down again and wiped her feet, as gently as I could. There were tiny cuts on her soles, one or two with green glass embedded which I extracted easily enough with a fingernail.

"I . . ." she said.

"Don't worry, we'll talk in the morning."

When I'd finished I sent her to bed. Then I kicked off my own shoes, found a fresh blanket in the airing cupboard and stretched out on the couch to sleep.

Chapter 22

Wednesday, November 9th, 2016

It was evening and the darkness around Seafield Cottage was thick with fog. We were sitting at the kitchen table when James came running in with a toy plane, flying it around us. Milly ran after him, flying a car.

"Take it easy." Georgina put her arm out to slow them down.

"Where's Daddy?" James stopped at her chair.

"He's up in heaven with the angels."

By the way she sang it at him, I could tell it was a much-repeated response, and was enough to satisfy him, but not enough for Milly.

"Do dead people ever come back to talk to us?"

"I don't think they do," Georgina answered. "They're more like Guardian Angels, invisible but making sure we're safe."

The little girl paused to think about that.

"Would you ever go out in the night and leave us?"

"Of course not."

"One time I woke up and I couldn't find you."

"Ah no, Milly, that must have been a bad dream. I'd

never leave you alone at night."

Milly looked up into her mother's face again, then nodded and ran out of the room, followed by her brother.

I was glad of the silence. Before the interruption, I had been trying to persuade Georgina to see a doctor. She was resisting and, to prove she didn't need a drink, she had not bought any wine at the supermarket. It was obvious to me that she now regretted that decision. She was as agitated as I'd ever seen her, incapable of sitting still.

I had agreed that I would stay for a few days. Emma hadn't minded giving up her room since she was already sleeping in her mother's bed at night. I got the impression she was glad to have another adult at the house. I had called Gabriel to let him know what had happened and that I would be away from Dublin for a while.

"What about work?" he'd asked me.

"I've nothing on at the moment, not until next week . . ."

"Right so, if you need me . . ."

"Thanks."

Now Georgina was insisting that all she needed was rest and my company for a while to steady herself.

"Have you been getting any help – I mean, a counsellor or something after all that's happened?"

"I don't need some shrink to tell me I've had a hard time, Bea." Her voice, as she spoke, was taut.

"I know but, sometimes, if you can say it all to a stranger . . ."

"Huh!" she scoffed.

"You know what I mean, Georgina – you get the truth

off your chest, doesn't matter what it is, you just say it and it's gone."

She squinted at me and tilted her head to one side. "Truth? Right, and did you do that after Laurence died?"

I felt the jab of the remark, but responded quietly, in as even a voice as I could muster. "It was different then. Things happened and you shut up and got on with life. People didn't go to counsellors, they went to confession."

"Confession?" Georgina stood up and the chair scrapped against the floor as she pushed it back. "Do you think I have something to confess, is that it? What are you up to? Tell me that. Why did you come down here anyway?" Her voice had grown louder and she began pacing the kitchen.

"You know why, Georgina. Come on now."

"Did that guard, McCann, send you?"

"What?"

"Are you here to get information on me for him?" She moved toward me, looming over me. "I see you on and off for years, then you're buzzing around like a – like a fly around shite. What do you want from me?"

She looked as though she might lash out. The transformation in her had happened so fast it took my breath away. I didn't know how to handle it and all I knew was I wanted to get away from her.

"I need some air." I went out the back door and into the garden. Outside the salty air was chill, the dark sky was filled with stars and I could hear the soothing rhythm of the waves on the beach nearby. I tried to figure out what had happened. I had seen before what an absence of alcohol could do to an addict, that inner desperation converted into outward aggression, aimed at whoever was closest. I wondered if the drinking had come after Andrew's death or before. And maybe if it was before, the marriage had not been as strong as I thought. What could I do now to help her? I felt like calling Gabriel for advice, but my phone was in the kitchen. So I stood instead and listened to the waves and thought of Laurence singing "Don't Stop" along to Fleetwood Mac on his record player until I could almost hear his voice and my feet were as cold as stones. Then I went back inside.

Georgina was sitting again at the table, a glass in one hand and a half bottle of whiskey beside it. "I hate this stuff," she said.

I poured a glass of water at the sink and sat opposite her.

"I'm sorry. I know you're only trying to help, Bea."

"Just tell me, what can I do for you?"

"Nothing. It's all such a mess."

"But none of it's your fault, Georgina, and you don't need to deal with it alone."

She put her glass down and hid her face in her hands and sobbed.

Emma came into the kitchen then and looked at her mother. "Did she tell you?" she asked me.

"What?"

"What he was really like. Is that why she's crying?"

Georgina lifted her head. "Stop." Her voice was steady and cold, emotion miraculously vanished, though her cheeks were still wet. "Stop it, Emma."

Emma looked at me, shook her head and walked out of the room.

"What was that about?" I asked.

"She has it in her head that Andrew was the enemy. Easier to think of him as a baddy, easier to bear his absence, I suppose." She rubbed her face with a tissue, blew her nose and sipped from her glass. She seemed to have entirely forgotten what she'd told me as I drove down to Ballymoney.

"What about her sleeping?"

"Much improved."

"That's good, anyway." My gaze settled on the whiskey bottle, though I didn't say anything.

"You're right, Bea, I do need it too much. I'll get some help when we go home."

"Good."

A phone rang then and it took me a few seconds to realise it was mine. I picked it up off the worktop.

"It's Gabriel." I nodded at Georgina and walked into the hall.

"Everything all right down there?"

It was good to hear his voice.

"Okay. A bit emotional."

"I wanted to let you know, let Georgina know – they've kept Sheils in custody."

"Why?"

"They found out Andrew did owe him the money but here's the thing . . ."

The phone made a crackling sound.

"Say that again." I walked toward the front of the house to try to improve the signal.

"He wasn't on the plane before Andrew died, he was on it two days later."

I remembered then how Sheils had told us in Georgina's kitchen that he was already on his way to Canada when the murder happened.

"The lads checked the flights. He was listed for travel on July 20th." He sounded delighted.

"Have they asked him about it?"

"He said he was embarrassed that he hadn't stuck around for the funeral once he knew Andrew was dead. Lied to you and Georgina because he felt guilty."

"Do they believe him?"

"You know Matt, doesn't say much. But it's a strong motive, isn't it? Couldn't get the money out of him so he clocked him on the head."

"And he didn't mind a bit of breaking and entering." I could hear Gabriel coughing loudly on the other end of the phone.

"Are you okay?"

"I'm fine. He has a record too. Done for grievous bodily harm a few years ago, spent eighteen months in the Joy."

"Thank God Georgina came down here – he might have hurt them."

"Fair chance he would have if he hadn't got his money."

I thought about that for a few seconds.

"What will happen if they let him go?"

"Early days. If they charge him he mightn't get bail. Tell Georgina to stay where she is, though, for the moment."

"Okay. Did they say anything about him knowing Billie at all? There'd have to be some connection, wouldn't there, if the pathologist is right?"

"They haven't found anything yet. I'll see you when you get back to Dublin?"

"Of course, thanks."

Relief flooded over me as I hung up. I had a sense that everything would be all right for Georgina and the children once the guards put someone away for Andrew's murder. And maybe, when it was over, Georgina would get herself some help, or maybe she wouldn't even need it once her questions were answered.

In the kitchen, she had topped up her glass. I sat down and told her what Gabriel had said.

"Jesus! It was him and I let him into my house." Her face turned white.

"They don't know for sure that it was him, but they suspect it."

"It makes sense though, doesn't it? It sounds like it." She began to shake and then cry again. When she had finished, she looked as though all the tears and emotion had been wrung out of her.

I thought what a burden it was to her, not knowing all this time why her husband had died.

"He killed him for money, just for stupid money. If he'd told me we could have raised it somehow."

"I'm sure Andrew didn't imagine it would go that far." I drank some of my water. "Gabriel said it would probably be best if you stay here for a while, just in case."

"In case what?"

"I'm not sure – it's just sometimes they have to release a person until the director of public prosecutions decides on a charge and sometimes, if there is a charge, the person gets out on bail." I hadn't wanted to frighten her but needed to be sure she understood the seriousness of the situation.

"Does he know I'm here?"

"No. How could he?"

Georgina nodded, suddenly all business.

"Okay. It'll be okay. We'll stay here until they decide about keeping him in custody. I'll let the schools know we'll be away for a while." She put the cap back on the whiskey bottle.

"Do you think I should tell the children? Maybe Emma, I'll just tell Emma." She called her daughter into the kitchen and Emma stood on the door saddle between the rooms.

"Come in and close it."

"What?"

"Sit down."

The child did what she was told. Georgina reached out and took hold of her daughter's hands.

"That man outside the house? They think he might be the one who killed Andrew."

I was shocked at her bluntness and Emma's face was all confusion.

"But – I don't understand."

"I know, it's very confusing." Georgina let go of her daughter's hands and put her two arms out to her.

Emma went into them and rested her head against her mother's shoulder.

"It's all over now, they have the bad man," Georgina whispered into her daughter's hair in a tone more suited to a four-year-old. "There's nothing to be frightened of anymore."

I wanted to remind her that it was nowhere near over, that Sheils could well be released tomorrow, that he might have some other alibi. But instead I slipped out of the kitchen quietly and left mother and daughter to comfort each other.

Upstairs in my room, I thought about Andrew and how hard it must have been for him to cope with his debts. Men, I decided, were strange animals. What was it that made them think they had to shoulder their burdens alone? I couldn't understand why someone married to a woman like Georgina could not have talked to her about his problems. Was it shame? Were his weaknesses so deplorable in his own eyes that he couldn't risk being exposed? I supposed if he hadn't been killed, he might have come round to sharing everything with her. Perhaps it was just that he had run out of time.

I thought about Billie Nichols then and whether the guards had asked Sheils about her yet. Perhaps there was no connection at all between the two deaths. The murder weapons were alike and it seemed the method was the same, but couldn't that just have been a coincidence? Bats of all sizes were easy enough to get hold of. Maybe someone had read about Andrew's death and simply copied it. It was, I supposed, a relatively easy way to kill. I felt I would be capable of inflicting enough damage to cause death if I were sufficiently provoked. But what would provoke me to that extent I didn't know.

I considered whether I might have been capable of killing Stephen O'Farrell. It was he who had swindled Laurence and, as far as I was concerned, driven him to suicide. I certainly had enough loathing in me to kill him,

had I met him in the days following Laurence's de,
But I was so weak with heartbreak I would not have ha,
the strength. And by the time my strength had returned, I
would not have been willing to sacrifice my own life to
take his.

By the time I went downstairs, Georgina and the
children were all on the sofa watching *Frozen*. Milly was
singing "Let it Go" at the top of her voice. She beckoned
to me to join her, but I shook my head.

"I'm going for a walk!" I called to Georgina who
nodded and smiled, looking happier than I'd seen her in a
long time.

Well wrapped up, I walked briskly down to the beach
and let the wind coming in over the waves blow into my
face and make my eyes water. I considered putting work
on hold, to stay at Seafield Cottage for a couple of
weeks, but knew that wasn't realistic. I needed to be
earning and Georgina, now knowing about the arrest,
probably needed nothing more for a while than to be
with her children. She would, I felt, get help for her
drinking when the time was right. I hoped that in a few
weeks' time, they would all be back in Dublin, the
children would be in school, Georgina would be back at
work and life could return to normal for everyone.

Chapter 23

Sunday, November 13th, 2016

I left Seafield Cottage at three on Sunday, earlier than planned because the house had been so calm and Georgina's mood seemed to have stabilised. She'd told me she'd had her first good night's sleep since Andrew died. Emma had slept quietly, for once, undisturbed by any of her usual terrors. And, Georgina said, knowing who had killed Andrew and why had helped something in her unwind that she hadn't known was full of tension. I had not contradicted her about the certainty. What did it matter if the position changed later and Lar Sheils was found not to have been her husband's killer? At least she was finding some relief. She had even been blasé when I asked her about Jason Armitage.

"His name sounds familiar," she'd said. "I think Andrew worked with him. I think he's a client of Techworld." She hadn't even pressed me about why I was asking. And I supposed it didn't really matter with Lar Sheils in custody.

Now, as I drove back to Dublin, I was five minutes into a call with Gabriel on speaker phone and I wondered whether, since they were holding Lar Sheils, the guards would stop their other lines of inquiry.

"They won't. Even if they're certain it was Lar Sheils. If they can get him at the location, they'll still need to find his connection with Billie. And they'll be talking to Jason Armitage as well."

I told him what Georgina had said about him maybe being a client of Techworld.

"That's the first real connection then, isn't it?" He coughed a bit then.

"Would you not get yourself something for that?"

"It's nothing, just a tickle. Matt'll be pleased with the Armitage link – the way he talks about that fella, you'd think he was public enemy number one. Says they think he brings trafficked girls into the country as well, though they haven't been able to catch him yet."

"Awful man."

I thought of Felicity Scott and wondered if she might know something about it that would be helpful. But I had said I wouldn't ring her again. The guards would have to do that.

"I meant to ask, did McCann say anything about CCTV from Spin?" I said.

"I think the lads got it all right, though I don't know if they've looked at it yet."

"And was Nikolai Strofsky any help to them?"

"Who?"

I checked my mirrors, manoeuvred into the left lane and took the slip road toward Loughlinstown, avoiding the M50.

"You know, Claire Davis – her boyfriend? The security

at Spin. I'm sure they must have interviewed him by now."

"Matt never mentioned his name, but that doesn't mean anything. I'm meeting him for a quick pint this evening. I'll ask him then. I'll see you tomorrow if that's okay?"

"Of course, why wouldn't it be?" It came out sounding snappy though I hadn't meant it to.

"Right so."

He ended the call abruptly and I jabbed the screen of my phone. Why had that irritated me so much? What was it I was supposed to say to him? 'I thought you were going to meet me?' I thought he'd said he was the last time we spoke, but so what? He could do whatever he liked.

I was so preoccupied I almost missed the turn for Clonkeen Road. It was ten minutes past four and dusk had settled on this part of the city, giving the three-bed semi-ds a winter-yellow glow. I drove past the car sales showroom and along the side of Deansgrange Cemetery. A flower seller parked at its gates was packing up his wares. I supposed there were not many visitors to the graveyard after dark.

I remembered when Laurence was only two weeks dead and I had taken the bus out to Sutton graveyard and sat on the grass by his grave and talked to him for hours. And the light had begun to fade and I'd been tempted to just lie down and sleep. A woman had approached me and asked for directions back to the city and I'd walked to the gate with her to show her where to get the bus. "Don't you think you should come with me?" she'd said and I'd known then her request had just been an excuse to get me away from the grave. I'd got on the bus and talked to the woman all the way home about Laurence without ever once asking who it was she'd been visiting there. The self-absorption of youth, I thought now.

As I passed Blackrock my phone buzzed with a message from Claire Davis.

"Can we meet you this evening?"

At the traffic lights, I quickly responded "Yes, same place at six?"

"Thanks," was the response.

When I opened the door to Sweetman's pub the smell of hops and Irish stew drifted toward me on warm air. Though it was early evening, there was already loud chatter in the bar and a group of men and women, some of whom I recognised from Store Street Garda station as off-duty officers, were talking with great animation. I thought I heard someone mention a promotion as I passed. I found Claire and Nikolai waiting for me at a table not far from the group. Nikolai went to the bar and brought back a tea for me and two beers. I took my coat off, settled myself on a stool and waited for them to speak. They seemed anxious about starting and were holding hands under the table.

"Go ahead," I said after I poured and milked some tea.

"Thanks for meeting us," Claire began. "We're hoping you might be able to help us."

"I can try. How?"

"You know the detective working on Andrew Dalton's case, don't you?"

"What makes you say that?" How could they know?

"It was just," Claire looked uncomfortable, "he came by the casino a couple of days ago and he was asking all kinds of questions and I had to tell him I worked at St Louisa's and then I told him about you calling in there, asking about Georgina's family."

So that was how McCann had found out.

"I described you to him and he said – well, he said 'Nosey type, was she?'– and when I offered him your name, he said he didn't need it, so I knew he must know you." She had flushed with embarrassment.

"That sounds like McCann," I said.

Claire hesitated. "We hoped, we thought, with you knowing him and all, you might –"

"We hoped you'd advise us," Nikolai interrupted.

"How? Is it to do with Andrew Dalton's death?"

"It is," Claire said. "We were both working in Spin that night but, well, the guards interviewed me but not Nikolai. They don't know he works there."

I didn't think it would look good that Nikolai hadn't come forward.

"Best to go to them before they come to you," I said.

Nikolai shook his head. "I can't – my work visa ran out last year. If I speak to police they'll send me home."

I wasn't sure how well connected the Garda National Immigration Bureau was with the rest of the force.

"What is it you need to tell them?"

"The night he was killed I saw him talking to a man outside. Then they walked off together."

McCann put his hand up. "Hold on, now hold on. You work on security at Spin? Why wasn't I given your name by the casino?"

Nikolai shrugged. "A mistake. They forget to put me on list."

"Right. So you worked security there for how long?"

"Eighteen months. My papers are in order."

He said it without flinching, though he knew I knew he was lying.

"Let me stop you there. My job is to find out who killed Andrew Dalton. As long as it wasn't you, I've no interest in your papers, okay?"

Nikolai nodded, still looking wary.

"Okay, then. You say you saw Dalton in the casino, how often?"

"Many times."

"And you say he pestered Claire?"

Nikolai looked at Claire again. "He always bothers her. I saw him one night – he wouldn't leave her alone. She was saying 'no' but he kept on."

"When was this?"

"A few nights before he was killed. They went into the park and she was saying no and he kept on and then she pushed him away and came out."

"And you saw this?"

"Yes."

"How?" The inspector made a steeple with his fingers.

Nikolai looked confused.

"It's a simple question. How were you in a position to see this?"

"I was afraid something would happen. I followed them."

"Okay. Are you two a couple?"

"Now, yes," Claire answered.

"But not then?"

"No, but I knew he had a soft spot for me." She smiled at the detective.

He didn't smile back. "You mentioned you saw him talk to a man?" he said to Nikolai.

"Outside the casino. This is what I want to tell you. The night he was killed I saw a man talk to him. The man, the one who talked to him, he was waiting outside."

"Could you hear what was said?"

"No. It was not loud."

"How did they seem with each other? Were they arguing?"

"I would say . . . they were like men talking business."

"Okay. Do you remember what the man looked like? How tall was he?"

He thought for a moment. "Not tall."

McCann nodded. He began to describe Lar Sheils.

"I can't be sure, but maybe yes," said Nikolai.

I didn't notice Gabriel until he was standing beside me.

"What are you doing here, Matt? I thought we were meeting in Mulligan's." He found a spare stool and sat down at our now overcrowded table.

"Just dropped in to buy a pint for one of the lads, got his sergeant's exam. You didn't mention you were meeting Beatrice . . ." McCann was trying to ascertain whether Gabriel already knew about Claire and me meeting up.

"No, he wasn't," I said, "but I texted him twenty minutes ago and asked him to drop by on his way to see you."

McCann nodded again and turned back to Nikolai. "You've been a help, Mr Strofsky," he said. "I might need to talk to you again later – maybe formally the next time."

Claire and Nikolai nodded.

"Can I just say this to you," he went on. "The visa situation isn't my bailiwick, but you might be wise to sort it out one way or another. I think you know what I mean."

Claire glanced sideways at Nikolai. They both looked relieved.

"Can I ask you one other thing, Mr Strofsky? When you followed Mr Dalton and Claire into the park, what would you have done if he hadn't stopped 'bothering' her?"

"I would have helped her get away."

"Would you have hurt him if you had to, like?"

"I would have, yes."

Claire picked up her coat and bag. "We should go now."

Nikolai stood up and shook hands with each of us in turn.

"Goodbye," I said. I couldn't help feeling that we might not see him again.

McCann must have felt the same.

"You won't go disappearing on me now, sure you won't, Mr Strofsky?" he said.

Nikolai shook his head.

We watched in silence as they left.

"Well now, Beatrice Barrington, aren't you something else?" McCann said.

"Pint?" Gabriel asked him. He nodded. "Anything for you, Bea?"

"No, thanks."

"You won't tell the Immigration Bureau, will you?" I asked when Gabriel had gone to the bar.

"Haven't the time. Not like you, Bea, with time to get your nose in everywhere."

I thought that was harsh but didn't feel like arguing with him at that moment. I suddenly felt tired.

Gabriel came back with two creamy pints.

"I'll leave you two to the rest of your evening," I said, standing and putting on my coat.

"Right so," said McCann. "And Bea, don't be telling Georgina O'Donnell about any of this, do you hear me?"

"Goodnight," was the only response I gave him.

On the way home, I thought about all the things I was not telling Georgina about her husband – the one-night stand with Claire, his treatment of her, his meeting with Lar Sheils at Spin, the Rohypnol found in his jacket. What sort of friend did that make me?

Chapter 24

Monday, November 14th, 2016

Mr O'Malley looked calm in Court 32 in a smart navy suit, pale-blue shirt and sober grey tie. As he stood to take the oath, it was evident from his lean frame and the fold of excess skin on his neck that he had lost weight. I wondered if he was one of those men who in middle age embraces an exercise regime to which he was unaccustomed or whether there was someone he had worked to get into shape for.

"I swear that the evidence I shall give shall be the truth, the whole truth and nothing but the truth, so help me God." He spoke slowly and with a clear voice, giving the impression he had been well coached.

"Now, Mr O'Malley," his barrister Ruby Clements said, "let's begin with your income."

She took him through the finer detail of his incomings and outgoings. He said the expense of having to pay rent on his Spencer Dock apartment as well as a mortgage on the family home was killing him.

"There are only so many hours in the day to earn money," he said.

"Do you have a new partner, Mr O'Malley?"

"Not at all – *she's* put me off women for life."

There was a noise from Mrs O'Malley like a stifled guffaw which she quickly turned into a cough.

"And the children, how would you describe your relationship with them?"

"Marvellous. They're the centre of my world. I love them all to bits."

There was another slightly louder sound.

"Robin is so clever for his age, you know? And good at football, much better than I ever was. Bluebell, she's eight, and so artistic, always drawing, and if she's not she's going over to her friends' houses, very sociable. And Petal, she's our live wire, I'd say she'd buy and sell you when she's older." He smiled while he spoke about them, all the way to his eyes.

"Can you address the claim that you forced the children to run up and down the stairs around the house at high speed when they didn't want to?"

"I didn't force them. I encouraged them. It was a game. And they asked me to do it over and over again because they were having fun. That's how kids are."

"Of course. Now, tell the court about how access has been since you moved out of the family home. Are there agreed times?"

Mr O'Malley pulled at his earlobe. "In theory, yes, but it really only happens when it suits *her*. She has to have complete control."

"And is it true that Robin didn't want to attend access with you last week?"

"No. She made that up. She's trying to turn them all

against me." He looked down the court in the direction of his wife. "Bluebell told me what you said, Rosemary."

"Direct your answers to the judge, please, Mr O'Malley," Ms Clements said. "What was it Bluebell told you?"

"She said her mother told them I didn't love them anymore and I was trying to find another family." His voice vibrated with emotion. "That's cruel, that is – not just to me, it's cruel to them." He drank from a glass of water beside him. "I haven't stopped loving them and I never will."

"That is very obvious here today, Mr O'Malley." Ms Clements spoke in a soothing tone and slowly so as to give her client time to compose himself.

"Have there been other examples when she's talked negatively about you to your children?"

"There was this one time when I said I'd collect them at two on a Saturday and bring them to the zoo, but I got a puncture and I phoned her to say I'd be delayed. But she didn't tell them. When they asked where I was she said she didn't know. She just let them sit there in the hall for nearly an hour with their coats on and their little bags. The look on Robin's face when I arrived. And he said to me in the car 'Mammy's right, we can't rely on you'."

"So she let the children suffer to punish you?"

"She did. There was no need for it."

Mrs O'Malley at the back of the room, finding it hard to contain herself, was sighing loudly and shaking her head.

"Do you think, Mr O'Malley, there's an attempt at

parental alienation here?" Ms Clements asked.

"I do, definitely."

"Judge, there are words being put in his mouth now," Ms Hollister interrupted. "That isn't an assessment he can make."

"No, indeed – that will be for Dr McArdle to assess. Can we move on, please, Ms Clements?"

Mr O'Malley's evidence-in-chief was completed by lunchtime and in the afternoon he was cross-examined.

"The truth is, Mr O'Malley, your children are afraid of you, aren't they?" Úna Hollister was less than ten minutes into questioning.

"No, they are not." His voice was tight, defensive.

"Did you know Robin has been having difficulties at school?"

"How would I? *She* never tells me anything."

"Have you been in touch with the school lately? Have you even asked Robin how he's getting on?"

"Of course I've asked. He tells me nothing, he just says 'fine'."

"Why do you think that is, Mr O'Malley?"

"I don't know. I'd say she tells him not to talk to me." He nodded in his wife's direction.

"Could it be that he's afraid of your reaction, Mr O'Malley?" Ms Hollister paused. "Tell the court what really happened the day Robin went home with a black eye."

"There's nothing to tell. There was a bit of horseplay going on. Robin was chasing his sisters, they ran into the kitchen and I closed the door too fast and he got a belt of it in the eye. It was just an accident."

The barrister paused to allow the picture to fully form for the judge.

"So the girls ran into the kitchen. Were they crying?"

"No, laughing, the way kids do when they're being chased."

"And you closed the door for what? To prevent Robin from catching them?"

"Exactly. It was a game."

"And you were in the kitchen and you pulled the door toward yourself to shut it, or away from you?"

Mr O'Malley paused as though trying to visualise. "It closes in, so towards me."

"Then how did you manage to hit Robin if he was on the other side and the door moved toward you?"

"What? Wait, you're confusing me now."

"Let's go through it again . . ."

"I pulled the door closed, yes, then I think I opened it again to see where he was and that's when it hit him. It was an accident."

"It couldn't have been the door handle – Robin would be too tall for that – so was it the edge of the door?"

"I suppose so. I didn't actually see." He moved in his chair as though he suddenly found it uncomfortable.

"Yes. Very painful for him, I'm sure. And what did you do next?"

"I got him some ice."

"Did you say sorry, Mr O'Malley?" She sounded like a head teacher now.

"I'm sure I did."

"Or did you say 'That'll make a man of you'?"

He stuttered and shook his head. "It's just a phrase."

Ms Hollister looked at the judge before moving on to finances.

"Now, you've told the court you can't afford both the rent and half the mortgage at the family home."

"That's right, it's a terrible struggle."

She handed a selection of photographs to the registrar who passed them on to the judge and gave a second set to the witness.

"These are images downloaded from your Facebook account, Mr O'Malley. Do you recognise them?"

"Yes."

"They are dated from May, July and September. Tell the court where they were taken?"

He checked each picture and reddened. "Abroad."

"Where exactly?"

"Mauritius, Sicily and Lanzarote."

"So three foreign holidays, Mr O'Malley, but you can't afford to provide for your own children?"

"My brother paid for them. He could see I was stressed and I needed a break. I only paid for the food!" His voice had grown louder.

"You have a very generous brother. And, tell me, did you take the children on holiday this year at all?"

"*She* wouldn't let me. I wanted to take them to Tramore for a week, *but she said no*!" He was almost shouting now.

"Tramore? Not Mauritius or Lanzarote?"

"She wouldn't let them out of the country!"

"Or you weren't willing to pay for them."

"No, I wanted to take them for a week, but she wouldn't hear of it!"

228

"So no holiday for your children and three for you, Mr O'Malley."

"That's not fair."

"Exactly, Mr O'Malley – you're not being fair to your children."

"You've made you point, Ms Hollister, move on," the judge said.

Shortly after four o'clock, when the cross-examination concluded and Mr O'Malley had been thoroughly flattened, the judge adjourned the case.

"Let the registrar know when Dr McArdle has completed her report, Ms Hollister, and we'll set a date to resume hearing."

"Yes, judge."

I got home around five, changed out of my work clothes into jeans and shirt and made myself something to eat. My head was filled with speculation about Andrew and Billie and the people who seemed to be involved in their lives. Jason Armitage seemed the only one to have a connection with both of them.

Gabriel had texted me early in the morning to say "the lads" had taken Armitage in for questioning. An officer in the cyber-crime investigation unit had found one of his films with Billie in it. The copyright stamp was from 2006, putting Billie at sixteen.

"Ignorance of age is no defence," Gabriel had repeated to me. He'd sounded as pleased as if he had made the arrest himself. "He'll struggle to get out of this one."

When he rang off I hoped they would find out if

Andrew had been involved with Armitage in some way – perhaps that he was more than just a client of Techworld. Maybe he'd been another person Andrew got a loan from. I thought Armitage was the kind of man who might be insulted if he was not being repaid – it would be more than just about money, there would be ego there, a need to show he was in charge and therefore, a need to punish. We already knew that Armitage had a motive to kill Billie. But then where did Lar Sheils, with his faulty alibi, fit in? Could he have been working with Armitage or for him? And I supposed, though I had ruled him out, the guards would be wondering about Nikolai Strofsky.

The questions were swirling in my brain and so when I'd finished eating I began doing my laundry. I felt there was more therapy in washing, drying and ironing clothes than in fashionable practices such as mindfulness. It was a question of finding a task that was soothing and absorbing, the rest was just pop psychology.

I was in my bedroom hanging up freshly ironed blouses when I heard my mobile ringing. It was downstairs on the hall table and I hated having to dash to answer it, but these days I was on alert in case anything happened to Georgina. I needed to be available for her.

I managed to get to it on the fifth ring. I picked it up, simultaneously noting that the number was unfamiliar.

"Hello."

"You called me." A woman's voice was on the other end. "I was over in Magaluf, only got back yesterday."

"Right." I didn't recognise the voice.

"I'm Billie's mother."

"Oh! I'm so sorry about what happened to Billie."

"Yes."

"Thanks for ringing me back."

"What did you want?" She was curt.

"I wanted to . . . I was hoping we could meet for a chat. Billie was a very special person."

She made a strange dry noise in her throat, like a croak. "I've a lot to do."

"I'm sorry, of course you do."

"Do you know Hanlon's, where she worked?"

"Yes."

"They still owe her a few bob and I'm going in to collect it. I can meet you there, I suppose."

"Good, great, thanks."

"I'll be there about nine tonight."

"See you then, thanks." It was a quarter past eight and I called Gabriel while finding my car keys and coat.

"Will I come with you?"

"I don't want to frighten her off. What about if you just sit somewhere nearby?"

He agreed and I hung up, put my coat and a scarf on and went out to the car. Turning the key in the ignition, I wondered what I was going to say to this woman. It was hard to know where to start. Did she even know everything about Billie herself? Did she know about Jason Armitage?

I found a parking spot on Marlborough Road, locked the car and walked the few yards to Hanlon's. A biting wind made me pull my scarf up over my chin for protection. The dark sky, heavy with cloud, threatened rain and it seemed to me that it almost touched the top of the red-brick chimney pots that were sitting on the grey slate roofs of the Georgian houses. The pub, by comparison, felt cosy. I sat at a table in the centre of a row so that Gabriel could sit nearby without being too close. When Piotr approached and asked what I wanted, I ordered tea. Gabriel arrived five minutes later and took up the seat I knew he would choose, two tables away, nodding discreetly in my direction as he sat down.

"You two are fighting?" Piotr placed the teapot, cup and milk jug in front of me.

"Of course not but we don't live in each other's pockets," I snapped back at him too quickly.

"None of my business." He put up a hand in surrender and walked away.

I was halfway through my tea when I noticed a woman approaching the bar, saying something and then turning to look around. She was older than I'd expected, and shorter, with grey hair in a stiff bob. There was that look of toughness about her that comes from deprivation in childhood and hardship in later life. As she moved closer, I could see the sinews in her neck, standing out like lengths of washing-line beneath thin, brown leather.

"Is it you?"

I stood up and offered the woman my hand. She took it, limply, unzipped a navy anorak, put it across one stool and sat down.

"Thanks first of all for meeting me, this must be a difficult time for you." I thought there was a slight sneer on her face, a kind of disdain in her eyes. "Can I get you something?"

Just as I asked, Piotr appeared with a tray containing

a glass of white spirit, a small tonic bottle and a sandwich. He unloaded it without speaking and waited to be paid. The woman did nothing. I reached for my purse and found a note.

"Thanks, Piotr," I said.

I waited for Billie's mother to empty the tonic into her gin.

"Mrs Nichols –"

"It's not Mrs – and it's not Nichols," the woman scoffed. She took a sip from her drink. "That was her – jazz mad. When she changed her name she put her favourites together – Billie Holiday, Herbie Nichols."

No wonder McCann had trouble finding background – she'd changed her name.

"What should I call you?"

"Joan, Joan Richmond."

The name sounded familiar to me though I couldn't place it. "Well, Joan, I knew Billie for only a little while, but I thought she was a fine person."

She bit into her sandwich, the kind of tentative nibble made by a woman who does not fully trust her dentures.

"You and she lost touch, Joan. May I ask what happened?"

She gave me a sharp look. "There's no use asking me, I don't know what I did wrong. I was a great mother, gave her everything. You wouldn't believe what I did to make sure she was looked after – singing lessons, nice clothes, everything. No gratitude though, not one ounce of gratitude." Her response sounded rehearsed. "But sure isn't that always the way with kids? The more you give them the less they appreciate it. Have you kids yourself, Beatrice?"

"No."

"You wouldn't understand so. The sacrifices you make for them from the moment you bring them into the world!"

I half expected her to spit on the floor with bitterness.

"You were a single mother then?"

Again, there was a half-sneer on Joan's face.

"My day you were an unmarried mother, that's what they called it, like you were half a person or somethin'. But no use tryin' to explain what that was like to your kid – no grasp at all of the hardship of it." She nibbled again. "All right now of course – you see the young ones pushing their new buggies down to the post office for the Social and nobody turning a hair. No shame in the young ones now. There was shame in it when I had her." She took a breath, let her shoulders drop in a heavy sigh and took another bite of her sandwich, washing it down this time with a mouthful from her glass.

"So when did she move out of your place?"

"Sixteen she was, and a right little rip. We had this massive row, called me some awful things. I said to her, says I, 'If that's how you feel why don't yeh feck off out of here?'. And she did." She looked off into the distance as though replaying the argument in her head.

I thought I saw a fleeting shadow of regret pass across her face, before she began to talk again.

"I gave her a few days, thought she was staying with one of her friends, but then when I went lookin' she was nowhere. Not even her best friend knew where she was gone."

"Did you ever find out what happened to her – before she ended up working here, I mean?"

"Sure I never got to speak to her again. I tried, God

knows, but I only found out by accident that she changed her name. Met a young one used to be in school with her, said she saw her in Hanlon's and she was calling herself something else, couldn't remember what. Do you know how that felt, some young one telling me my daughter changed her name?"

She swallowed back the remains of her drink and I asked if she'd like another. She nodded her head, not in gratitude, but as though she was acquiescing as a personal favour to me. I signalled to Piotr who brought the same again.

"Do you know, I came here lookin' to talk to her and she wouldn't even speak to me?" Her tone was filled with fresh incredulity. "Do you know what I believe, Beatrice?"

I shook my head.

"She got mixed up in some nasty business, maybe drugs or somethin' and she was so ashamed of herself, she was afraid to come near me." She paused again, as though waiting for some sort of approval.

I could not force myself to agree and felt only a wave of sympathy for the bright girl who had served behind the bar and had lit up Oxmantown Road.

"Do you know what she said the last time I saw her? She said I didn't keep her safe. Would you believe that? And all I ever wanted was the best for her."

"I'm sorry, Joan. It must be very hard."

The woman took a deep swallow from her glass. Her pale, bony cheeks were crimson and I thought she might have been drinking before our meeting.

"She could've been big, did you know that? She had the voice of an angel. But she just threw it away." Her eyes filled with tears and she covered them with her left hand, the glass still in her right. "Oh God, Jess, what happened to you at all?" Her shoulders began to shake and the hardness in her seemed to momentarily dissolve.

I rummaged in my handbag for a tissue and handed it across to her.

She blew her nose. "She was only young – she had everything still ahead of her."

"She was lovely. I'm so sorry."

Joan composed herself then. "Anyway, I've got to talk to the guards again." She paused. "Would you come to the funeral?"

"Of course."

"Okay, then." She swallowed the last of her drink, stood up and carefully found the sleeves of her anorak into which she slipped her arms. She stood with her feet apart, wavering slightly and focusing on the coat's zip. It took her a couple of attempts to slide the two parts together then she tugged the pull-tab upwards to her chin. "I'll see you tomorrow so."

"Tomorrow?"

"Yes. Not decent to leave her any longer. Eleven o'clock. St John Vianney, do you know it?"

"I think so."

"Right then."

She turned and walked over to the bar again. She had a few words with Piotr and he handed her an envelope. I supposed it was Billie's wages. She left then, without looking back.

A mixture of pity and revulsion overcame me when she had gone.

Gabriel picked up his pint and moved to my table.

"Did you hear all that?"

"I did. Poor woman."

"Poor woman? There was a lot of self-pity there, a lot of self-justification."

"What did you expect? She's the one left behind. She has to tell herself some story to make it bearable."

I stirred the remains of my tea, though I didn't intend to drink it.

"I wonder what Billie meant about not keeping her safe," I said.

"Who knows? Tough as old boots, though, wasn't she?" He said it with a hint of admiration.

I couldn't feel the same.

"Took the guards long enough to find her though, didn't it? They must have had her phone number a couple of weeks."

Gabriel didn't answer me or try to defend "the lads" in the way he normally would. We both knew there were resource problems and that McCann was under pressure. I let it go.

There was something niggling at me. I pushed the cup away.

"I should order some flowers for tomorrow," I said. "Would you like me to get you some, a wreath maybe?"

"Please, but not a wreath – a big bunch with lots of yellow."

Yellow would be just right for Billie, I thought, and for a moment I wanted to take his hand in mine. I wanted to tell him that I thought he was a lovely man.

Then something dawned on me. Joan Richmond, Jess

Richmond. I had heard those names before. I had read them. Where though? Where? I closed my eyes and then I pictured the name, in handwriting on a page . . . on a page in a diary, the diary I'd found in Gabriel's. It hadn't belonged to some long-ago case of his. It had belonged to Billie. Why hadn't I thought of that?

I stood up abruptly and grabbed my coat.

"We need to go back to your house."

Gabriel followed me out to my car.

On the way to Oxmantown Road I explained as clearly as I could about how I'd come to read the diary and what was in it. He listened without speaking until I'd finished.

"Why didn't you tell me, Bea?" he said then. He looked completely puzzled.

"I'm sorry . . . I never imagined it was Billie's. I thought maybe it was evidence from some old case that you somehow mislaid or something." It sounded ridiculous, when I said it out loud, that I would think Gabriel could be so unprofessional.

"If you say so." He didn't look pleased with my excuse.

In Number 9 I went straight to the bookcase and pulled out the diary.

We sat on the sofa and I flicked through the pages. I gave him the gist of what each page said.

"God almighty, there's some right bastards out there."

"I know. Poor Billie."

He turned the diary over in his hand. "I'll give this to Matt. We'll tell him I only just found it, okay?"

"Okay."

He went out to the hall and called McCann. I looked again at the writing in the diary, Billie's writing, Billie's story. It made sense now that she'd left home, that she'd blamed her mother for not protecting her.

"He's asked me to hand it in at the station," Gabriel said when he'd finished on the phone.

"I'll drop you off, and order those flowers," I said.

Chapter 25

Tuesday, November 15th, 2016

St John Vianney Church on Ardlea Road in Artane was typical of a 1960s creation, a simple shape with grey brick and plaster painted walls and row after row of wooden pews with red leatherette kneelers. Its size had rightly anticipated a local spurt in population, but had not foreseen a drift away from Catholicism. It meant that, though there were more than 100 people gathered for the funeral Mass of Billie Nichols, or Jess Richmond, the church looked barely populated.

Joan Richmond sat alone in the front row looking pitiful in a black wool coat that seemed too big for her.

Behind her, rows of people sat, young and old, neighbours, friends and relatives. On the way in, Gabriel had nodded at two lads, sitting in the back row wearing plain clothes and the spotless white runners of undercover gardaí. We had taken up a position halfway down the church from where we could see all who came and went, many passing by us and up the aisle to place white envelopes on Billie's brown coffin close to the altar. It was adorned with carvings on each side of what looked like the Last Supper. There were brass handles, a brass plate on top, and sitting upright a photograph of a teenager, fresh and lovely, with long brown hair and Billie's smile beaming out at the congregation. There was, I thought, nothing sadder than a young person's coffin.

The service was simple. The priest spoke of the bright young woman he thought might have joined the school choir and the terrible loss of hope that had manifested when someone had cruelly taken her young life. The congregation prayed collectively for Billie's mother, for the troubled people of the world and for the gardaí that they might apprehend the perpetrator and bring justice to the community.

"Of course, there is a higher justice, that will manifest in the afterlife and even if the perpetrator of this terrible deed is never known on earth, he will be found out and judged in the Kingdom of God."

I couldn't help thinking what little comfort that would bring Joan. It was on this earth that she would want to see justice done, not in some hereafter conjured up as a sort of eternal courtroom. I wanted to say what I thought to Gabriel, but knew it wouldn't go down well. He was a Mass-goer, and despite, or perhaps because of, his experiences with crime and criminals, he believed in the justice and comfort of the Almighty.

It was not long until a wave of incense drifted down the aisle toward us and the coffin was being lifted and then shouldered by half a dozen young men. I spotted Piotr from Hanlon's, and Gabriel quietly pointed out Dewain Babangida, from the house share on the North Circular Road, among the pallbearers. For the first time, music filled the church as the coffin moved slowly down its centre. It was Billie Holiday singing "God Bless the Child". Gabriel cleared his throat and when I turned toward him he was blowing his nose into a big white handkerchief.

Joan walked behind the coffin, with a woman of about her own age linking her arm. Behind them, a group of young people clustered and I noticed one young woman, in black jeans and black faux-fur jacket, who was sobbing wholeheartedly.

Outside, in a cold, misty drizzle, people hastily shook hands with Joan before making for their cars.

We joined the queue to tell her we were sorry for her troubles. She thanked us for coming, but it was clear she didn't know who we were – her eyes were glazed with grief.

We followed the hearse and the black limousine that carried only Joan out to Glasnevin Cemetery in Gabriel's car. Mourners' cars snaked on a slow detour, behind the hearse and round by Castletimon Lawn to pass the door of Billie's childhood home. Then we picked up a little speed to navigate the Oscar Traynor Road, and the M1, through Whitehall and Botanic Road to the Finglas Road.

Billie was to be buried in the newer half of the cemetery, on the opposite side to the Parnell monument and museum.

We parked on Claremont Crescent and made our way with the other mourners into the cemetery. It seemed many of those who were in the church had continued on to witness the burial. We stood and watched as Billie's coffin was lowered into the plot, nestled at a side wall, out of the breeze. Joan threw a yellow rose down into the grave, weeping as she did so. The priest said a few prayers and then passed on Joan's message requesting all those present to return to the "Roundabout lounge" near the church, for soup and sandwiches and a final farewell to her daughter. Mourners drifted back to their cars, weaving their way between headstones until they were out again on the busy road.

Though we hadn't intended to, we both felt it would be rude not to follow the others back to the pub in Artane. I told Gabriel it was the same pub that had hosted the long-ago singing competition that Billie had spoken about in her diary.

"I wonder how different Billie's life would have been if she hadn't entered that competition," I said as we drove back.

"That's how life is though, isn't it?" Gabriel said. The car was quiet – he mustn't have felt like listening to Johnny Cash. "All those little decisions, and none of us can know how things might have been if we'd made a different choice."

"It wasn't all of her choosing though, was it? She was only a child. And the person who should have been protecting her was too gullible."

"I know. It kept me awake last night, thinking about it. If I could put my hands round the neck of that man, do you know, Bea, I think I could kill him." He pulled up on Ardlea Road and we got out.

I led the way into the lounge side of the pub. There were ten tables reserved for the funeral, with folded triangles of paper on each saying "*Friends and family of Jess Richmond*". There were plates of sandwiches, brown and white, mixed fillings, all cut in little triangles sitting in the centre of each table. And a waitress was working her way around with bowls of soup. We took two empty seats at a table already half-filled.

I found myself sitting next to the young woman I'd noticed at the church, wearing black faux fur. She had shed her outer garment and underneath it a black, sequined top clung to her, accentuating the white of her neck and the narrowness of her waist.

"I'm Beatrice."

"Leanne."

"You were a friend of Billie, I mean Jess, weren't you?" I hoped she was. I hoped she was the girl mentioned in her diary.

The young woman sighed. "Great friends when we were kids." She cut into a white bread roll and began to butter it. "I still can't believe it."

I turned my teacup, which had been face down, the right way up. "It's very cruel."

"I knew her all the way up from Junior Infants. We used to sit together at the back of the class giggling. She was lovely, so she was. Thanks." She smiled as a bowl of vegetable soup, its steam swirling upwards, was placed before her. She raised a spoonful of soup and blew gently on it before tasting.

"Nice."

"I only met her shortly before she died," I said. "But I thought there was something, I don't know, special about her." I shook my head when offered soup and chose instead a brown bread and salad sandwich from the platter.

"Definitely special. Ever hear her sing?"

"No."

"She was fabulous. Like, when we were kids, she used to say she'd be a star on Broadway when she grew up. An', you know, we all had dreams like that, but she was the only one I ever thought could do it."

The bar was buzzing with conversation but above the general noise I could hear Joan, at a table of men and women, talking about her "beautiful Jess" and how much she had tried to do for her.

Leanne could hear her too and made a coughing, choking sound as she swallowed her soup.

"She's unbelievable."

"What do you mean?"

She tilted her bowl to collect another spoonful.

"I know she's Jess's mother an' all but . . . Do you smoke?"

"No."

"Come out with me anyway, if you really want to know." She finished her soup and left.

Gabriel nodded toward me as I got out of my seat, leaving him to chat to a young man in a three-piece suit, who looked like he might have been a banker. As I walked through the pub, I spotted Piotr with his boss Derek Johnston and, in the far corner, though I didn't acknowledge him, I saw Matt McCann nursing an orange juice.

We stood just outside the door, and I was glad I'd taken my coat off the back of my seat. I pulled it round me and buttoned it up. Leanne had taken her jacket and she zipped it up to her chin, then took a cigarette out of a pack, lit up and began to puff.

"That woman – Jess's mother, she was a wagon when Jess was a kid – a soak for starters. Jess used to have to do everything around the house, the cooking and cleaning and that, and this was when she was still in Primary." She sucked in and blew out a short burst of grey fumes. "When she was a teenager, she had this voice. God, you'd kill for it. She won this song contest, in here it was. Then that stupid woman let her go off to sing at a competition in London with a slimebag who said he was a record producer. Fifteen she was, only fifteen." She inhaled again deeply, this time letting the smoke escape through her nostrils. "When she came back and told Joan what he did to her, do you know what that cow said?"

"What?"

"'You must've been asking for it' – instead of calling the guards, she blamed her own daughter. What sort of a mother does that?"

"That's awful." I thought then that if I had looked closely enough at Billie I might have been able to see the hurt she was carrying.

"Of course it was guilt – she couldn't face it. It was easier to blame it on Jess." She drew again on her cigarette. "Stuck it out at home a few months, she did, till after her sixteenth birthday, then she just disappeared. Never even told me she was going. It used to annoy me that she left without saying anything. Now I think she had to cut us all off so she wouldn't have to keep remembering. Know what I mean?"

"I think I do." I thought of my own
sending me away after Laurence died, p
hope I could make a new life for myself.

She stubbed the cigarette out on a meta
the pub door for that purpose.

"The man, do you know his name?" I asked the
question as we walked back through the door of the pub.

"No – but hang on." Leanne walked toward the bar.
"This fella's worked here for years. *Ollie! Ollie!*"

The grey-haired barman took his time getting to us.

"Do you remember the year you did the song
contest?"

He leaned closer. "Say again."

She spoke louder. "The year you did the song contest
and Jess was singing on it?"

"God, yeah, I do."

"Do you remember the fella did the judging? Record
producer or something?"

"That's right. An old school friend of mine. Fella by
the name of Andrew Dalton."

I felt suddenly light-headed and I think I swayed a
little on my feet. I thought there was a chance I would
pass out or vomit.

"You okay? Sit down." Leanne put her hand under
my elbow.

"I'm okay, I just . . . That's definitely the name?"

"Yeah. I booked him myself, sure." Ollie moved away
to serve another customer.

I looked over to where McCann had been sitting, but
he was gone. I made my way back to the table. Leanne
followed and sat down.

found my handbag and leaned close to Gabriel. "I have to get out of here," I muttered.

I said goodbye to Leanne and waited while Gabriel gathered his coat.

Once we got outside, I said, "I know the connection."

"What?"

"Between Billie and Andrew Dalton," I said rapidly. "All this time we couldn't figure it out, McCann couldn't figure it out. We thought it was us, we thought it was the weapon or Jason Armitage."

"Slow down." Gabriel unlocked the car and we both got in.

"Kevie Baby – the man in Billie's diary – it was Andrew. God, I can't believe it, Gabriel."

"Leanne told you? Was she sure?"

"It was the barman who actually said his name. She'd forgotten it." I thought about the Andrew Dalton I had known, a family man who adored his wife and doted on his children. And yet he was a gambler and worse, he was this man too, it seemed. He had never been happy to talk about his life before Georgina, and polite enquiries had been diverted to other things. I had taken that as modesty. There had never been a whisper of darkness about him. I thought of my friend. Had she known what he was capable of? I felt sick and sad, and angry on her behalf.

We drove out onto the Malahide Road, the wipers fighting against sleety rain that had only just begun.

"Do you think," I asked, "I mean, is it within the realm of possibility ... could Billie have killed Andrew?"

"If you mean was she physically capable, I'd say she

248

was. But even with a motive like that … I'd have to say no."

"What if she took your cosh from the house?"

He was silent as we drove past Donnycarney Church, and on by Clontarf Golf Club.

"Ah no," he said then.

"Sure?"

"If she killed him, then how could she have ended up dead herself?" He indicated left, onto the coast road. "And what about Lar Sheils? He's been telling lies. And Jason Armitage?"

When I considered it, I couldn't really imagine Billie killing anyone.

Gabriel continued. "There's that Derek Johnston as well. Matt said he has no alibi for the night Andrew died."

"You never told me that."

"Did I not? Must have forgotten." He indicated for Clontarf Road.

I thought about all those people, all with a connection to Andrew, and was perplexed that Georgina, a woman I had always thought had her life in good order, could not have known about any of them.

"I'll ring Matt and let him know what you've found out."

"I noticed him in the pub with his orange juice."

"Yeah, he was never great at keeping a low profile."

We pulled up outside my house, and Gabriel turned off the engine. The wipers stopped and rain began to obscure the glass.

"Coming in?" I asked.

"No, I've a few things to do . . . I'll talk to you later."

I opened the car door. "I'm going to ring Georgina."

I felt his hand on my arm.

"I don't think you should. That sort of thing is better coming from Matt, officially like."

A part of me knew he was right, but I didn't like it. "What's this, are you putting your Garda cap on? She's my friend."

"I know that, Bea. But at least let me talk to him first. I'll call you straight after."

"I suppose so." I turned and got out, closing the door quickly and dashing toward the house, horizontal raindrops spraying me all the way.

Chapter 26

When I'd put away my wet coat, I defrosted a portion of stew that I'd made in a big batch. I forced myself to eat it though I was nauseous and agitated waiting for Gabriel to phone. I carried my phone with me from kitchen to living room, glancing now and then at its blank, silent screen.

It was ten past five. I switched on the TV and hit a wave of adverts, for funeral insurance, stair lifts and incontinence pads. I turned it off again quickly.

The radio wasn't much better – there was news of the dullest sort – political infighting in the Fine Gael party.

I cursed myself for agreeing not to call Georgina without speaking to Gabriel first. It felt like hours since he'd dropped me off at the house and in that time I had tried to think of all of the reasons why I shouldn't ring her. The longer I waited, the fewer real reasons I could find. She was my friend. Surely that was what mattered, not what McCann or what Gabriel thought?

I was just about to pick up my mobile when its screen lit up and it began to ring. Georgina's name was on the caller ID.

"Beatrice, is that you?" She sounded tense, panicky even.

"Yes. How are you, Georgina?"

"I don't know how I am. I just got a call from the guards. That man McCann, he says he wants to come down for a chat." Her voice quavered. "I asked him if it was about Lar Sheils and he said no, it was something else . . . What could it be?"

I wanted to explain it all there and then but held myself back.

"Did he say what time he was calling?"

"Eight o'clock. Do you know what it's about?"

"I don't." I hated lying to her. "Try not to worry."

"Do you think, would you mind, I mean, I know it's a long drive, but could you come down? You could stay over. I don't want to have to face them alone."

I checked the time. I would be able to make it before eight. I had a case next day at the commercial court, but if I got up early I could drive straight to the Four Courts and beg a spot in the car park.

"Yes, of course I'll come down."

I would have to brace myself, I knew, for the disapproval from McCann at my presence. Well, pity about him.

"See you as soon as I can," I said.

When I got to Seafield Cottage, Georgina opened the door before I could ring the bell.

"Thanks, thanks so much."

She hugged me and I could feel the tension in her, her shoulders rigid despite the embrace. I took off my coat, slung it over the banister and left the overnight bag I'd packed on the floor beside it. I tried to think of soothing phrases that might help.

"It'll be all right. There's nothing to worry about, they probably just want to let you know how the investigation is going."

"Do you think so?"

We went into the kitchen and sat at the table. From the other room, the sound of Milly and James shouting at each other while playing a computer game drifted through the opened connecting doors. I got up, shut them and sat down again.

"You have nothing to fear from the guards. You've told them everything, you've done your best."

"I thought it was all over, though. They have Lar Sheils, what more could they want?"

As she spoke, she scratched the back of her left hand with her right repeatedly and I could see the skin was raw from her nails. I wanted to put my hand out and stop her, but didn't.

"They won't want anything, I'm sure. They probably just need to tell you a few things." I wanted to ask her about her drinking. I glanced around the kitchen. There weren't any glasses or bottles. She had either put them away or she hadn't been drinking and was struggling with that. The latter would explain her extreme agitation.

I stood up, desperate to find some way of calming her.

"Will I make some tea?"

"I'm sick of tea. Sit down, will you?"

I sat and my surprise must have shown because

Georgina got up, filled the kettle and switched it on.

She put a hand on my shoulder. "Sorry. You've driven all the way down here. I should have offered."

"It doesn't matter, Georgina. And it was no trouble, really."

"I don't think I can take much more of this."

I thought of all the murder trials I'd worked at over the years, how long-drawn-out the process had been in each case, the painstaking gathering of evidence, the initial charge, then various adjournments, before families had to endure the trial itself. Georgina really had no idea what was ahead, how much more she would have to take before a final verdict.

"It all goes round and round in my head. All the things Andrew said, everything that happened and what might happen. It's like I can't stop it. I can't switch it off."

"But you're doing well, Georgina, you're managing. Just try not to think too far ahead. Try to take it one day at a time." I almost winced at the sound of my voice, drifting into the lyrics of a Kris Kristofferson song.

The kettle boiled and Georgina made tea in a cup and pot set and put it on the table. She made nothing for herself.

"Thanks."

We sat in silence for a while, listening to the now muffled sounds of the children.

"How's Emma doing?"

"Good, better anyhow. She's up in her room. Needs a bit of space from them sometimes." She indicated toward the living room, from where singing could now be heard. Then the doorbell rang.

"God."

"It's okay. Deep breath and answer it."

I stayed where I was. I could hear the door be opened and the low, Cavan "Ms O'Donnell" of Detective Inspector Matt McCann. Then introductions, and a lighter "hello" from what must have been a woman officer. They walked through to the kitchen and I braced myself for his reaction. He didn't disappoint.

"Lord above, Beatrice. Is there anywhere you're not?"

"Georgina asked me to come down. She wanted the company."

He pulled out a chair without asking and sat down. The uniformed garda, who introduced herself as Francine Gibson, sat beside him. She took out her notebook and a pen and placed them on the table, her pale-pink nail polish, incongruous with the dark navy uniform, catching the light.

Georgina went from the sink to the worktop with the kettle, and made no effort to talk while she prepared a large pot of tea and a plate of biscuits. There was something about the way she moved from cupboard, to fridge, to worktop and back again that reminded me of a jaguar I'd seen once at London Zoo, pacing behind a glass screen.

"Are you down for a couple of days, so?" McCann asked me.

"I'll go back in the morning."

I felt I should add something more, but I didn't know what and we sat in uncomfortable silence until Georgina served McCann and the garda, and sat down, moving her chair a little closer to mine.

with milk and stirred in

_____ a drink. "I have news for you.
_____ ...ody for Lar Sheils. He still has a
_____ ...swer." He reached toward the plate
_____ ...ture of plain, chocolate, and jam. He
_____ ...bit into it, nodding his appreciation.

_____ ...e Georgina's hands in her lap, one scraping
at the ...er.

"We've also picked up a man called Jason Armitage – do you know him?"

Georgina glanced at me. "Yes, I told Bea, he was a client of Techworld. Andrew worked with him."

"You told Bea? Right." McCann shot me a look. "And did you tell her your husband owed him money, by any chance?"

"I didn't know that," Georgina said.

"We've had him in for questioning. €15,000 he says he was owed."

"God." Georgina put her head in her hands.

"I'm afraid your husband was mixed up with some not very nice people, Ms O'Donnell." His tone was hard, too hard, I thought, for someone dealing with a grieving widow.

"Go easy," I said.

He drank from his cup, giving me what felt like a warning look.

"The other thing is, we think we have a connection between your husband and a woman who was killed in Dublin. Have you ever heard of Billie Nichols?"

"Only in the news and what Bea told me, about the murder weapon."

McCann took a big breath in and let it out noisily. "Will you take a look at this then? Tell me if the face is familiar." He nodded to Garda Gibson who produced a photograph.

It was the one of Billie as a teenager, the one that had been on her coffin.

Georgina took it in her hand, looked closely at it and shook her head.

"This then?" Another photograph was produced, this time of an older Billie with her blonde spikes. It looked as though it had been downloaded from a social media account and then enlarged. Her eyes and the surface of her skin were pixilated.

"I think I saw this one on the telly, but otherwise no, sorry." She handed both photos back.

"Did Andrew ever mention Billie?"

"No."

"Or a woman called Jess Richmond?"

"No, I don't think so."

"It's believed he and she knew each other in the past."

"Which of them?" She looked puzzled.

"They're one and the same person."

She shook her head again. "Andrew was in his forties when I met him. I didn't grill him about his past, or about other women he may or may not have known."

McCann put his hand up to her. "All right, we're just trying to gather as much information as we can." He poured himself more tea. "Is there anything else at all that you might remember?"

"I've told you everything I know." She sounded weary.

257

"Okay, but if you think of anything –"

"I'll call you."

"Please do. Call *me*, not anyone else." He looked in my direction again.

Garda Gibson began to close her notebook but stopped when McCann spoke once more.

"There was just one other thing – routine, you understand?" He looked at her and waited for her nod before he continued. "On the night Andrew died, July 18th, I never asked you where you were. Where were you, Ms O'Donnell?"

"At home, of course, with my children, asleep until your lot woke me."

Garda Gibson wrote that down.

"Of course, I just needed to ask. Thanks for the tea."

"Is that everything?"

"It is."

I watched McCann's face throughout the questioning and knew he was holding back. Was it just the nature of the connection between Billie and Andrew that he didn't want to go into? I supposed I would have to hold back on that too. But it wasn't just that – there was something he wasn't satisfied about. If I phoned Gabriel later he might be able to tell me.

We all walked to the hall.

"I suppose I'll be seeing you shortly, Beatrice," McCann said, a note of sarcasm in his voice.

I didn't respond.

"Ms O'Donnell, try not to worry – we'll have answers for you soon."

"Okay, thanks."

She closed the door behind them, a combination of relief and anguish mixing on her face.

"What did he mean, where was I?" She went back to the kitchen and began opening and closing presses. "Why did he ask me that?" She found what she was looking for, a bottle of red wine already open and half-empty. She pulled out the cork, poured a generous glass and sat down.

"You heard what he said, it's routine. He has to ask."

"And what was all that about Andrew knowing this Billie woman? I mean, how am I supposed to – God, my head hurts."

I was tempted to point out that the red wine would not help that.

"Have you painkillers somewhere?" I asked instead.

"Painkillers, yes, upstairs I think, on my bedside locker." She began to move.

"Let me get them for you."

I went upstairs, collecting my overnight bag on the way, and found the master bedroom. I flicked on the light switch and crossed to the locker. A lamp sat on top of it and a novel by Nabokov, but no painkillers. I thought perhaps she had put them in her drawer, so I opened it. Inside there were packets of them. I counted them out onto the bed, twelve boxes. What was this? Could she be planning to take them all? I had known she was struggling, but not that she was this desperate. Should I call a doctor? I was about to shut the drawer when I noticed what looked like a letter. I paused, weighing up whether or not to look at it. Was it possible Georgina had written a suicide note in preparation for the time when she would swallow all of those pills? Better then to look at its contents and try to get a glimpse inside her head and gain some understanding of her anguish.

I reached into the drawer, but when I pulled out what I thought was one letter, it was actually four envelopes with letters inside them. Each had Georgina's name and address handwritten in capitals on the front, with a stamp on each one imprinted with a Dublin postmark. There was a neat slit across the top of each envelope, the kind made with a paperknife. So these were letters to Georgina, not from her. I put them back and as I did I heard footsteps on the stairs. I tipped the painkillers back into the drawer, closing it as quickly and quietly as I could. Then I flicked the light off, picked up my overnight bag and walked out just as Georgina reached the landing.

"I'm sorry, I couldn't find any painkillers . . . I'll just put this away." I held up my bag and felt my cheeks flush at the lie as I made for the guestroom.

Georgina brushed past me into her own room. "They're in here somewhere."

While I emptied the contents of my bag – a suit and blouse for work in the morning, pyjamas and pouch of toiletries – I could hear Georgina opening her locker. I sat on the edge of the bed and worried about what I should do. There was no good reason I could think of for an accumulation of so many drugs. I would have to find a way to talk to her about them. But how would I? I'd just said I couldn't find any painkillers.

I closed my eyes and thought of Georgina when I knew her first – fresh-faced, full of fun, a focused person, brimming with enthusiasm. And here she was now, secretive, stressed to the brink of breaking. I couldn't let that happen. I would have to find some way to get through to her.

Chapter 27

When I'd settled myself I went back downstairs. It was after ten o'clock and Milly and James were only now ready for bed.

"Can we not watch one more cartoon?" James was saying as I walked into the living room.

"We've no school tomorrow," his sister chimed in.

Georgina was tolerant at first, humouring them, but when they failed to move, her patience ebbed away.

"Up you go, now," she said sharply.

They didn't budge.

"*Bed now, I said!*" she shouted at them, standing over them, blocking the TV, her face contorted with anger. "*Brats!*"

They ran out of the room and up the stairs.

I tried to hide my shock, but Emma didn't.

"Really?" She scowled at her mother. "You're a disgrace." She went after her siblings and I could hear her calling as she ran up the stairs, "*It's okay! I'll do the story!*"

Georgina went into the kitchen and came back with a freshly opened bottle of wine and a glass.

"Want some?"

I shook my head.

"Of course not – Legion of Mary." She poured herself a full glass and took a gulp from it.

I wasn't sure what to do. She was in pain, I could see that, and it was making her drink too much. She wasn't the sort of person who mellowed under the influence. This couldn't go on, but how could I stop it? How could I help her?

"Back in a minute," I said.

I wanted to think. As I went into the kitchen I could hear her topping up her glass. Perhaps if she fell asleep on the couch I could dispose of the medication. And I could think of who I should contact. She needed help urgently.

I tidied around the kitchen, wiping down surfaces, putting cups and glasses in the dishwasher. I felt pity for Georgina, but I was sorrier now for her children, particularly Emma, who seemed to be trying to deal with the worst of it. Her mother had become dependent on alcohol, there was no point in pretending otherwise, and as the eldest Emma was trying to keep everyone safe, including her mother.

I had wrung out the dishcloth and taken off the yellow gloves I'd worn to clean the surfaces, when the kitchen door opened.

Emma came in.

"You see?" she said to me.

"Yes, I'm sorry, I didn't realise it had got this bad. It must be very hard for you."

"I wish I was back at school and I wish I could take Milly and James with me."

"It wasn't easy there either, though, was it?" I was remembering the night terrors that Georgina had told me about.

She sat down at the kitchen table.

"Would you like a coffee or something?" I asked.

She shook her head. "I'm not allowed that – it makes my nightmares worse, the doctor said."

"Juice?"

"Okay."

I gave her the juice and sat opposite her with a glass of water. "What's it like, a night terror?"

She thought for a few moments. "Night terrors? I don't know."

I was confused. "But I thought you had sleep trouble?"

"I do, I have nightmares, very, very bad nightmares."

Hadn't Georgina called them night terrors? Perhaps I was mistaken.

"So you remember them then?"

"Yes, bits of them, but they're hard to put into words . . . Really intense, more of a feeling than anything else, but with pictures. Do you know what a meme is?"

"Is it some sort of Facebook thing?"

She gave me an indulgent smile, as though about to explain the internet to a granny who had lived under a stone for the last twenty years.

"It's like a picture or a short video, really short, usually funny, and if it's sent to you, you can play it again as many times as you like."

"Right."

"That's what it's like for me when I'm asleep sometimes, these little videos and pictures get played in my head over and over again, except they're not funny and I have no control over them. And sometimes they make me scream. I try to stop them, but I can't, so I just keep screaming."

"That must be exhausting. And these memes – are they always the same?"

She drank more of her juice and began twirling a piece of her hair round her right index finger.

"I think so, only lately they've been growing a bit and there's sounds in them." She twisted the lock of hair tighter.

"What are the sounds like?"

She glanced at the dividing doors. There was only the noise of the TV inside. "You won't tell?"

"No."

"It's Andrew's voice saying my name over and over again." She shivered. "It scares me."

I wasn't sure what to say to her that would be of any help.

"I suppose when people die, that kind of thing can happen – our minds bring them into our dreams." I knew that was true. But I always felt comforted when the voices of Laurence or my parents visited me while I slept. Emma seemed to feel only fear.

"It's more like – I'm remembering something," she said.

Georgina appeared in the doorway then, swaying slightly.

"What? What is it you think you're remembering, Emma?" I asked.

"I don't know." Emma looked down at her glass.

I thought she might cry.

Her mother crossed the kitchen and put a hand on her shoulder.

"It's okay, go on up to bed now. You must be very tired."

The child got up and left the room.

"Thanks for that," Georgina said harshly as soon as the door was closed.

"What do you mean?" I was surprised at the tone of her voice.

"You got her all upset with your prying. You're to leave her alone, do you hear me?"

"The child is obviously distraught and you are too wrapped up in yourself to see it." I knew I shouldn't have let that fly but I couldn't help myself. "Damn it, Georgina, you're drinking too much and she's suffering."

"*How dare you!*" She was screaming now. "*What would you know about anything, you dried-up prune of a woman?*"

Emma reappeared then at the door. "Mam, stop shouting."

Georgina turned to look at her, blinking. "Sorry, sorry, love." She crossed the room, opened a press filled with cleaning solutions, reached into the back and took out another bottle of wine.

"Mam, no. I swear if you open that . . ."

Georgina ignored her and reached for the corkscrew. Emma banged the kitchen door loudly and I could hear her stamping up the stairs.

"I need some air," I said.

I got my coat and my phone and went out the door and down onto Ballymoney beach.

It was after eleven, the sky was clear and a full mo⌣ had silver-tipped the waves coming gently up the strand. I stood in the centre of the small beach and looked out to the horizon, a thin charcoal line dividing dark sky and dark sea. A trawler with a red hull was moored to one side. Did they fish at night? I imagined fishermen in oilskins pulling in their nets, steadily, hand over hand, hoping for a good catch. Good physical toil, tiring, I supposed, but satisfying in its own way.

I found a large rock to sit on and contemplated ringing Gabriel. His steady voice, his sanity would be soothing, but it was late. It would only worry him and more than likely he would feel obliged to drive down from Dublin to help. That would be unfair. I could only hope that Georgina would fall asleep soon and that, in the morning, sober, I would be able to persuade her to call a doctor. I regretted that I had gone back to Dublin after the last episode and left her with the children.

"Beatrice." I turned and Emma was beside me, in pyjamas and dressing gown.

"You'll catch your death, Emma," I said. "Let's go back inside."

"No wait, please." She put her hand in her pocket and took something out. "You need to ask her about these."

She handed me the four envelopes I'd seen in Georgina's bedside locker.

"Did you take these from your mother?"

"Just read them, please, and then ask her about them. I've been too afraid to." She shivered then turned and ran back to Seafield Cottage.

I looked at the envelopes closely and held them in my

ong time. I thought of Georgina. There was something she was hiding even from me, that was keeping her trapped. I could walk this whole mess in the morning if I wanted to and her down here to suffer with her children. Or I could find out the truth and help her deal with it. Was it right to read them? Maybe it wasn't, but I did.

The first envelope had a date stamp of June 10th, 2016, and was posted in Dublin. I slipped the note out of it. It had been folded in half – a clean, sharp crease in thin lined paper that looked as though it had been torn from a notebook. I opened it.

The writing was neat and in block capitals. There were only a couple of lines.

GEORGINA, YOUR HUSBAND IS NOT WHAT HE SEEMS. MEET ME AT SHOE LANE COFFEE SHOP ON TARA STREET AT ONE O'CLOCK ON THE 18TH. I MEAN YOU NO HARM.

The second note was dated July 1st and written in the same hand.

GEORGINA, WHY DID YOU NOT COME? I AM ONLY TRYING TO HELP. YOUR HUSBAND IS NOT A GOOD PERSON. HE HAS DONE A TERRIBLE THING. I WILL WAIT FOR YOU AT SHOE LANE COFFEE SHOP ON THE 5TH AT ONE.

The third note was dated July 6th and, when I read it, I thought it must have made Georgina's stomach turn over.

GEORGINA, I HAVE SEEN YOUR LOVELY CHILDREN. THEY DESERVE A BETTER FATHER THAN THEY HAVE. YOU DESERVE A BETTER

HUSBAND. MEET ME PLEASE. AT SHOE LANE
COFFEE SHOP 2PM ON THE 10TH.

And then the fourth, July 12th, the week before
Andrew's death, more worrying still.

GEORGINA, I KNOW WHERE YOU WORK. I
WILL WAIT FOR YOU IN THE UNDERGROUND
CAR PARK AT FOUR THIRTY ON FRIDAY. DON'T
BE AFRAID. PLEASE JUST HEAR ME OUT.

The letters took my breath away. I felt as though they
had opened a door into a darkened room and let the light
in just a little bit. I could see shapes inside now, but I
didn't know what they meant. Who were the letters
from? Who knew bad things about Andrew Dalton? Lar
Sheils did – at least, he knew he owed him money. Jason
Armitage did too. Or what about Claire Davis? She'd
seen a nasty side of him. So had her boyfriend Nikolai
Strofsky. He might have thought telling Georgina about
her husband's affair would be a good way of getting rid
of him.

Or what about Billie? It was she who knew his ugliest
side. Could the letters have been from her?

I would have to speak to Georgina. I needed to know
whether she had met the writer and why she hadn't told
the guards about the letters. Why had she brought them
with her to Seafield Cottage? There were so many things
I didn't understand.

What I needed to do first, though, was to find a way
to put the letters back tonight. In the morning, when she
was sober, I could ask her about them and convince her
to give them to the guards.

When I got close to the house, and the light from the

kitchen, I took out my phone and took photographs of each envelope and each letter, then put them in my pocket and approached the door.

Chapter 28

I let myself in the back door as quietly as I could. The kitchen was empty and in the living room Georgina was asleep on the couch, the bottle of wine she had taken from the cupboard empty on the table. I took the bottle and glass into the kitchen and rinsed them both. Should I try to get her to bed? I supposed that would probably be the best thing, but the thought of waking her, not knowing what state she might be in, put me off. Instead I fetched a blanket from the hot press, slipped off her shoes and covered her.

It was after midnight when I went upstairs. I sat on the edge of my bed and thought about what I would need to do. I would return the letters to Georgina's locker. I would try to get some sleep and then I would get up early in the morning. I would need to make contact with an acquaintance who worked for a stenography firm and see if she could find someone to take on my commercial court assignment. There was no way I could leave Ballymoney in the morning. I would be calling a doctor first thing, whether Georgina liked it or not.

I took out the letters, opened the door of my room and stood still on the landing. There was no sound from downstairs so I made my way to Georgina's room. I opened the door quietly, knowing Emma would be asleep in her mother's bed, as she had been every night since she came home from school. I left it slightly ajar so that I would have enough light to see by and I inched my way around to the bedside locker where I'd found the painkillers. I intended to replace the letters and remove the medication. But when I opened the drawer the drugs were gone.

My first thought was that when Emma took the letters, she must have taken them away – she'd been trying to protect her mother for so long, poor thing, it was probably automatic for her. I put the letters in the drawer, closed it quietly and inched back across the room, glad I had not disturbed her. She was lying still in the bed and a thin column of light, from the open door, shone across her. It was then that I noticed them – the blister packs of painkillers on the floor, emptied.

I stopped breathing for a moment. Emma had taken them, not her mother. My pulse raced and I couldn't think straight. What was it I was supposed to do? I couldn't remember. Wake her up? Make her vomit? Give her coffee? I ran first to my bedroom for my phone and dialled for an ambulance.

"I think she's overdosed," I told the voice on the end of the line. Then I gave the address and quick directions to Seafield Cottage.

"Try to wake her, if you can, and talk to her – that's all you need to do – we'll be there soon," a calm woman said.

272

I put the lights on in the bedroom, opened the curtains and the windows and began to shake Emma by the shoulders.

"*Come on, come on, Emma!*"

Her head flopped around on the pillow. I checked for a pulse – it was there. I put my ear close to her face. I could hear her shallow breathing.

"*Emma, Emma!*" I shouted at her.

"No, stop, please stop," she said.

But she didn't open her eyes and I realised she was having one of her nightmares.

"*Emma, Emma, wake up!*"

"Get away from me!"

"What's happening?" Georgina came into the room.

I pointed to the blister packs on the floor.

"*Jesus, no!*" She ran across to the bed and scooped Emma into her arms. "*Come on, pet, come on, Emma, you're all right, come on, wake up!*"

"There's an ambulance on the way," I said.

"Go the other side of her." Georgina seemed perfectly sober now. She pulled back the duvet, and we manoeuvred Emma to the side of the bed. We put her arms around both of our shoulders and we got her to her feet.

"Come on, come on, love," Georgina said.

Emma's head lolled but then straightened. She opened her eyes.

"What? What?"

"It's okay, love, you need to wake up," Georgina said. "Come on, just walk."

Emma put one foot in front of the other and we

walked her round the bedroom, from window to door and back again. We were still walking her when we heard the ambulance arrive, its sirens cutting through the quiet night. Georgina sat on the bed with Emma and I went down and opened the door. Though she was now conscious, the paramedics insisted on taking her downstairs on a stretcher. They said they couldn't tell whether she'd done herself any long-term damage.

"You're lucky you caught her when you did," I heard one of them say to Georgina as he helped her into the ambulance.

"Don't worry about Milly and James," I said as the ambulance doors shut. But I could see there was only one person she was worried about at that moment.

I stood at the door and watched until the blue lights had faded, and my heart began to return to its normal rhythm. What a mess, what a terrible mess.

I got a glass of water and went up to bed. I lay under the duvet but I knew I would not sleep. The panic of finding Emma like that had not yet fully subsided.

What had possessed her? Had she hoped to get rid of the nightmares by drugging herself to sleep? Was she so tormented by them? Or was it coping with her mother that got too much for her? I supposed Andrew's murder must have been deeply traumatic and, given Emma was the eldest, she had heard too many of the details of how he was killed. Perhaps it was that image that warped her sleeping mind and tormented her.

I longed to call Gabriel then, but it was three o'clock in the morning. I told myself I would have to wait until at least eight. He wouldn't be awake before that.

Gabriel. It was always Gabriel I needed when I was in trouble. And he was always there. After the Stephen O'Farrell trial and then Alastair McAuliffe's murder conviction we had seen each other at least three times a week. He had felt like the best friend I ever had.

I thought back to the lunch when that had changed, in the little restaurant in Duck Lane. When was that? Last January or February? We'd both taken our trays to a table, unloaded our food and I had been teasing him about the lovely Italian woman who had served him his Irish stew. "I think she has her eye on you," I'd said. And he'd looked at me in his straightforward way and put his hand over mine and said, "Do you honestly think there could be anyone else for me?" I can't remember what I'd said in reply, but I know I couldn't hide my – I wasn't sure now what – my fear, I supposed, of being that for him. He saw it in my face and he looked down at his plate and didn't look up again until he'd finished. Then he'd said a cool goodbye. I tried afterwards in phone calls to explain, but it was hard to put into words what I didn't really understand myself. No man wants to hear how special he is but how the person saying it isn't capable of giving him all that he wants. It was as though a door had been firmly shut between us then, and I had shut it, though I didn't mean to.

The last few weeks had been good, being around him. We'd got on. Had I been wrong to think I was not capable of giving him what he needed? Was this the time to test that out? No, I couldn't go there again, I couldn't risk hurting him like that again. He didn't deserve it.

My phone pinged at five o'clock with a text from

Georgina. "She's going to be okay."

I felt relief pass through me.

"They're keeping her in for a few days to be sure."

"She's in the best place," I replied.

"I'll be down in a few hours."

"No rush."

I hoped they'd keep her in for more than a few days. Someone needed to get to the truth about what was wrong with Emma. She needed help to sort out Andrew's death in her head, to separate her nightmares from what actually happened to him. And, I knew, she needed support to cope with her mother. I would speak to Georgina plainly when she got back. I would tell her to see a doctor. If I had to, I would threaten to contact the Child and Family Agency. Doing that, I knew, would probably make her hate me, but it might be enough to force her into action. Though perhaps Emma's actions would be enough. Maybe the fright she got would make her change.

Chapter 29

Wednesday, November 16th, 2016

I forced myself to stay in bed until seven, then got up, put on some clothes and went down to the kitchen. At seven thirty I texted Siobhán from Bloom Stenography and told her I was really stuck and asked if she could find someone to replace me at the commercial court. She said it would be no bother.

I made tea and ate some expensive-looking muesli. Then I heard a car outside. I went to the door in time to see Georgina getting out of a taxi. She stepped into the hall and immediately put her arms around me.

"Oh Bea, if you hadn't been here I might have lost her."

She looked exhausted and I led her into the kitchen. I made coffee for her as she talked about the journey up in the ambulance to St Vincent's Hospital in Dublin, the nearest one on duty.

"They had her on a drip – she looked so helpless, Bea," she said. "When we were at Bray she threw up, and the doctor said that may have saved her kidneys."

"Poor thing." I poured out a cup of coffee and put it in front of her. "Will you eat something?"

"No, thanks."

"A bit of toast even? You have to eat."

"Yes, toast then. They're going to keep her in until at least Friday, they said."

I stood by the toaster, waiting for it. "And will she get some other help? I mean a psychologist or something?"

"They said someone will come and talk to her later today. That's why I came down. I want to pack up and get back to Dublin. It makes no sense to be this far away from the hospital." She drank the coffee.

The toast popped. I buttered it and gave it to her.

"Can I ask, did she say why she did it?" I said.

She shook her head.

"Do you have any idea?" I spoke as gently as I could.

"I don't know, Bea, I just don't know."

When she'd finished eating I suggested she have a short rest.

"You're not fit for driving by the look of you."

Her eyelids looked weighted down and there were dark circles below her eyes. She hesitated.

"Don't worry, I won't let you sleep beyond ten."

She nodded and dragged herself wearily upstairs.

I checked the time, quarter past eight, before sending a message to Gabriel.

"Are you up? Can you talk?"

"Am now," was his response.

I phoned straightaway. He answered in a groggy voice. "Bea?"

"Sorry, Gabriel, for waking you, it's just . . ." I poured it out, what had happened to Emma and the ambulance and the dash to hospital.

"Jesus, that's dreadful," he said when I'd finished.

I told him Georgina intended going home to Dublin and he promised to let McCann know so the lads could keep an eye on her.

"What do you mean, keep an eye on her? Have they let Lar Sheils go then?"

"For the moment. He hasn't been charged yet, but they've sent a file on to the Director of Public Prosecutions."

"That doesn't sound like they think he's a murderer, does it?"

"They haven't enough on him yet – the file is for trespass and demanding money with menaces." He yawned loudly.

"I'm not looking forward to telling Georgina that. As though she hasn't enough to worry about." I wondered whether I should keep it from her for a while anyway. Perhaps I would let McCann tell her on his next visit.

"Try not to worry too much, Bea. Lar Sheils isn't stupid. He knows the lads would pick him up if he goes anywhere near Georgina."

"I hope you're right – are you free later, could you meet me?" I felt I needed to talk over everything that had happened face to face.

"Of course, ring me when you're back."

I said I would and then said goodbye. I went upstairs and woke Milly and James. I gave them breakfast then told them we had to play a game of tiptoe so that we wouldn't wake Georgina. They didn't seem to mind as we crept quietly around their bedroom, packing their things.

279

"We're going back to Dublin?" Milly asked.

"Yes."

"And what about Emma?"

"She's there already. She had a tummy ache last night and had to go to the hospital, but she's fine now."

She looked puzzled but I didn't want to say any more – that would be up to her mother. James had no questions to ask about the trip at all. He was happy once I told him he could keep his aeroplane with him in the back seat.

I put a video on for the children, packed up the car and then went up to wake Georgina.

She looked so peaceful that I hesitated by her bed, hating to disturb her. I knew that once she awoke, the anguish of what happened last night would come back to her – not just Emma in hospital, but her drunken behaviour too. I knew she would be filled with remorse for that. I waited a full minute and then shook her gently.

"What time is it?" she said, blinking and then sitting bolt upright.

It didn't take long for her to pack her own things and we drove away from Seafield Cottage shortly afterwards, Georgina ahead, with me following.

She had arranged with the children's regular babysitter to come and mind them, so that once she'd dropped them off at Belford Avenue she would be able to go straight to the hospital. I would be lying if I said I wasn't relieved – I had feared I might be required to babysit the children. And though I was willing to do it to help her, I didn't really want to.

I followed her all the way to her home and helped her

unpack. She fed the children and I waited with her until the babysitter arrived.

"Do you want to come to see Emma?" she asked, once she was ready to leave for the hospital.

"Maybe tomorrow, when she's a bit stronger," I said.

"Thanks for everything, Bea." She hugged me before we both got into our cars and drove away in our separate directions.

I had just enough time to shower and change before Gabriel called by about an hour after I got home. I found some scones and toasted them and made a pot of tea. We sat in the kitchen. He asked how Emma was and was glad to hear she was on the mend.

"It was a tough night," I said.

"It must have been."

"Even before that, though. Georgina was in a state. She'd had too much to drink again and she got very difficult. Honestly, I'm really worried for her and the children." I told him about the things she'd said and how Emma had confided in me about her nightmares.

He showed no surprise. "Murder can have a terrible effect on people, Bea – even just investigating it – I wasn't the only guard who had nightmares about some of the cases we dealt with."

"I didn't realise." I knew he'd dealt with some awful cases but hadn't thought they'd distressed him too much.

"It's the way the brain works, I think. It tries to comprehend the incomprehensible while we're sleep. Sometimes it reminds us of things we're trying very hard to forget."

"Do you think that's what's happening to Emma, that there's something in her nightmares that's real, that actually happened? I mean, could she have seen something?" I said that, but it didn't make sense. How could she have seen Andrew's murder when she was at home in her bed?

He shook his head. "If there is something, some memory, it'll come out eventually."

"She must be so frightened."

"Yes, poor girl."

"Do you want more tea?"

He said he was fine and I poured the dregs of the pot into my cup. When I put a drop of milk in it was almost the same colour as the dye my hairdresser Marcia used to mask my grey roots. I sipped it and my teeth ached.

"Tell me about Lar Sheils, Gabriel – did McCann get anything useful out of him at all about the murder?"

"Mixed bag really. He has a record, GBH, but he also has another alibi – not that he was in Canada, but he was with a stag party at the Brian Boru pub. Matt couldn't get an extension to hold on to him with only the trespass and demanding money against him."

"So he has an alibi. But the Brian Boru isn't far from Spin, and didn't Nikolai Strofsky say he saw Sheils outside that night?"

"He did, but the lads said the CCTV isn't very clear and Sheils has six friends who all swear he was at the pub the whole time."

"Did you speak to McCann about keeping an eye on Georgina's house in case Sheils comes back?"

"I did, but as I said it's unlikely he'll go back there."

I felt a little reassured. "What about Jason Armitage, is he still being held?"

"For the moment. Matt says he has no alibi for when Billie was killed, says he was at home alone, but he does have a good solicitor. And the other thing is, I keep thinking about what Barney said after he'd found Billie in the cellar."

I couldn't remember what and I said so.

"He told me he saw a man walking away from the pub just before he found Billie. Said he was wearing jeans, a navy padded jacket and a hoody. Doesn't sound a bit like Armitage from that description."

"No, more like Lar Sheils. But the man he saw leaving may not have killed Billie. Or Armitage could have paid someone to do the job for him. He doesn't seem the type to get his own hands dirty."

He said nothing for a few minutes. He appeared to be contemplating the half scone left on his plate. He picked it up and took a bite.

"The lads are looking into Nikolai Strofsky as well." He licked his fingers where jam had dripped. "Matt says he's in touch with Russian police and they're seeing if they have anything on him."

"If they have I'll be disappointed." I couldn't help recalling the look of complete adoration he had bestowed on Claire Davis, the gentle way he had touched her. What a pity if he turned out to have a shady past or, worse, had been involved in Andrew Dalton's death.

"I like him," I said.

"Do you now?" He finished what was left of his tea. "That's neither here nor there really though, is it?"

283

"I'd hate it if they sent him out of the country – I mean if there's nothing on him, but someone finds out about his visa. That would be an awful shame for the two of them."

"Are you feeling okay? It's not like you to be so sentimental."

I wanted to say that I could recognise a good match when I saw it, but I didn't know what reaction that might get, so I didn't respond.

"Meant to say to you, the foster parents, Andrew's that is, both of them are dead a few years. They were old enough when he lived with them."

I recalled having asked him to check them out, but that was before we knew about Billie and what Andrew had done. His foster parents seemed irrelevant now.

Then I remembered the letters that Emma had given to me.

"I forgot to tell you about the letters." I explained where I'd found them and how I hadn't read them, but then Emma had given them to me. I told him what they'd said.

"That's very important."

"I know, and I never had a chance to ask Georgina about them." I was certainly not going to ask her now.

"Where are they?"

I thought about it. I had put them back in the drawer and they were probably still there. Was it likely that Georgina had remembered to take them with her in her haste to leave Seafield Cottage? I supposed it depended on how important they were to her. Important enough for her to take them to Ballymoney in the first place anyhow.

"I don't know."

"They could be from Lar Sheils – he might have been trying to intimate Georgina," he said. "Matt will have to ask Georgina for them."

I squirmed at the thought of McCann asking her about the letters when she probably thought no one else in the world knew about them.

"Not yet, Gabriel. Don't tell him yet. It wouldn't be fair to Georgina with Emma in hospital." The truth was I knew once McCann asked for the letters, Georgina would know I had told him about them and she would probably never forgive me. It would bring an end to a friendship at a time when, I really believed, she needed me.

"Let me talk to her first, will you, so she's at least prepared for it?"

"Okay," Gabriel reluctantly agreed. "We can't hold off too long though."

"Fine."

"Right then, I'm going to call into Hanlon's on my way home, there's a few things I wanted to ask Derek Johnston." He carried his cup and plate to the sink.

"Want some company?"

"Would you not be better off getting a bit of sleep?"

I said I wouldn't. I didn't feel like being alone right then. There were too many conflicting ideas swirling in my brain. At least with Gabriel, I could voice them, no matter how ridiculous they might sound.

Chapter 30

Rain began falling heavily just as we pulled up round the corner from Hanlon's at about three thirty.

"Hang on, I think I have an umbrella in the boot."

Gabriel jumped out of the car, opened the boot and began rummaging. When he came back, he sat into the driver's seat with a wide grin on his face.

"No umbrella, but look what I found." He held up his old garda-issue cosh. "I forgot I left it there. I was going to bring it up to Donegal with me the next time I visit Bernadette." Bernadette was Gabriel's youngest sister. She lived in Glenties in what was the family home with her husband and children. "The nephew, Eugene, says he wants to be a guard. I thought I'd give it to him."

He sounded so relieved at having found it. I was glad for him.

We made a dash for the pub. By the time we got to the doors, we were both out of breath, Gabriel more so and his cheeks were bright red. We shook the rain off us and removed our coats. Hanlon's was quiet. Barney was sitting at the corner of the bar and Piotr Gromczewski was cleaning away after the lunchtime carvery.

"Boss around?" Gabriel asked him.

"Down in the cellar – I'll send him over to you when he comes up. Pint, is it?"

"Please – and, Bea?"

"Soda water and lime."

"I'll bring them over."

We took our usual seats and Piotr was quick with our drinks.

"How're things?" Gabriel asked him.

"Okay." Piotr put his hand out for the €20 note Gabriel was proffering.

"Are people staying away because of what happened to Billie?" I asked.

He shook his head. "You'd think that, but no – we get people we've never seen before, coming in and sitting up at the bar and asking questions."

"Go 'way?" Gabriel said.

"When I tell them I was at home in Poland when it happened they are very disappointed. But they still sit there and they stare at the door into the office. I think if I offered, they'd like to go down to the cellar and see where she died."

Derek Johnston appeared then at his shoulder. "Dark tourism, they call it," he said. "There's a lad drives a bus around Dublin and points out the places where people were murdered."

"That's very ghoulish." I shivered at the thought.

"Have you time for a quick chat, Derek?" Gabriel asked.

Derek sat down. "What's up?"

Piotr returned from the till with Gabriel's change and went back behind the bar.

"Do you remember you told us about the day Billie moved out?"

"Yes."

"Have you remembered the date yet?"

I wasn't sure what Gabriel was getting at.

"I've been trying to remember and I think it was the day before I went on a trip to London." Derek took out his phone and began scrolling through his calendar. "Look – see, I have the flight time marked in." He tilted the phone in Gabriel's direction. "I went to London on the 16th, so then Billie moved out on Friday the 15th of July." He tapped the screen of his phone with his finger to confirm his certainty.

"And you mentioned Billie went out that day, didn't you, in the middle of packing?" Gabriel took a sup from his pint.

"That's right, drove me mad, I told you that."

"You did, and what time did you say?"

He thought for a moment. "Late afternoon I think it was, around four maybe."

My heart began to pound. Gabriel had been a step ahead of me, but I'd caught up now.

"Thanks, Derek."

"Right, well, is that all you wanted?" He had already stood to leave.

Gabriel nodded, I thanked him and he went back to work.

"Do you think it was Billie who wrote the notes?" I asked as soon as Derek was out of earshot.

"Seems likely, doesn't it?"

We both fell silent, thinking of the young woman who had been behind the bar less than a month before.

"The question is, did Georgina meet her?" Gabriel said. "You'll have to ask her now, Bea – we can't keep Matt in the dark about those letters much longer."

I knew I would, but I didn't relish it. How would I explain having seen the letters? And she'd been so definite when she'd told McCann she'd never met Billie and didn't know anything about her. What if she'd been lying?

I took my phone out of my bag and texted Georgina.

"Would it be okay if I dropped by the hospital later?"

She took a while to reply, then answered that she'd be there again at six thirty if I wanted to visit. I said I would.

"I'll drive if you like," Gabriel said. "I can chat to Emma while you take Georgina for a coffee or something."

That seemed like a good plan. I certainly didn't want to be having a conversation about the letters within Emma's hearing.

We went back to Oxmantown Road to put in some time. Gabriel insisted on making me a ham and cheese toasty and, though I'd been reluctant, it turned out to be delicious. We ate in his living room, where he'd lit a fire, and I followed his example by taking my shoes off and resting my feet on his coffee table.

"A while since you've done that," he said.

"I missed it," I responded without thinking.

He looked at me sideways and made a kind of harrumphing noise. "You're a terrible woman, do you know that, Bea?"

"I don't know what you mean."

He shook his head. "Never mind . . . You look very tired. Would you not go up and stretch out on the bed for half an hour? I'll call you in plenty of time."

I was going to say no but, with the warmth of the house and the comfort of the food, I felt heavy and drowsy.

"I will then," I said and went upstairs.

Billie's room felt bare and sad. The mattress was stripped of sheets. I heard Gabriel call up from below "*Use my room!*" and I didn't argue.

I didn't get under the duvet though, I just lay on top and pulled his dressing gown, that had been lying at the foot of the bed, over me. It was rough, and a bit shabby, but its scent was deeply comforting. I drifted off quickly and when I awoke the room was pitch dark and I could hear knocking at the door.

"Are you right, Bea?" Gabriel came in with a cup of tea. "It's half five."

"Thanks." I sat up and took it from him.

"The traffic will be rotten getting across town," he said as he left.

"I'll just be a minute."

I gulped back the tea, splashed water on my face at his bathroom sink and went down.

He was already standing by the hall door. I found my shoes in the living room, got my coat and we left.

He was right about the traffic. It was fine going into town, but once we crossed the Liffey from Church Street, it was gridlock. Johnny Cash growled 'Sunday Morning Coming Down' as we stop-started through Baggot Street.

Gabriel didn't sing along.

It took us until quarter to seven to get to St Vincent's Hospital.

I bought chocolates from the ground floor shop. Emma was in St Charles' Ward on the third floor. I have never cared for hospitals, with their particular smell of antiseptic and disease, and since my involuntary stay at St Lucian's two years previously even the sight of a medic in a white coat made me want to run. Still, we were right to come, I knew.

We found Emma in the corner of a four-bed ward, her mother sitting in a chair beside her. Georgina stood and put her arms around me.

"Bea, you're here. And Gabriel." She shook his hand.

Her voice sounded strangely high, as though her vocal cords were being held tight. I thought she was nervous.

Emma was sitting up in bed, her head resting back on her pillows. She smiled for a second when she saw me and then closed her eyes as though that was as much as she could manage.

"Good to see you," I said, putting the chocolates on her locker.

"Thanks."

Gabriel borrowed a chair for me from nearby and then stood a little awkwardly between Emma's bed and the window.

"How are you feeling?" I asked the patient when she opened her eyes again.

"Very tired. They keep asking me questions, but I don't want to talk to them." She looked over at her mother.

291

"It's okay, love, you don't have to answer them if you don't want to."

I thought it an odd thing to say. I felt Georgina should be encouraging her daughter to talk as much as she could.

"Never mind, I won't ask you anything, except – can I get a cold drink for you from the shop downstairs?"

She smiled weakly. "Something cold would be lovely – Fanta if they have it."

I asked Georgina if she'd like to come with me.

"Gabriel will keep Emma company."

She hesitated, but then stood up.

"We'll only be a few minutes," she told Emma.

As we walked out of the ward I could see Gabriel moving from his place by the window to the seat I'd been in.

We travelled in the lift to the ground floor. I took change from my purse and got Emma's drink from a vending machine.

"Let's have a coffee before we go back," I said to Georgina.

I indicated the nearby café and she reluctantly agreed. I bought the coffees and carried them to a table in the corner. Around us, patients in dressing gowns and slippers sat with relatives or friends.

I put the cups down and took a seat, feeling uneasy about having to bring up the letters. "What have the doctors been saying?"

"Depends which one you talk to." Georgina sounded fed up. "To be honest, I just want to get her home – one doctor says yes, the next says no. Her system is clear of the drugs, it's not clear yet. The ward sister says we have to wait until the consultant psychiatrist assesses her."

"Don't you think that would be best?" I was picking my words as carefully as I could.

"But you see how she is, Bea – talking to them just upsets her more. She'd be better off in her own bed."

I stirred the milky coffee, cutting into the frothy heart on its top and dispersing it. "Have they found out why she did it yet though, Georgina?"

She looked at me, and I thought she seemed angry that I'd asked.

"When I get her home I can find that out. She'll talk to me."

I wanted to remind Georgina of her state in Ballymoney, and how it was Emma who had been trying to look after her. It seemed she had forgotten that. She spoke as though she believed she had no part in Emma's overdose, as though her drinking was not an issue. I could have pointed all that out, but I didn't. I was sure that under the facade she was presenting she was well aware of her own contribution to Emma's condition.

"There's something I have to tell you." I could feel my stomach flip over. I was dreading saying the words. I took a sip of coffee. "Emma gave me something in Ballymoney when I went out for some air, while you were . . . while you were in the house."

"What?" Her brows knit as she looked over the top of her cup at me.

"The letters, she gave them to me."

I thought there was a flicker of panic across her face. But then she shook her head.

"What letters?" She sipped at her coffee and dabbed her upper lip, removing a bubble of foam that had caught there.

I hadn't expected to have to explain. "The ones you got before Andrew died, the anonymous ones."

"You read those?"

"Emma wanted me to and, under the circumstances, I thought I should." I felt uncomfortable, realising how it must look from her perspective.

"Circumstances? You had no right to do that, Bea." She said it in a low, cool voice, tinged with anger, but then her tone softened. "I know you worry about me, Bea, but you don't need to. Everything is going to be all right."

I was struggling to think of what to say. I needed to know if she'd met the person who wrote the letters.

"The last one said something about meeting you after work – did that happen, Georgina?"

"Of course not! That would be a stupid thing to do, to go and meet some crank who wrote those letters!"

Relief flooded through me.

"Honestly, Bea, I didn't take those seriously at all. I showed them to Andrew and we just laughed about it. He said it was probably some prankster from work." She shrugged. "Poor Emma, maybe they were what had bothered her."

She looked as though she thought she'd found the answer to a very perplexing puzzle. She had identified a culprit for her daughter's troubles.

"I'll give them to Matt McCann the next time I see him if that's what you want," she said.

"Yes, that would be best."

I was glad I hadn't had to ask her to give the letters to McCann but at the same time I was worried. All the stress she was under. How would she cope once Emma came home from hospital?

Chapter 31

When we left the hospital, I told Gabriel what Georgina had said about the letters.

"And she said she'd give them to Matt?"

"As soon as she sees him."

"Strange though, isn't it?" We were on the Merrion Road and he was concentrating on the traffic lights ahead, which had just changed from green to amber. He kept going.

"It is and I'm worried for her. Do you think she's having some sort of breakdown?"

"It's possible."

He said no more but I knew what he was thinking – that Georgina had something to hide.

"How did you get on with Emma?" I asked.

"She's a clever girl." He glanced over at me and then back at the road. "I told her about a pal of mine who had post-traumatic stress after witnessing a murder, got terrible nightmares. She said she wasn't the type to get drawn out by a bit of 'me too' nonsense."

"Did she?"

"She did. Said the doctors were forever giving her examples and waiting for her to explain what happened to her, only she couldn't, she said, because she doesn't remember anything."

"Did she mean she didn't remember taking the pills or did she mean something else?" We were back on Church Street now and seemed to be heading for Stoneybatter. "You're not forgetting me, are you?"

"I nearly was, Bea." He half-smiled to himself and indicated right onto North King Street then. "I'm not sure what she meant. And I didn't get to say anything else to her – a nurse came along to take her blood pressure and then you came back. As soon as she spotted you both at the door, she closed her eyes. It was like she didn't want to have to talk to you or Georgina."

"I'm not surprised. I'd imagine she's glad of the rest in hospital. Since she came home from school she's been the one doing the looking-after."

"Did you mention to Georgina about going to the doctor herself?"

"No, I didn't get a chance." The truth was I felt I'd asked her enough questions for one day.

Just as we arrived at Clontarf Road, my phone rang. It was Claire Davis.

"We're in town – would you join us for a drink? We're celebrating."

"Celebrating what?"

"It's a surprise."

"I'm with Gabriel at the moment."

"Great! Please bring him with you."

I was surprised at her enthusiasm, given her last

297

meeting with Gabriel, and thought she might have already had a few beers. She said they were in Sweetman's again.

"See you there," I said.

Gabriel was happy to go along.

When we got to my house, I suggested he leave his car there, knowing he would enjoy a pint.

"We can walk up to the DART station."

"I will so," he said.

The evening was cold and clear with a tingle of frost in the air, but no breeze. Dublin Bay was almost smooth and, though the full moon was on the wane, it was still beautiful.

"Do you ever think how privileged you are to live here?" he asked as we took the footpath along the low stone wall at the sea's edge.

"When I stop for long enough to consider it, I do."

We paused just before the old Clontarf baths to look at the view. A Stena ferry was making its way slowly out into the Irish Sea and seemed to be gliding on a mirror. I thought of the day I took the ferry from Dun Laoghaire and left my mother and father on the quay. I was never to see them alive again and, if I was being truthful, they were hardly even alive then. They had died with Laurence, only more slowly.

Gabriel seemed to sense my thoughts.

"Come on," he said, "we'll try and catch the quarter past nine."

We walked briskly to the station and arrived on the platform as the train pulled in. I took a window seat and Gabriel sat opposite. We didn't talk but watched the bare trees of Fairview Park as they passed us and the slate-roofed, red-bricked houses of Stoney Road and Hyacinth Street and Shamrock Terrace. At least I did, but when I glanced over at Gabriel he was watching me. He had a wistful look on his face that made me, for some reason, want to hide.

We passed the Royal Canal and paused at Connolly Station with its busy platforms and its diesel smell. Then over the Liffey to Tara Street Station where we got off and walked up to the pub.

Claire Davis and Nikolai Strofsky were on the top floor and they were not alone. There were about a dozen people around them, laughing and drinking and eating cocktail sausages and chicken wings.

Claire was wearing a red lace dress, with an asymmetrical neckline and long sleeves. Beside her there was a small posy of cream roses and on her ring finger a gold band.

"Congratulations," I said, leaning in to kiss her cheek.

She beamed at me. "Mad, isn't it?"

I extended a hand to Nikolai, who was wearing a dark-blue suit, the jacket sleeves straining over his biceps.

"Thank you, thank you," he said, squeezing my hand and reflecting his new wife's smile.

Gabriel had gone to the bar and brought back a pint for himself and a soda and lime for me. He put them down on a nearby table.

"Let me get you a drink," he said to the couple and went back to fetch two pints of Brother Bowen.

I found a stool and moved it close to Claire.

"How on earth did you manage it? I thought you had

to give three months' notice?" I couldn't help asking.

"Didn't you know?" She looked into my face, perplexed for a moment, then nodded in Gabriel's direction. "Your friend knows someone who works in the Registrar's office."

"Of course he does."

"We were able to get our application back-dated." She looked worried suddenly. "You won't tell?"

"Of course not. I hope you'll both be very happy."

"Do you know, I think we might." She sounded as though that had just occurred to her and she laughed a bit. "We're happy tonight anyway, aren't we, Nikolai?"

Her husband, who had been talking to friends, turned back to her.

"What did you say?"

"I said we're happy tonight."

"Oh yes, very happy." He kissed her then and the people around them cheered.

It was lovely, and I felt uplifted, seeing their joy.

Gabriel came back with their drinks and put them down. There was a small queue of pints forming in front of them both.

Gabriel sat down. I leaned toward him.

"Did you arrange this?"

"I don't know what you're talking about."

"I just hope McCann doesn't find out anything about him from the Russian police."

He shook his head. "Ah no, I checked first – that came back all clear."

I smiled at him.

"What?"

"You're a lovely man sometimes, did you know that?"

He took a drink from his pint.

At another table, someone began to sing, the tune was familiar, but the words were in Russian. Nikolai joined in.

Gabriel lifted his glass up and clinked it against mine. "Cheers," he said.

We hadn't intended staying late, but it was good to sit for a few hours surrounded by people jubilant with celebration and we found it hard to leave. The noise level in the pub had contributed, too, to my inability to think, which was refreshing.

Gabriel's ability to think, however, had been enhanced by the pints he'd had and he spoke at length to anyone who would listen about his theories on life and politics.

By the time we were leaving at one o'clock though, he had moved on to a more contemplative state and he told me, in the back of the taxi we'd agreed to share, that friendship was, above all else, the most important commodity on earth. I'd suggested that he should be dropped home before me because Stoneybatter was closer to the pub, but he insisted on seeing me to Clontarf and said he'd collect his car in the morning.

"We're good friends, aren't we, Bea?" he said, sitting close to me on the back seat. He took my hand in his and examined my fingers. "I've a few things on my mind, Bea."

"That was a nice night, wasn't it?" I said.

"Very nice, a very nice night. And fair play to them for making a go of it. People do, you know?"

"Do you think, does it happen often here?"

"What?"

"People getting married to get around immigration laws?"

"It does, of course. There's a steady trade in sham marriages, couples don't even know each other. But not them, not Claire and Nikolai." He gestured vaguely back in the direction of the pub. "Do you not recognise it when you see it, Bea?" His head was on one side and he looked baffled.

"What?"

"The real thing – do you not recognise it?"

I squeezed the hand he was still holding mine in and didn't tell him I had spotted it a while back. "You're just an old romantic."

"Right, folks." The driver had pulled up outside my house.

Gabriel insisted on paying the fare. I got out and so did he. The taxi drove away.

"Oh," Gabriel said. "I should have held on to that." He stood and watched the taxi's tail-lights disappearing.

"Come on, I'll make you a coffee before you go." I took him by the arm and guided him up the path to the front door. I opened it and let us into the hall. I took off my coat and put it over the banisters. When I turned around, Gabriel was next to me, our toes almost touching.

"Bea," he said, and leaned down and kissed me.

It was a warm kiss, and familiar, so lovely and familiar.

I melted into it for a moment. Then I tasted the Guinness and pulled away. I couldn't do this.

"Don't. Not now," I said, putting my hand on his chest and pushing just a little. "Coffee?"

I walked into the kitchen, expecting him to follow me. Then I heard the front door close. I went back into the hall and out the door, fearful he might try to drive home. When I got outside though, his car was still parked and he was across the road, getting into a taxi.

I found my phone and texted him. **"You okay?"**

He didn't answer.

Chapter 32

Thursday, November 17th, 2016

I was back in Court 32 having been summoned by Ruby Clements. Dr Rita McArdle had completed her report and was ready to give evidence. She sat at the back of the room until she was called. She had the pink cheeks of a just-ripe apple and a figure to match, contained in a green shift dress and jacket. I had seen her in court before and knew I would have to strain to hear her voice, which was firm but low.

Ms Clements was the first to question her since it was her client who had initiated the legal separation.

"Could you begin by taking us through your findings, Dr McArdle?"

"Yes. Firstly, I just want to make it clear that I accept both parents want the best for their children and the children are loved and well cared for by both Mum and Dad." She paused for breath. "The children are coping as well as can be expected with their parents' separation, given the level of animosity which neither Mum nor Dad have tried to hide from them, from what I can see."

She paused and took a sip of water.

"Mum made a number of allegations to me around Dad's treatment of the children and his behaviour towards them at access. They're detailed there on page six, judge."

The judge turned the pages of the report. "Yes, thank you."

"I observed the children with their father at two access visits and my experience is at variance with Mrs O'Malley's allegations. The children showed great affection for Dad and I could see no evidence of fear there. Robin, the eldest, has a healthy relationship with Dad. There is a degree of horseplay and a level of natural competitiveness, which I would expect to see at his age, but not to any harmful extent."

"Can you take us to your assessment of the black-eye incident?"

"I specifically addressed this with Robin and his recounting of it, that it was an accident, concurs with Dad's and I believe it is credible."

Mrs O'Malley whispered intensely to her barrister.

"It is my opinion that Mum has a tendency to catastrophise Dad's behaviour. And, I believe Mum, perhaps unintentionally, is undermining Dad in her discussions with the children. There is a distinct danger that over time this could lead to alienation of Dad. And this can only lead to suffering for the children."

There was a sound of further, slightly louder muttering from Mrs O'Malley.

"Please continue, Dr McArdle," Ms Hollister said.

"Yes. Turning to page ten of my report, there were a series of complaints made by Dad, including, you'll see there, excessive drinking on the part of Mum while in charge of the children. I could find no evidence that Mum drinks to excess. She holds a responsible job and tells me she drinks only occasionally. The children's schools tell me they have never been late, they are collected on time, either by Mum or their minder. They are clean, are provided with lunches and generally have completed their homework. They are reasonably well behaved in school. All of these things point to a regulated home life, very often not evident in cases of alcohol misuse."

It was Mr O'Malley's turn to mutter.

"In terms of her relationship with the children, Mum is obviously loving and caring, though overprotective, stemming from a fear of loss," Dr McArdle continued. "Dad is also devoted to his children though he does lack some parenting skills, including negotiation at a child level and boundary setting, which can lead to confusion for the children."

She stopped again to take a drink of water, oblivious to the reaction of the O'Malleys to her report. They were both scowling in her direction as though she was the cause of all their difficulties instead of themselves.

"In terms of the children and how they view their parents, the girls largely take the lead from their brother. Robin articulates a desire to split his time 50/50 between Mum and Dad while recognising the logistical difficulties that might entail. He has asked that I make it known that he doesn't want to have to choose and he would prefer if Mum and Dad could be friends, if they can't be together anymore."

The judge nodded.

"Petal and Bluebell expressed much the same sentiment in their own ways. Bluebell told me she just wants everyone to go back to being happy."

Sniffling was audible from Mrs O'Malley and Mr O'Malley had his head down.

"Perhaps this might be an appropriate time to adjourn for lunch, Ms Hollister?"

"Yes, judge."

At lunch, it was Gabriel who preoccupied me. My stomach churned with regret at how I had handled last night but, at the same time, I couldn't figure out what it was I was supposed to have done. He'd had too much to drink. He probably wasn't thinking straight, if he was thinking at all. I had to be the one to think for both of us. If we were going to start up again, it should be a definite decision, not something we stumbled into because he'd been drinking too much and I was intoxicated with the atmosphere at Claire and Nikolai's party.

In the morning, I'd expected him to at least knock at the door and let me know he was taking his car but he didn't, and when I checked it was gone from where he'd left it the night before. I took my time considering whether or not to phone him. Would I apologise or something? Had I anything to apologise for? As far as I was concerned I hadn't.

I sent a brief text. **"Everything okay this morning?"** He didn't answer.

Why did I let him leave me home? If we'd gone

straight to Stoneybatter I could have just dropped him there and nothing would have happened. And if I hadn't got so caught up in Claire and Nikolai's celebration, I would have left earlier and Gabriel would have had less to drink.

I was still kicking myself when the phone rang. It was McCann.

"Bea, we need a chat. Will you come to me or will I come to you?"

Though he said "chat", it sounded like he meant "interrogate" and he didn't wait for me to answer.

"I'll be over this evening if you're at home."

I said I would be. "What's it about?" I asked.

"We'll talk then," was all he said.

My brain raced as I made my way back to court. I wished I could contact Gabriel so that he could be there when McCann called, but knew I would have to resist. I had texted him twice and he hadn't responded. If I sent a third message he would definitely believe that I thought I was in the wrong.

It was difficult to switch on my focus for the O'Malley case, but of course I did. Dr Rita McArdle was making her recommendations.

"For the sake of their emotional wellbeing and mental stability, it would be best if they continued to attend their local schools and that would be logistically challenging were they to live part of the week with Dad. So I'm suggesting Monday to Friday with Mum. They are also entitled to quality time with Dad, and so I believe they should spend every weekend at his home."

She emphasised her findings were focussed on "the best interests of the children" and not on the competing interests of the O'Malleys.

Ms Hollister was the first to challenge.

"What this effectively means for my client is that she will be the disciplinarian, the school-run, homework-done, get-to-bed-early parent while Mr O'Malley will be the weekend fun, trips to cinema, relaxed and easy-going one." She took a breath. "Mrs O'Malley has deep misgivings about any overnight stays at her husband's apartment. Given Dr McArdle's conclusions, she concedes they must occur, but she believes she should be allowed every second weekend with the children as well as Monday to Friday."

The judge arched his eyebrows. "Ms Clements?"

"That would be deeply unfair to my client, who Dr McArdle acknowledges is a loving and caring father. He wishes to be involved in the children's lives more often than just weekends. Though he had hoped Dr McArdle would recommend some overnight stays midweek, he accepts her findings that this would be logistically difficult, and he has no desire to disrupt the children's school attendance. However, he could not agree to only every second weekend, judge. That would be deeply unfair."

"At this point, would there be any value in adjourning for a short time so that you can both discuss whether an amicable arrangement on custody might be reached between you?" The judge leaned forward and looked at the barristers, briefly hopeful.

They both shook their heads.

"Very well." He sat back in his chair.

The debate about custody and access continued until three thirty when both parties finally exhausted their arguments.

The judge looked tired. "I want to give all matters my due consideration in this case and so I will reserve my judgment."

The barristers nodded.

When McCann arrived at about seven o'clock, I looked over his shoulder, expecting to see one of his juniors with him.

"Just myself," he said.

I led him into the kitchen where he sat down at the table.

I made a pot of tea and set out a plate of biscuits. He immediately helped himself to a chocolate biscuit. I poured tea for both of us, sat opposite him and waited.

"I'm told you saw some interesting letters."

"Gabriel told you?"

He didn't deny it.

"Yes, I did. Georgina said she'd give them to you. You should ask her."

"I already have." He paused to gulp some tea and reach for another biscuit. "She says she doesn't know what I'm talking about."

I didn't know what to say. "She couldn't have understood what you meant."

"I was very clear."

"What did she say exactly?"

"She said 'There aren't any – Emma told Beatrice

about letters, but she was only making it up to get attention'. Could that be right?"

"But . . ." I was confused. What was Georgina thinking? "She promised she'd give them to you."

"Could Emma have made them up?" He dunked the last of his chocolate biscuit in his tea and a piece fell off. I recoiled involuntarily.

"*No!* I saw the letters myself, I read them!"

"What happened to them then, after?" He picked up a spoon and fished out the biscuit clump and put it in his mouth.

"I put them back where Emma took them from, in the bedside locker in Ballymoney. I didn't want Georgina to know I'd read them." I was having trouble trying to understand what had happened.

"They're not in Ballymoney and they're not in Belford Avenue either."

"How do you know? Did you get a search warrant?" It seemed like a bit of an overreaction to me. I pictured gardaí turning over both houses, poor Georgina and the children looking on. And it happened because I had read private letters and then told Gabriel about them.

"Not at all – she let me have a look around her house and gave permission for one of the local lads to check out Ballymoney. There was nothing."

He had come to the end of his mug and I topped him up from the pot.

"Just so I can get this straight, Beatrice: you read four letters, all anonymous, you got your handprints all over them, you recognised the importance of them, then you gave them back and now they've disappeared."

When he put it like that it sounded as though I'd interfered and then deliberately botched things.

"She's my friend – you don't steal letters from a friend," I said. At the same time I was thinking you don't spy on a friend and read letters she didn't give to you.

"Beatrice, I don't know what to make of all your carry-on. You seem to want to help, then you do this sort of thing."

He looked exasperated and I felt guilty and wished I had not seen the damn letters.

Then I remembered.

"I have photographs!"

"There were photographs too?" He gave me a look of incredulity.

"No, I forgot, I took photographs of the letters."

His expression changed, as though someone had told him there was a picture to prove the existence of unicorns.

I got my phone. "I'll text these to you."

I scrolled down until I found them and sent them to the number he gave me. He squinted at them.

"Very dark, but still good. Thanks, Bea."

I was so surprised I thought I might fall off the chair. "Am I back in the good books?"

"For the moment maybe." He looked up from the phone. "But mind yourself, do you hear me?"

I nodded. "Can I ask you something?"

"If you must."

"Are you still holding Jason Armitage? Do you think it could have been him?"

"Are you going to tell this to Georgina?" He raised

one bushy eyebrow at me and I felt yet again that I was betraying my friend.

"No. She has enough to be worrying about with Emma at the moment."

"We're still holding him. He'll certainly be charged with child pornography and there's a whiff of money laundering in there as well if we can just nail it down."

"What about Andrew Dalton's murder, can you link him to that?" I thought how good it would be to have a definitive answer to that at last.

"He's got motive, certainly. Dalton owed him, and no alibi, but it's early days."

"Is it?" It didn't feel like early days to me, it felt like a lifetime.

"There's others too, Bea. Derek Johnston has a criminal record, GBH. And he found out about the porn films, admitted he argued with Billie about them."

I hadn't heard that. I thought of Johnston in his apron, ladling curry.

"But has he a link to Dalton?"

"Not that we know of. Yet. But there are other lines we're following, too."

"Like?" What other lines could there be?

He gave me a long look. "I'll talk to you another time."

I went to the hall to see him out, then sat in the living room thinking of Georgina. I knew she was under pressure, but why had she lied to the guards?

I texted her – "How's Emma?" and she responded, "Getting out tomorrow at ten". I answered "Marvellous". I would give it a few hours tomorrow, I decided, so that

313

Emma was home and settled and then I would have to call over and speak to her. I had to know what was going on.

Chapter 33

Friday, November 18th, 2016

I waited until two o'clock to drive over to Georgina's. It had been difficult to fill the morning. There was nothing from Gabriel and only one other message – from Úna Hollister. She'd asked if I was available for Monday when the O'Malley case would be back in court. I'd been surprised the judge was ready to deliver his decision so quickly, but I'd said yes.

It was a full three minutes before Georgina answered the door and when she did she looked distracted.

"It's you," she said, hesitating before letting me in.

I stepped into the hall, handing her a bunch of flowers I'd bought for Emma and a novel I'd got help choosing for her from a bookshop assistant.

"You're very good – she's in here." Georgina led me into the living room where Emma was lying on the couch, a blanket over her, looking weak and pale. I gave her the gifts, she thanked me and Georgina took the flowers.

"I'll just . . ." she said, leaving the room.

I sat on an armchair.

"Mam says you were the one who found me." She wasn't looking at me, she was looking at the book I'd given her. She turned it over, glanced at the back and then dropped it on the floor. "I suppose I should thank you for what you did." She had lowered her voice so that I had to lean forward to hear her. "So thanks for nothing."

I was shocked, unsure of how to respond. "I know you feel bad now, Emma, but it will get better."

"How would you know? You haven't a clue what went on in this house." Her lip curled with disdain. "I wanted to escape and it's your fault I didn't." She closed her eyes then.

I hadn't expected her to still be in such distress. I had thought, once she got to a hospital, they would help her enough to bring her back a little from the dark place where she seemed to be.

"Did you get to see the – the specialist?"

"You mean the psychiatrist? I've an appointment next week."

In a week – anything could happen in a week.

"Is there something I can do to help?"

She shook her head.

I looked around the room, the four cream-painted walls, the perfectly positioned flat-screen TV over the fireplace, the tasteful art-deco lamp in the corner, the two Marquet prints stylishly displayed. It looked like something from a show house.

Emma followed my gaze.

"This place is suffocating me, I can't stand it," she said.

"But why, Emma? What is it I don't know about what went on here?"

She lifted herself up on one elbow.

"Before I took the pills, I was lying in bed, not asleep yet, *and then I remembered.*"

The door opened and Georgina reappeared, with the flowers in a crystal vase. "Do you want these here or by your bed, Emma?"

"Don't care." She turned on her side to face the back of the sofa and brought the blanket up, almost covering her head.

"Sorry," Georgina said to me, putting the vase on the windowsill.

"Where are Milly and James?" I was thinking of them running by the vase and knocking it to smithereens.

"They're staying with their aunt – you know, Tracy, for a couple of days, so Emma can get some rest."

So it was just the two of them in the house.

"How are you doing?" I asked Georgina, not wanting to refer to her drinking, but meaning it.

"Okay. Tea?"

I picked up on her signal to follow her out to the kitchen. She obviously didn't want to talk in front of her daughter. When I sat down at the table she checked the kitchen door and dividing doors were closed before putting the kettle on. She looked worn out.

"Are you managing okay?"

"It isn't easy, you see how she is. I've called the GP and he says he'll be over sometime this afternoon. I'm hoping he might give her something, just until she sees the psychiatrist."

"Didn't they offer anything in the hospital?"

"No, they said she'd have to wait for a full assessment."

I found it hard to understand how a teenager who'd overdosed could be let go home from hospital with no help.

"What do you think happened, Georgina? Did she say why she did it?"

She had her back to me, wetting a pot of tea, and I could see her shoulders shake as she began to cry. I couldn't imagine how hard it must have been for her to lose her husband and then almost lose her daughter. I got up and put one arm around her and guided her to a chair.

I carried the pot and cups to the table and found a jug of milk in the fridge. I poured for both of us and sat down.

"The things she's been saying," I said. "That she remembers now. What does she mean?"

She wiped her face with her hands. "I've no idea, none of it makes sense."

"What is it she thinks she remembers?"

She looked at me a little more sharply than I expected, then shook her head. "I don't know – some nonsense about Andrew, about him being in her dream."

I felt she wasn't telling me the truth, but I didn't say so, I just waited.

She sipped her tea. "Emma never liked him, you know? Right from the start. And now that he's gone she can say anything she wants about him and he can't defend himself."

"But what has she been saying about him, Georgina?" I felt as though we were going around in circles.

"Rubbish, that's all, just rubbish!"

The dividing door opened and Emma came into the kitchen.

Georgina said quietly, "You mustn't listen to her."

"Tell the truth, Mother." Emma stood there, the blanket wrapped round her shoulders.

"Go and lie down," Georgina said.

The teenager stood defiantly. "You tell her or I will."

"*Stop it! Be quiet!*"

"I won't be quiet! Say it, Mother! *Say the words*. He tried to rape me – your husband tried to rape me!"

"*No!*" Georgina stood, pushing back her chair with such force that it flew to the floor with a crack, and lunged at her daughter. She put one hand over her mouth and pushed her back against the fridge.

Emma squirmed under her grasp, dropping the blanket. I got to my feet and put my hand firmly on Georgina's arm.

"You're hurting her, stop it."

She stopped and drew back, taking in as she did the red marks left by her hand on her daughter's mouth. She gasped. They both looked at each other. Emma began to shake all over, as though she'd been plunged into freezing water. Georgina started to wail and slid to the floor at her daughter's feet.

Emma knelt down beside her. Then she put her two arms around her and whispered, "It's okay, it's okay."

I wasn't sure what to do, how to react. I hadn't imagined such a thing could happen in that perfect home. The nightmares she'd been having, the visions of Andrew – they hadn't been some awful apparitions of his murder, they'd been true. And so horrific for her, I supposed, she had blocked them out of her consciousness. Is that what had happened? Is that how it worked? The memories had

319

sat there, deep and buried, until her mind insisted she recall them. She must have told Georgina about it at the hospital after she woke up. How devastating that must have been for them both.

Mother and daughter still clung to each other on the floor, rocking slightly against the fridge door. I picked up the chair that had fallen over.

"Come on, love, you should lie down," Georgina said after a while.

Emma got to her feet, stretched and yawned. "I'll go to bed." She hugged her mother and left the room.

Georgina sat at the table, her chin in her right hand. "Now you know, Bea." She looked resigned. "God, I need a drink." But she didn't stand up.

"I'm so sorry, Georgina. I can't imagine how you must feel. I can't believe a man like Andrew could . . . his own stepdaughter." I couldn't bring myself to say it. It seemed impossible. He wasn't some shadowy stranger, some predator in a dark alleyway. He was a husband and father. I thought about Billie then, what she'd said in her diary.

"When did it happen?"

"A few days before we were due to go on holiday, Emma said."

"You mean just before he was killed?"

"She told me about it in the hospital. I couldn't accept it, well, you saw . . . But if I'm being honest, I had a sense there was something."

She didn't look at me as she spoke and she held her voice steady with great effort.

"I think I sensed it the Saturday before he died. I

remember standing at the kitchen sink, washing salad leaves and looking out at the garden. Andrew was putting away the lawnmower and Emma was lying on a blue-striped beach towel on the grass." She paused as though she could see the scene before her. "You see how she is, Bea, so beautiful, and she was stretched out in her bikini, eyes closed, her lovely limbs brown already. Andrew had locked the garden shed and was walking back up to the house. I'm sure he didn't notice me watching, and he turned his head and looked at her and . . . It wasn't a good look, Bea, it was . . . I thought it was ugly." She shuddered. "I thought I'd be sick right there at the sink. But then it vanished from his face and he was smiling at me and I told myself I'd imagined it. I went out for a drink that night with the girls from work. It happened then, Emma said."

Poor Georgina, what a burden of guilt she must carry.

"You'll both need help to cope with this."

"I know. I'll speak to the doctor when he comes."

"I need to ask you something." I was cautious, unsure whether it was right to ask now, but desperately needing to know. "What happened to those letters? The ones Emma showed me."

She sighed. "I'm so sorry, Bea. I told the guards I didn't know what you were talking about because I lost them. When we packed up that morning after Emma was taken to hospital I put them somewhere, and then forgot about them. I would have let the guards have them, and I said they could look for them, but they didn't find them either."

I thought that very strange, but I didn't think there

321

was any point in saying so. "And are you sure you didn't meet the person who wrote those letters?"

She took her time to answer. She looked at me oddly, I thought, as though we were never friends.

"You read the letters?"

I nodded.

"So on that Friday, the day we were to meet in the car park, you can imagine, it was on my mind. I thought about taking time off and going home, in case the person did show up. But a part of me didn't want to avoid it. I wanted to hear. When I got to the car there she was, this girl, leaning against a pillar, jeans, runners, a blue sweatshirt, hood up."

She paused and drank a little from her cup and topped it up from the pot.

"When I saw her I thought she wanted money, right? But the first thing she said was 'I'm not looking for anything', like she'd read my mind."

"Did she give you her name?" I spoke carefully, afraid that a wrong word from me would stop her talking.

But she didn't stop, it seemed to come as a relief to her to talk.

"No, and I didn't ask. I thought there was something vulnerable about her. I didn't feel threatened at all. So I opened the car and let her sit in the passenger seat."

I wanted to say how risky that had been.

"She said 'I knew Andy before you did'. 'Andy', she called him. Then she told me she met him when she was fifteen and she'd longed to be a singer and he said he'd help her, but he took her to London and – *raped* her." Georgina made a gulping noise at the word. "She said to me 'I was a child'. I asked her had she been to the guards and I said, if it was true, she would have. She said when it dawned on her that she could, it was too late."

It was definitely Billie, then, who had written the letters and who had met her.

"I told her I didn't believe her for a moment and she said there was nothing she could do about that. 'I promised myself I'd warn you, now you've been warned,' she said and then she got out of the car and walked away."

Poor Billie. "And did you believe her?"

"I pitied her, to be honest. I thought she could've confused Andrew with someone else. But some of the things she'd said were so familiar. Then I thought maybe she'd known him in some capacity, at some time. But no, I couldn't imagine him being capable of such a thing with a child not much older than Emma." She started to cry then. "I drove off after she left and the nearer home I got, the less I believed her. I convinced myself Andrew had disappointed her in some way or rejected her. I thought she must have decided to make up lies about him to hurt him and maybe to come between us, so I didn't even mention it to him when I got home. He didn't know about the letters. I just put it out of my head. I wish to God I hadn't."

"And when you saw that look, Georgina, that Andrew gave Emma in the garden, did you not worry then?" I felt I would have if it was my child. But then how would I know? Perhaps the desire to preserve the status quo was stronger than the fear of what might happen in the future.

She shook her head. "It's hard to understand now, I know, but I didn't. I didn't put those things together at all."

"What a mess." I said it out loud though I hadn't intended to.

"Don't you think I know that? It's all my fault. If I'd challenged him then, when I got back from meeting that girl, or if I'd called him out when I saw the way he looked at Emma . . . I did neither. I just went out with my friends like nothing was wrong and let it happen." She sounded bitter and angry with herself.

"He did it, not you." It was difficult to find the right words.

She got up from the table and began to tidy.

"I'm really tired now, Bea," she said.

I took the hint and stood up to leave. "I'd imagine McCann might call over at some stage. It'd be best if you tell him the truth about the letters."

She said she would.

"Do you mind if I go up and say goodbye to Emma? I won't disturb her if she's sleeping."

She looked at me wearily. "Go ahead."

Chapter 34

I went upstairs and opened Emma's room as quietly as I could. She was lying under her duvet, eyes closed. She looked peaceful and I thought that she might improve now that it was in the open.

I was about to leave when she called my name.

"Sorry, I didn't mean to wake you." I went over to the side of her bed.

"You didn't. I was just thinking about everything. Sit down for a minute."

I sat on the edge of her bed and she took my hand.

"I was rude when you came in first, I shouldn't have been. I'm glad you found me in time."

"I'm glad you feel that way." I could see already the difference speaking out had made. "You're going to be fine now that it's all out in the open. The doctor will come and your mother will get you the right help."

"She's told you everything then?"

"Yes."

"Good. You know all the times I had those nightmares, it was only *his* face I was seeing. I only remembered the look on her face when I was in hospital. It came back to me then."

"On her face?" I was confused but didn't want to show it.

"When she came into my room that night and saw what he was doing. She was so horrified."

"Of course she was." My heart began to thump. So Georgina had been there. She had lied to me about not knowing.

"I didn't remember any of it for a long time, you see, only I knew there was something bad."

I didn't know what to say. My mind was racing.

"You'll be alright now," I repeated and stood to leave. She closed her eyes and I left the room and shut the door behind me. I stood frozen on the landing. Georgina had known all along that Andrew had tried to rape Emma. She had interrupted him. That was why Emma had said "tried". Georgina had caught him before he could. But she hadn't told the guards and she hadn't sought help for her daughter. What had she done then?

What had she done?

I walked down the stairs as quietly as I could, planning to just slip out the front door without disturbing Georgina. I needed time to think clearly away from the house. I needed to be able to piece it all together before I told McCann.

I was about to open the door when I heard footsteps behind me. Georgina was coming downstairs. She had been up there then, when I was talking to Emma. Had she heard?

She answered my question before I asked it.

"It's true, I did see it," she said. "I was too ashamed to tell you."

"But why didn't you tell the guards?" I couldn't keep from showing my bewilderment.

She sat down on the third step, her elbows on her knees, her face cupped in her hands.

"He'd given her something – Rohypnol he said it was. He cried and said he was sorry and promised me she wouldn't remember anything because of the drug."

I gasped at the horror of that, the premeditated nature of his attack.

"I let her sleep and the next morning she said nothing about it, only that she felt a bit sick. I gave her paracetamol and one of my sleeping pills. I thought if I said nothing she wouldn't remember. I thought it would be the kindest thing, just to let her forget. I didn't know it would come back to her."

"Oh Georgina, I can't imagine how awful that was."

She stiffened and stood up and began walking down to the kitchen.

I followed her.

"That's not everything though, is it, Georgina? What did you do?"

"You don't understand. You'll never be able to understand." She was twisting her hands, one over the other now, as though washing them under a hot tap. "I knew there was something wrong with him, I just . . . I didn't let myself believe it until that night. I came home early, about half eleven, and I went upstairs and I heard noises and I opened the door and he was there, on top of her." Her face was twisted with anguish.

"It must have been unbearable." I was afraid now of what she was going to tell me, but I needed to know. "What did you do, Georgina?"

"You know what I did, Bea, what any mother would have done. I waited for the right time. I knew he'd go to the casino on Monday night, his last chance until after our holidays. I waited for him and when he came out I followed him into the Blessington Basin. I only had one chance. I gave it everything, Bea, as hard as I could." She clenched her teeth as though remembering the physical effort. "He fell forward into the lake."

Her voice was flat now, and cold.

"It was the best way, Bea, it was the only way to protect my family."

I stared at Georgina. Who was this woman? Not the person I knew, surely? I thought of Billie then. What happened to Billie? There could only be one answer.

"Why did you have to kill Billie?"

When I looked directly at her eyes it was as though there was a stranger peering out through them.

"You can understand my problem, can't you?" She waited for me to agree.

I stayed silent.

"She was the only one who knew what he was capable of. After he was gone she phoned me. I didn't give her a chance to get beyond hello. She would have asked me for money in exchange for her silence and kept on asking. I couldn't have that."

"She wasn't that sort of person, Georgina."

"Don't pretend you knew her. Even if you're right and she didn't ask for money, if she just told the guards about

Andrew and about meeting me, where would I have been then? I couldn't let that happen."

Billie had been Andrew's victim and then the victim of his wife, only because she had tried to warn her, only because she wanted to help protect her children. I didn't know what to say. I was unable to hide my shock.

"You're the only one who knows now, Bea," Georgina said then. Her tone had shifted.

I felt frightened for myself for the first time. This person standing in the kitchen, her back to the countertop, looking at me with a steady gaze, this was not the Georgina I knew. I couldn't predict what she would do next. There were questions still in my head about what had happened and I thought perhaps if I asked her, she would answer them and I would have time to think of a way to get help.

I summoned up a sympathetic voice.

"I can't believe you had to go through all that, Georgina. It must have been awful for you."

"It was, Bea, really." She looked desperately sorry for herself.

"Can I ask you something?" I was playing for time. "I know it's an odd question, but did you use the same weapon on Andrew and Billie?"

She smiled then, as though reminiscing. I shivered.

"I thought it was best – it worked fine the first time."

I was struggling to keep the judgment and fear out of my voice. Despite my pounding heart, I knew I needed to appear as calm as possible.

"Where did you hide it, then, in between times, I mean?"

She laughed a little. "The best place to hide something is in plain sight, didn't you know that, Bea? It's been here all the time." She gestured at the worktop where her large, grey granite mortar and pestle sat. She picked up the pestle, which had a long handle and a bulbous head, and pressed it into her left palm.

"These things are surprisingly heavy."

Looking at it, I could understand how a pathologist might have thought a bat was used for the killings.

"We brought this back from our honeymoon in Egypt – fitting in a way, don't you think? To end our marriage with something we had when it started?"

I recoiled at the thought of the weapon being so close by all the time, but tried not to show it.

"It's neat, isn't it?" she said, holding it out for me to admire. "I could just pop it back in my shoulder bag when I was finished, bring it home, wash it and then go on using it as normal. I made you lunch once with spices, didn't I?"

I remembered eating sandwiches she'd made with spiced chicken. I remembered her telling me she'd ground the spices herself. I felt as though I might vomit.

The doorbell rang then and it was Georgina's turn to look frightened.

"Who is that?" She opened the kitchen door slightly and peered round it.

"You called the doctor, didn't you? I expect that's him."

"That's right, I did." The doorbell rang again. She closed the kitchen door. "We'll just ignore it – he'll go away."

"Don't you think he should see Emma?"

"He should, but not now. I have to figure out what to do. I'll call later, tell him we were both asleep."

The bell rang for a third time.

"For God's sake – he'll wake Emma!" She seemed exasperated now.

We waited, but Emma didn't wake and the doorbell didn't ring again.

Chapter 35

I was sitting at the kitchen table looking at her, trying to keep my nerve. Should I just try to push past her and run out the front door? But what about Emma?

She was still holding the pestle, tapping it every now and then against the palm of her left hand. I could read in her face what it was she was considering.

"You're not going to do anything with that, Georgina, not here. It would be too messy."

She considered that. She put the pestle back in its mortar, opened a kitchen drawer and took out what looked like a large boning knife. The blade was long and narrow. I breathed in sharply.

"There's no need for any of this. There's only you and me here." I held her gaze and tried to project confidence.

She put the knife on the worktop.

"How long have we been friends, Georgina?"

"I don't know – fifteen years?"

"More like twenty – that's a long time. I've always been a good friend, haven't I?"

I could feel sweat at the back of my neck.

"You did your best," she said grudgingly.

"Do you think I'd betray you?" My palms were sweaty too. I tried to keep my breathing steady.

"I don't know, Bea. Would you? You told McCann about the letters, didn't you?" Her fingers were on the handle of the knife.

"I thought I was helping you and that was before I understood – if you'd told me the truth from the beginning we could have worked it out between us." There was nothing I could do about the warble in my voice now.

"How do I know though, Bea? How do I know you won't call McCann as soon as you leave? You think you understand people, you think you can trust them, you believe what they say and then they let you down." She was shaking her head as though she was having an argument with herself and not with me.

"There've been good people in your life, Georgina. You can't let what Andrew did colour everything. If you do then he's won, hasn't he?"

She looked confused and I thought I was making some progress, but I was wrong. She picked up the knife and pointed it at me.

"I'm sorry, Bea, I have to protect my family." She pointed the knife in the direction of the patio door. "Out."

I stood up slowly, my knees wobbling beneath me. "Just tell me," I said as I walked toward the door, "does Emma know what you did?"

"Of course not." She reached for the key which was sitting in the lock, turned it and then slid the door along

333

its frame. There was her black slate patio, with its pretty garden furniture and beyond that a lawn with shrubs bordering it. At the end of the garden was a small wooden shed. It all looked so orderly and normal.

"It will be easier out here," she said, holding the blade now close to my throat.

"Emma will know. If you kill me, she'll know." I was getting desperate. "Let me leave, I promise I'll go straight to the airport, get a flight to London and I won't come back."

"That would never work, Bea, and you know it. You'd tell them, you couldn't help yourself." She pushed me ahead of her down the garden toward the shed. The air was cool on my face, but I was sweating. I could feel the blade against my skin.

"Don't do this, Georgina. You know you don't want to."

"I must, don't you see?"

We were at the wooden door of the shed now.

"This is madness, Georgina."

She reached around me with one hand and slid the bolt.

"Move." She flicked the blade to the right to make me move out of the way.

Then she swung open the shed door and signalled for me to go inside. I stood on the threshold, aware that if I did not act, then I was looking into my own coffin. What a strange place to end, among the deck chairs and lawnmower and garden tools. There was no point in going on talking to her now, I knew. I wouldn't be able to convince her, it had gone too far. This was the last chance

I would have to get away. I put one foot into the shed and at the same time reached for a spade propped up against one wall. I grabbed it, turned and rammed it – handle first – into her stomach with all the force I could manage. She fell backwards onto the grass, the knife falling from her hand. I dropped the spade, ran past her into the house and locked the patio door. Panting, I ran round the house checking all the downstairs windows. I put the dead bolt on the front door, in case she had her house key in her pocket. Then I found my phone and called for help.

While I waited I could see her from the kitchen. She stayed sitting on the grass, holding her stomach, then picked up the knife and ran toward the door. When she found she couldn't open it, she dropped the knife and pounded on the glass with her fists, screaming my name, until she no longer had the energy. Then she sat down on a patio chair and began to weep. Despite everything, I felt sorry for her. She looked like a child who had just had a tantrum. I wanted to open the back door and let her in and put my arms around her.

They weren't long in coming, McCann and half of Store Street. I could hear their sirens as they drove up the avenue. So could Georgina. She got to her feet, looked in both directions then ran around to the side entrance of the house. When she came back she was accompanied by a uniformed officer, holding her by the arm.

I opened the door and let them both in. McCann followed with half a dozen other guards.

"You all right?" He put a hand out awkwardly and touched my elbow. "Here, sit down."

I sat at the table and as I did a mixture of relief and shock flooded me. I began to shake.

"Emma's upstairs."

McCann signalled to one of the woman guards who left the room.

"She did it, she killed them both." I said the words but I could hardly believe them. Georgina, normal, lovely Georgina had done that to her husband and to Billie.

"You don't have to tell me now, there'll be plenty of time for that," McCann said. "Has she family we should call?"

"The younger children are with their aunt. Emma should be brought there. I'm sure there's a phone number around here somewhere." I got up and started opening drawers, looking in them for an address book or something.

McCann put his hand on my arm again and encouraged me to sit. I sat.

"Don't worry, we'll find it."

Georgina sat opposite us at the table, staring ahead, her face as empty as a mannequin's.

"Bring her to Store Street," McCann told two of the officers.

"I think she might need to go to hospital," I said.

"There's nothing wrong with me." She almost spat the words.

McCann nodded and the two officers got her to her feet and walked her out.

"Once she's in the station we'll get her assessed," he said. "Did she hurt you?"

"No, but she intended to. I managed to get away."

"Thank God for that."

"Andrew tried to do to Emma what he did to Billie . . . that's why Georgina killed him."

"We were catching up with her, Bea. But I hadn't expected this to happen. I should have been more direct with you."

Had he been thinking of her children, I wondered now, while he was "catching up".

"She could have hurt the children." Why hadn't I seen the truth? I had been so blinkered, so certain in my views. I suddenly missed Gabriel and wanted nothing more than to see him walk into the kitchen.

"Have you spoken to Gabriel at all? Does he know what's happened?"

He looked surprised. "He didn't tell you?"

"Tell me what?"

"There's nothing to worry about. But he took a bit of a turn on Thursday night on his way home. He's up in the Mater."

I felt my head spin. "Is he okay?"

"He'll be fine – they put a stent in, he said."

All this time I'd been thinking bad things about him and he was in a hospital bed. "But that can't be right – his car was gone yesterday morning." Was it only yesterday morning? It felt like days had gone by with Georgina in the kitchen.

"I got one of the lads to pick it up for him. He was worried about it being left on a main road."

I felt suddenly angry with him. "So he told you about his damn car and he couldn't be bothered about telling me?"

McCann saw through me. "Now, Bea, stop worrying, he'll be grand."

I got up again and began searching for my bag. "I need to see him."

"Now?"

"Yes, now." I found my car keys.

He sighed and signalled to one of the guards who came over. "Bea, give Eamonn here your keys – he'll drive you over."

"There's no need." I said it but I knew there was a need – my hands were shaking and I felt weak. I handed over the keys.

"I'll talk to you later," McCann said. "And don't worry about Emma."

I nodded.

Then he addressed the guard. "See she gets home safely, will you? And I'll see you back at the station."

Chapter 36

The drive from Belford Avenue seemed to go on forever. I sat silent in the front seat worrying about Gabriel and trying to unscramble all that had happened. Emma, Milly and James had lost both parents now. Georgina would be gone for a very long time, either in prison or in a psychiatric unit. I didn't think I was in the best position to judge which one it should be – all I knew was she had killed two people and had been on the verge of killing me. I trembled at the realisation.

When we got to the hospital, the guard drove into the underground car park and came up in the lift with me to the first floor. The Mater was a melding of old and new buildings with lifts and corridors linking one with the other. McCann had told me Gabriel was in the Sacred Heart Ward. The guard pointed me in the right direction and said he'd wait for me at the first-floor coffee shop. I walked down the hospital's wide, modern corridor, turned left into an old part, to another bank of lifts and went up to the seventh floor.

I located the Sacred Heart Ward, asked a nurse for

Gabriel Ingram and found him at last lying on a bed in the corner of one of the rooms. His eyes were closed and I lifted a plastic chair from the foot of his bed, placed it closer to him and sat down as quietly as I could. He looked helpless lying there, his arms straight down on top of the stiff white sheet and blue hospital blanket, his head propped on three pillows. I had an urge to pat down his iron-grey hair, which was standing up at the back, into its usual neat arrangement. But I let it be. I thought about the first time we'd met, at retirement drinks for a tipstaff. What was it – ten years ago? We were both at our peak then though we didn't know it. And now we were like two late-flowering plants, just going over.

I placed my hand ever so lightly over his. He sighed and opened his eyes.

"I thought I was banjaxed," he said.

"How are you feeling?"

"Okay now." He spoke as though he was testing out his body for discomfort. "I'm a bit stiff." He rolled onto one side and manoeuvred himself up in the bed. I fixed his pillows.

"That's better."

I gave him a glass of water poured from a jug on the locker beside him and he sipped from it.

"What happened? How did you end up here?"

He thought for a moment. "It was all very quick." He sipped again. "I got a taxi outside your place, I remember. I was sitting next to the driver and he was talking about football and I got this terrible pain in my chest and down my arm and I think I put my hand to my

340

chest. I could hardly breathe. And the driver said to me, 'You need to get to hospital', and he drove me here. That was it really. They just whipped me in, hooked me up to these machines. Did a few scans. I was having a heart attack, they said. Narrowed artery."

"Oh, Gabriel." I felt so guilty that I let him go out into the cold night in the way I did. What if he hadn't got a taxi? He might have decided to walk. It wouldn't have been the first time. And he could have keeled over on the footpath.

"Don't look at me like that now, Bea, I'm going to be grand. They put in one of those stents and the doctor says I could be out in a day or two."

"I wish you'd told me you weren't feeling well." I felt as though I should have known. Hadn't he been off-colour, breathless? And that cough.

"There was nothing to tell – I was a bit tired maybe, but . . ."

I thought of how we'd parted. "I wanted to say, Gabriel, about Wednesday night, when you came into the house . . ."

He shook his head and looked very uncomfortable. "Please, Bea, don't."

I stopped talking.

"I'm lucky the way it happened – if I'd been at home in bed I might have been a goner."

He might have been a goner. The words sank in and before I could stop it a wave of emotion flooded me and I began to cry.

"Here now!" Gabriel reached for a box of tissues on his locker and handed me a bunch.

"Sorry," I said, wiping my eyes. "It's just . . ." It was no good, I couldn't even speak until I'd let all the tears out. All the things that had happened. And Gabriel had always been so strong and now here he was, mortal. But I couldn't say that.

"Better?" he asked after a few minutes.

"I'm supposed to be asking you that."

He laughed and I took another tissue and tried to decide whether I should tell him about who killed Billie. It didn't seem right to foist it on him when he was in this condition, but I knew it would come out soon in the media. Georgina would be charged and the world would hear it. Gabriel would find out from the hospital TV, clamped to the ceiling above the door at the entrance to the ward. It would be better if he heard it from me. He didn't need to know all the details, just the facts.

I composed myself and put my hand over his.

He looked at me.

"What?"

"It was Georgina." I said the words quietly and firmly.

"What was? What?"

"She killed them both."

His face registered confusion. "But how? Why?"

I explained as best I could what had happened, that Georgina had met Billie who had warned her about Andrew, that she'd caught him then abusing Emma and that she'd murdered him. And poor Billie had been a casualty of her own concern for Andrew's children. I didn't tell him what had happened in Georgina's kitchen.

I felt as though I was talking about a stranger. I had

342

thought I knew her as well as you could know any friend. In my head she had been labelled "hardworking woman, great mother, contented wife, good friend". I had no idea what she was truly capable of.

"That must have come as a terrible shock, Bea. How did you find out?"

I hesitated. I wasn't ready to relive it all and I didn't think I would be helping him by telling him all the details now.

"We'll talk about that another time – you must be tired." There was no point in saying I didn't want to worry him. He would have dismissed my concerns.

He yawned, stretched a little, winced.

"Are you in pain? Will I get a nurse?"

"No, no. I'm grand."

"Is there anything I can get you before I go?"

He said there wasn't, that McCann had brought him in shaving gear and pyjamas. I wanted to ask him why he hadn't let me know he was in hospital. But I wasn't sure I wanted to hear the answer.

"I'm so glad you're going to be okay, Gabriel." I stood, and bent toward him and kissed his cheek, and then, remembering Thursday night, I kissed him lightly on the lips. He grinned.

"I'll be in again tomorrow – text me if you think of anything you need."

He said he would.

In the corridor outside, I met McCann on his way in.

"How is he?"

"He says he'll be fine."

"And what about you?"

"Me? There's nothing wrong with me." As I said the words, it was as though my legs turned to liquid beneath me and I thought I would collapse.

"Come on."

He led me into the lift and out again to the third-floor café.

"Your officer is downstairs," I said.

"He can wait. Have you eaten at all?"

I didn't answer him because I couldn't remember.

"Sit down, I'll just be a minute."

I sat at a table near the door. Around me mostly medics were eating and chattering. I thought how strange it must be for them to see life and death every day, and to treat it as though it was just a part of their working lives. I supposed that was how it had to be for them to function.

"There now." McCann put a tray down on the table with brown-bread sandwiches and tea. "Eat up."

I opened the packet and tried to eat.

"It's rare, you know, women killing their partners," he said.

I wondered why he was telling me that.

"Compared to men killing women, I mean. I'm not using that as an excuse though."

"An excuse for what?" I couldn't grasp what he was getting at.

He looked uneasy about having to spell it out for me.

"In case you thought . . . we weren't doing our jobs right."

"I didn't think that."

"Because there was a lot of evidence pointing in other

directions, Bea. We thought we were looking for a man, for Billie's murder certainly."

I remembered what Barney had told Gabriel about the man he'd seen leaving Hanlon's.

"Did you ever find that man?"

He pointed his finger. "There now, that's what I mean. Barney said it was a man and we assumed he was right. But he only saw the person from behind and the hood was up. It could have been Georgina."

The reality of that, of Georgina putting on jeans and a hoody and walking into Hanlon's and going down into the cellar and then . . . I put my sandwich down.

"How did she know where Billie worked?" The thought had just occurred to me.

"She told us she followed Billie after that meeting in the car park, and then a few other times, till she found the best place."

I thought back on all our conversations. Every time I had confronted her about something she'd lied. I couldn't believe she had been so calculating.

"And do you remember that tin box, the one Gabriel found in Billie's room?" McCann said.

I recalled it now, with its handwritten notes and photos.

"Did you notice the lid? A London bus – she must have got it on that trip with Dalton."

I felt heavy with sadness at the thought of it, the young Billie on her trip to England, buying her souvenirs, filled with hope.

"So you can see how it took a while for us to get there, can't you?"

He was looking at me intently and I realised then that he felt guilty because I'd been in danger.

"You could never have known what she'd do. I didn't think that for a moment."

He nodded. "Right so." He looked down at the sandwich he'd bought me, with two bites taken out of it.

"Are you finished?"

"I am, thanks."

He picked up the untouched one, folded it in half and put it all in his mouth. I wondered when he'd last eaten.

"It's time for me to go," I said.

We both got up and walked to the bank of lifts.

"You'll be in to make a statement over the next few days, Monday maybe?" He pressed the up arrow.

"Tomorrow, I'm working on Monday."

"Work? Would you not take a few days off?" The first lift arrived going up.

"I've had too many days off."

I thought he was going to berate me, but he didn't.

"I'll see you tomorrow then." He stepped in and the door closed.

I turned and walked down the stairs.

Chapter 37

Monday, November 21st

Court 32 was quiet at twenty past ten as I set up for
O'Malley v O'Malley again. I felt drained and still a little
shaky and thought McCann had probably been right and
I should have taken time off work. But I didn't want to
let Úna Hollister down.

So much had happened since last Wednesday that I
felt almost as though I was a different person. I'd been
thinking about it over the weekend – the assumptions I'd
made about Georgina and her marriage. I'd thought I
knew her well, but I had no idea.

I could understand that she would have wanted to be rid
of Andrew once she found out what he'd done. But why
didn't she just go to the guards and tell them what had
happened? They would have arrested him immediately, I
was sure. And then she could have divorced him. It wasn't
as though she was living in the 1980s. She could have come
here to the family court and put an end to their
relationship. No judge would have allowed him near
children again so he would have been cut out of their lives.
What made her choose to kill him instead?

Ever since I'd known her she had striven for the perfect life. Had she wanted to go on pretending that was what she had? Did it seem to her better to be rid of him entirely from the world? I had to admit that if she had killed him on the night she caught him with Emma, I might have found it easier to understand, the blind horror of it. But to wait and to calculate, what did that make her? And hardest of all to understand was her ability to move on to killing Billie – lovely, bright Billie who had only tried to alert her.

The media had been full of her arrest at the weekend. The red-tops were already calling her the Spice Killer. They reported she'd been charged and then transferred to a secure psychiatric unit. One paper showed her picture with "Mad or Bad?" written beneath it. And there were articles discussing the treatment of women charged with murder compared to how men were treated. All I could think of was Emma, Milly and James, effectively orphaned. I hoped they were being protected from it.

I had set up my stenograph in the usual spot, to one side of the court registrar. The barristers arrived and sat at the table, facing the judge. They talked quietly to the solicitors who were sitting opposite them. Their clients sat as usual at the back.

When Judge Peter Hadley-O'Toole arrived Ruby Clements addressed him.

"Judge, there is something my client wishes you to hear before you make your judgment."

"This is most unusual, Ms Clements, I am halfway through drafting my judgment at this stage."

"Yes, judge, and he's very grateful to you for agreeing to hear him."

"Very well."

Mr O'Malley made his way to the stand and took the oath as before, though I thought I detected a humbler tone.

"Now, Mr O'Malley, there is something you want the court to know?"

"Judge, it's that I don't want the separation, I want to go home. I've realised over the last while, and especially after speaking with Dr McArdle, that I don't want to break up our family."

It was he who had initiated proceedings – it was he who had moved out of the family home. "I still love Rosemary, you see." He turned toward his wife. "Rosemary?"

Mrs O'Malley sat at the back of the court, her mouth wide open.

"Well, Ms Clements," the judge said. "Do you think you might want to speak to your client outside?"

"Thank you." Ms Clements nodded.

The judge looked at his watch. "Right. Back here at two, please." He rose and left the court to a cacophony of voices.

As I got ready to leave, Mrs O'Malley, her solicitor beside her, remained seated, holding a tissue to her face, her shoulders shaking. She didn't look up as her husband walked out with his legal team.

"He's playing another game," I heard her say as I passed. I felt sorry for her.

I called Gabriel, still in his hospital bed, when I left the court.

"Do you remember the O'Malley case?"

349

He said he did and I told him about Mr O'Malley's declaration.

"Whatever he's up to, he's certainly shocked her," I said.

He whispered something then and I had to ask him to repeat it.

"The trouble with you, Bea, is you don't believe in second chances."

Did I not?

"I'll see you later," I said.

Back in court, I waited for the parties to arrive. Ruby Clements walked in first with her solicitor, then Úna Hollister followed by the O'Malleys who to my surprise took seats together at the back wall.

"All rise."

When the judge came through the door from his chambers he appeared to look twice at the back of the court, before sitting down.

Ruby Clements stood to address him.

"Judge, on consent, I am applying to strike out the case. My client no longer wishes to pursue his action."

The judge's face was a mixture of astonishment and pleasure. "Well, I must say, this is not something we see here very often. Are we certain?"

He looked at Ms Hollister.

"Yes, judge, my client is agreeable to the case being struck out."

He nodded in the direction of the couple. "In that case, let me wish you both all the best for the future."

"Thank you, judge," they responded in unison.

"I assume costs have been agreed," he said before getting up and leaving the court again.

The O'Malleys left together shortly afterwards. The barristers tidied their papers then Úna Hollister approached me.

"Thanks, Beatrice. Will you send us your invoice so we can settle up?"

"I will. It's hard to believe, isn't it? All those terrible things they said about each other." I couldn't hide my scepticism.

"I know, first time it's ever happened in one of my cases, anyway." She spoke quietly in the now empty court. "He told me he just woke up last Saturday and it dawned on him that he'd made a terrible mistake. He thought the only way his wife would believe him was if he swore it under oath. And, apparently, she never wanted him to leave in the first place."

"Amazing." I packed my stenograph away and said I'd put the invoice in the post.

I went back to my office to drop my equipment off, organise the transcript and print up the bill. I was glad the case was over so that I could visit Gabriel early. Despite his claim that he would be out in two days, doctors had held on to him over the weekend and he wasn't sure when they'd let him home.

I thought about the O'Malleys on my way back to Clontarf, all that they had been through together and separately, all that seeming hatred in the courtroom and yet behind it there had still been a bond. How complex human relationships were, how strange the emotions on which they were built.

I bought a box of dark chocolates to take in to

Gabriel. I knew he would have to watch his diet now, but he had a sweet tooth and I'd read that dark chocolate was healthy in small doses. I bought a large bottle of Diet 7up too, and a pair of earphones he could plug into his mobile so that he could listen to the radio.

All the time I was shopping I was thinking about him. He and I had so much history. It was not all good, I knew, but there was something there, at the back of it, that had some value. While I put on a little lipstick before visiting the hospital, I looked in the mirror and saw myself clearly – a frightened woman. I had been too afraid, too wary of being hurt to be willing to make any sort of promise to him, to give him the kind of commitment he needed. But what was it I had been so determined to protect? My wonderful single life? My peace? My autonomy? What good was any of that really?

It had struck me, when I saw him in the hospital bed, that he needed looking after now. And he was fundamentally a man who should not be alone. Did he know himself well enough to know that? I wasn't sure. I would be taking a risk, asking of him now something I'd refused to give before. But then it needn't be so momentous. Couldn't I start by suggesting he stay with me for a while until he felt stronger? Would his pride allow him? I didn't know, but better to speak than regret my silence. I drove to the Mater hospital having made up my mind. I would set my natural reticence aside and make the offer.

I left my car in an underground space and navigated my way to the Sacred Heart Ward and to Gabriel's room. And there he was sitting on a chair beside his bed, fully clothed and with a small bag at his feet.

"Well, now." I smiled at him and he grinned back.

"They're letting me out. I'm just waiting for a prescription from the doctor."

"That's great. You probably don't need these now." I gave him the things I'd bought anyway.

"Thanks, Bea. You shouldn't have." He put them on top of his bag.

I sat on the edge of the bed, close to his chair. I reached out and touched his hand lightly and readied myself to ask him the question.

"How are you feeling, Gabriel?" I began.

"I'm grand now, really I am."

I took a deep breath and tried to hide my nerves. "I wanted to say, I mean, I wanted to ask you . . ."

Before I could continue, I heard a woman's voice behind me.

"Are you telling people you're grand again? You're not grand at all."

I turned and the woman put her hand out to me.

"I'm Bernadette, Gabriel's sister." She looked a little older than him though I knew he'd told me she was younger. She had the same straight nose and firm chin and the ruddy cheeks of a country farmer. "He's a terrible man," she said.

She told me she had driven from Glenties that morning and spoken to the doctors who said Gabriel needed rest and a bit of minding. He squirmed a little in his chair while his sister talked about him as though he wasn't in the room.

"So I said to him, I won't take no for an answer.

You're coming up home with me and that's an end to it. So he's coming." She looked in Gabriel's direction and nodded firmly.

He nodded too. I could see he had resigned himself to it.

"For a few days," he said.

"For at least a fortnight, till I see the colour back in those cheeks."

The Donegal air would do him good, I knew. And his sister would most likely spoil him.

I managed to smile.

"What were you going to ask me?" Gabriel said.

"It'll keep. Maybe you'll give me a call when you're back?"

"I will, of course."

I left him then to wait for his prescription. I drove home, parked the car and went for a walk along the seafront. There was a salt-filled breeze blowing in across the bay and the gulls were squawking as they swooped.

My head ached. My heart ached. There would be rain soon.

THE END

Acknowledgements

Thanks to all at Poolbeg Press especially Paula and Caroline, for their willingness to investment in me and in this book. Thanks to editor Gaye Shortland who has an unfailing eye for detail and a typo and error guidance system like a polite Exocet missile.

My thanks to barrister Katie Dawson for the legal pointers, and to Gwen Malone Stenography Services, the initial inspiration for Beatrice Barrington's world. Also a special thanks to Michael and Deirdre Small – they know why.

I want to thank my sisters and brothers, as well as extended family and friends, for their many words of encouragement and for buying and talking about the first book in this series, *In The Court's Hands*. And thank you to all the kind people at work, in *The Irish Times*, who bought the first book and said nice things about it.

Thanks to my children for cheering me up when I needed it and interrupting my internet browsing to tell me to write. And finally, thanks to my lovely husband Paul, my champion and encourager-in-chief, as always.

Now that you're hooked why not try
In the Courts Hands
also published by Poolbeg

Here's a sneak preview of the first two chapters.

IN THE
COURT'S
HANDS

FIONA GARTLAND

Chapter 1

Friday, April 25th 2014

If it had rained on the 25th of April at least one woman would not have died. Not that I bear any responsibility for that. Nothing I did intentionally caused anyone's death – though the fact remains, people did die.

It began with an innocent change of plan. I'd intended eating at the office, but the sun was so bright by one o'clock, and the Phoenix Park looked so attractive in its spring costume, that I decided to leave the Dublin Criminal Courts of Justice and take my lunch with me.

People have said to me how envious they are of the view from my office window in the glass cylinder that is the country's newest and tallest court building. I can see the Wellington Monument, a nineteenth-century granite obelisk, rising from the park. "Wonderful," they say, "so tranquil, so picture-postcard", and the monument is "powerful" and "inspiring". To me though, that phallic symbol is a reminder of the things I do not have.

I visited the ladies' toilets before I left, to tidy my chignon. As I re-pinned it, I frowned at the roots beginning to show up the red dye; no matter how hard hairdressers try, they can never match my original shade. Still, it's better than conceding to the ribbons of grey.

I reached into my handbag and dabbed a little extra make-up on. Fair skin, prone to freckling, becomes more vulnerable with time and I like to protect my vulnerabilities. I smoothed down my Size 14 pencil skirt and congratulated myself again on the cut of the navy jacket.

I took the glass elevator to the ground floor – some of my colleagues take the stairs, their vertigo a constant torture to them. I like to stand at the back of the transparent lift so that I can watch the cream triangles of the marble foyer rush toward me.

If it weren't for the security checks at the entrance, the Criminal Courts of Justice or CCJ, with its pleasing circular walls, sweeping staircase and neat reception desk, could be confused with a spartan, well-designed hotel. It's won all kinds of architectural awards and yet it is simply a place for processing criminals.

I nodded to Mike the security manager. He had an earpiece in his left ear, index finger pressed against it, making him look like he was communicating about a serious security breach. We both knew he'd actually agreed to take two sugars in his skinny latte.

Outside, I turned right, up toward the gates of the Phoenix Park. I've heard it described as Europe's largest walled park in a city. How we struggle on this little island to have the largest something.

I walked up Chesterfield Avenue in the centre of the park and chose a bench beneath a chestnut tree that was already almost in full leaf. The dappled shadows gave pleasant shade from the sun, yet held its warmth. I unpacked my lunch, of goat's cheese and rocket on focaccia bread, and opened my bottle of sparkling water. I was pleased with my decision to take the air. I find food always tastes better outside. I chewed slowly, relishing the richness of the cheese and the bite of the rocket.

It was then I saw him on the opposite side of the wide road, sitting on a bench the mirror of mine. He had that way some men have of dominating the space, with his arms outstretched along the back of the bench and his legs wide apart. He was wearing the blue-grey suit I had seen on him so many times in court, on this occasion with a pink shirt and dark blue tie. His silver hair, abundant and with a wave, was pushed back from his forehead. It was Stephen O'Farrell – the accused in the high-profile Signal Investment case.

I took another mouthful and wondered if he could see me. I felt that even if he could he would not recognise me. Few people notice the stenographer.

As I watched, from his left, a woman approached. He sat up straight, ran his fingers through his hair, folded his arms and brought his knees together. She sat beside him – a slight woman of indeterminate age, with a sharp nose and a red, A-line skirt, too short for her shapeless legs.

They did not greet each other or even appear to make eye contact, but not long after she sat down, he glanced around him, reached into the inside pocket of his jacket and took something out. It looked to me like an envelope. He passed it to her, and she placed it in her handbag. They made no eye contact, but words were exchanged. She nodded, stood up and walked away.

I watched her as she made her way toward the centre of the park. Before the Phoenix Monument, she got into a car. When I looked back at the bench, its occupant had gone.

I had been the stenographer on Stephen O'Farrell's case for weeks and had become accustomed to the terms used in the world of investments and property – flipping, options and acquisition fees. That's what happens in my business, you learn a new language with each new case. On my next assignment, I could be back to asphyxiation or induced myocardial infarction. There are other things I hear too. The words come out of my fingertips, but I try very hard to ensure that they do not lodge in my brain. Other courtroom participants get counselled when they've had to listen to disturbing experiences, but not stenographers. We are merely the vessels through which experiences flow, to come out on a transcript in 12-point Times New Roman.

When I'd finished my lunch, I packed up the detritus, put a stick of dental chewing gum in my mouth and walked back to the courts. I don't care much for gum, and baulk at the sight of other people masticating like farm animals, but my dentist recommended it post-meal. I chewed rapidly, mouth closed, before depositing it in tissue paper in the bin.

I would be lying if I said I didn't speculate on the encounter I'd witnessed. A romantic meeting? Hardly, unless the lack of physical contact was a disguise for hidden passions. It certainly wasn't his wife. I had seen her sitting at the back of the court, perfectly coiffured and in a beautifully cut dress and jacket, elegant and understated – Louise Kennedy probably. She was at least fifteen years his junior. I supposed it could have been a member of his staff, though the deference I'm sure he would have required seemed absent. I decided it was better to put the meeting out of my mind. It was ten minutes to two, just enough time for me to reapply a layer of lipstick in the bathroom and take up my position in Court 19 on the sixth floor. Judge Reginald Brown was nothing if not punctual. He'd said he would be ready to begin again at exactly ten past two and he would be.

To him, at least, I am not invisible. And he sometimes takes the trouble to stop a barrister in mid-flow to remind him to speak up, so I can hear. He is among the few judges that retain the wig since it became optional. A handful of barristers continue wearing it too. Judge Brown seemed undecided about his wig: wearing it in the morning, taking it off most afternoons and frequently slipping his hand between wig and head to scratch his scalp.

My powers of concentration are immense, but when they wane, my colleague Janine Gracefield takes over. Janine is a reliable sort, despite her youth and relative inexperience. She is in her early thirties, a slight person, with fair hair and the delicacy of a fawn. We have worked together for five years and have become friends.

At five minutes past two, I settled myself in my spot, visible but invisible, from where I could survey the entire courtroom. I find it amusing that, although the new criminal courts were designed for the twenty-first century, they hold on to the eighteenth-century structures of the older Four Courts. The highest bench is reserved for the judge, to the judge's right, one level down is the witness box and, below that, the place where the defendant sits. To the left is the jury. The registrar and assistants sit below the judge on the same level as the witness box. This is where I am, placed discreetly to one side. Solicitors are lower down again and sit facing the body of the court, with a long table between them and Senior Counsel. The next row is for juniors and the benches beyond are for the press and public.

The legal teams get cushions under their rumps, while the rabble must endure the hardwood of bare benches. The privileged must always have their comforts. I cannot complain of course, since I have a decent chair, with a straight, supportive back and comfortable cushion, with space for the stenograph to rest neatly between my knees.

I watched as the different parties made their way into the courtroom.

Leona O'Brien, Senior Counsel for the prosecution, walked calmly in, with her team scurrying around her. I'd worked at her cases many times before and we'd become friends. She'd been the talk of the Law Library when she'd had her baby, Grace, that January, after fifteen years of childless marriage. I'd overheard hushed discussions about how motherhood would spoil Leona's chances of progressing to the judicial appointment she'd looked destined for. I hoped they were wrong.

Her daughter kept her awake at night, she'd told me but, with her blonde bob neatly clipped and curling perfectly just below her ears, she still looked fresher than Raymond Rafferty, Senior Counsel for Stephen O'Farrell. He strolled into court, kicking the ends of his black gown out before him – an old-school, barrel-shaped barrister. His black, slicked-back hair, accentuated an open-pored nose, tinged with the plum colour of a drinker.

The media took up two rows and the public filled out the remaining seats. There was a knot of court watchers, mostly men, retired or unemployed. I had seen them rubbing their chins and nodding to each other in appreciation of a cogent point, occasionally allowing themselves a short laugh at one of Rafferty's witty flourishes.

"All rise," the judge's assistant intoned, and the room got to its feet.

Judge Brown smiled, sat and nodded at the jury minder. The twelve jurors entered, stage left.

I had become fond of this jury. They'd sat through six weeks of evidence already, some of it technical, much of it dull, yet most of them had remained awake. There were two jurors, a man and a woman, who struggled to keep their eyes open in the afternoons, succumbing, no doubt, to the lunchtime meat and two veg; while another two, both men, sat forward in their seats and took copious notes. It is often the way with juries – there are one or two at each end of the enthusiasm spectrum, with the remainder in the middle. They generally reach predictable verdicts, though once in a rare while they go astray in a way that makes me wonder if they've been infected with outside influence.

Leona O'Brien got to her feet.

"The next witness is George Reilly," she said.

"Very good," the judge responded.

A man in a blue double-breasted suit, straining at its

buttons, made his way to the witness box and the afternoon's evidence began.

When court is over for the day, I generally go back to the office and work through my transcript for rare, typographical errors. On this occasion, I had an appointment with my hairdresser, so Janine agreed to stay behind and carry out the necessary work.

"Bea," she said, "there's no need to apologise. I owe you one from last Friday."

She did.

"I wouldn't ask, only it's a special occasion," she'd said. "It's Alastair's birthday and I want everything to be just perfect for him."

Alastair was her boyfriend, or perhaps partner is the correct term, since they've moved in together.

"We have a reservation at Chapter One," she'd told me. It was one of the city's few Michelin-starred restaurants. "Alastair likes good food."

I'd met Dr Alastair McAuliffe only once, when I'd called over to Janine's apartment to collect a transcript she'd brought home to work on, after a particularly long day in court. The forty-two-year-old had the excellent bone structure Janine had so enthusiastically described to me, with the chestnut-brown hair of a young Sean Connery, as well as the accent.

"So, this is Beatrice," he'd said, as he shook hands with me. He'd smiled with his head to one side, as though he was viewing a patient or a specimen.

The way he looked at me made me feel foolish. Many medics have a habit of doing that – it's a kind of condescension that I expect is bred into them during training.

Without taking his eyes from me, he said, "You've been a stenographer for some time, I believe." His accent was Edinburgh soft, rolling on his Rs. "Janine says you're the best in the business."

"Janine would say Mass," I responded, joking.

He hesitated before deciding to release a short, dry laugh. Janine squeezed his arm, delighted.

"Well, thanks for this," I'd said, putting the transcript under my arm. "I'll see you at work." I was glad to get away – Dr Alastair McAuliffe made me feel uncomfortable, as though I'd been peered at through a microscope.

The following day, when Janine asked if I liked him, I said he was every bit as handsome as she'd described. She was so pleased, she didn't notice the evasion. I was sorry that I hadn't warmed to him. Janine had a good heart and, if she was fond of him, Alastair had to have something. I promised myself I'd try harder the next time we met.

It was unusual for me to find myself leaving the CCJ just after four o'clock on a weekday, at the same time as the jurors and witnesses.

The forewoman, a twenty-something with a hungry face, exited beside me and I saw, ahead, the heavyset man who sat in the back row of the jury box. We were all making our way toward the Luas tram stop to get into the city centre. The forewoman, a neat, thin person who appeared every morning with her long brown hair firmly controlled in a ponytail, was beside him. They turned at the traffic lights to cross over the Liffey and catch the tram at Heuston Station. I walked further on to the stop outside Collins Barracks, which I preferred.

As I approached the stop, the ding of a bell told me a tram was approaching. I could hear the Luas woman intoning "Museum: Ard-Mhúsaem". I pressed the door button and got on.

I took a seat beside a young man, too skinny for his tracksuit, with the pallor of heroin on him. A few seats up I noticed the jury forewoman, who must have got on at Heuston. She was facing toward me, with her back to the driver. A woman in a red skirt was standing beside her, bent towards her a little as she spoke. I couldn't place her at first, but then I recognised the sharpness of the features, the unattractive legs. She was the woman who'd met O'Farrell in the park. She put her hand on the juror's shoulder.

"Smithfield: Margadh na Feirme," the tram-voice said.

The doors of the carriage opened and the woman in the red skirt got out. I noticed as she passed me outside that she glanced in the window, looked away and looked in again. A line developed between her brows.

At that moment, I believed she recognised me and I felt uneasy and frightened, though I was not sure why. I looked quickly away as the doors of the carriage closed, and the tram slid on.

Chapter 2

Sunday, January 18th 1981

The rain hit the window at an angle, carried on a strong north-westerly wind. It was four o'clock and the bedroom was in semi-darkness. We hadn't got out of bed all day. At least Leo hadn't. I'd been into the kitchen to make us breakfast and then lunch.

The radio was on. 'Woman' was playing and Leo, sitting up in bed, was singing it at me. His two arms were stretched out straight in front, the blankets at his waist.

"I'm sick of that song," I said.

The newspapers had been full of the gunning down of the pacifist musician before Christmas. They'd released 'Woman' after Lennon's death and the stations kept on playing it, over and over again.

I carried two mugs of coffee across the room. Leo took them from me, put them on the bedside locker and pulled me toward him.

"I can't believe you missed Mass, Bea."

It was our first time to spend the entire weekend together. On Saturday, we'd gone to Glendalough and then Leo had got us reservations for dinner at Le Coq

Hardi in Ballsbridge.

"Are you trying to impress me?" I'd asked, doing my best not to sound impressed. It was Dublin's most exclusive restaurant, a place my parents had only read about in the newspapers. I'd fussed over what to wear, anxious not to let Leo down. I'd finally settled on a green floral-print dress, tight at my small waist, and piled my red hair up into a soft bun.

"You look sweet," he'd said, and I'd thanked him, though I'd been trying for sophisticated.

The rain on Sunday morning had put an end to any plans for another outing. I wasn't sorry.

Leo kissed me on the mouth, his lips sweet and firm.

"What would your mother say if she found out?" His grin showed the sharp white points of his eye teeth and accentuated his square jaw.

I punched him gently on the shoulder. "You're a bad influence."

My parents wouldn't have approved of my missing Mass or of anything else about that day. Mother would take one look at Leo, with his broad shoulders under his double-breasted suit, and his dark hair pushed back from his forehead, and lecture me about older men. Father might take him aside and ask him, man to man, to leave quietly. And the idea of me taking him into my bed would horrify them. They clung to their 1950s' morality like a sinking ship. But this was 1981 and their rules didn't apply to me anymore.

Neither Mother nor Father had siblings, and their parents had passed away long before my brother and then I arrived. The two of them were late to marriage.

When I was growing up, I thought it made them too careful. I used to envy classmates whose packed, busy homes I visited. Their families seemed carefree and filled with fun. I would return to my mother in our neat and quiet living room, with the cushions plumped and perfectly positioned on the settee, and I'd want to toss them all on the floor. I never did, of course. When other parts of my life were in chaos, I even appreciated the calm sense of order in our house. And the love there too, though it was never spoken. My parents had been baffled by my decision to take a flat in the city centre after I got a job in Melmount Secretarial, instead of remaining with them.

"But why, Beatrice? You're only nineteen and you've only just started that job," was all my mother could say back in March when I'd told her I was moving out and had found a flat. She'd always assumed I'd stay at home until I found a suitable man to marry. My older brother Laurence hadn't moved out and there was no sign of him finding a girl.

"Because it's what women do now."

I was patient with them, explaining how convenient it would be for me and how I'd learn those domestic skills my mother so valued.

"But won't you be lonely?"

"I'll be fine."

What I'd meant was that I longed to be alone, to run my life my own way, without answering to anyone.

"I can't see the wisdom in that at all," was my father's contribution.

"Even so, I'm going." I used my firmest voice and

looked directly at him.

He'd stared at me for a few moments, then got up from the table, walked into the sitting room and turned on the television.

They couldn't have stopped me, but a part of me still wanted their approval, so when my father had agreed to drive me and my belongings to the new flat I was pleased and relieved.

It was a small place on the third floor of a Georgian building on Westland Row.

"That's not practical," he'd said, waving in the direction of the pay phone in the hall. He'd urged me to put my name down for a private telephone. "What if you have to get up late at night and come down to take a call?" He'd almost shuddered at the thought of me creeping downstairs in my nightclothes. "And every dog and divil will be able to hear what you're saying."

I'd promised that I would get on to the phone company, though I knew I'd be waiting for months.

I loved my three-roomed flat, even if it wasn't exactly up to my parents' standards. Father had been shocked when he saw the paper peeling from the walls of the living room. His brow had furrowed at the sight of what passed for my kitchen. He'd switched the cooker on and off again.

"Do you hear that buzzing? That's not safe." As he'd opened the small fridge, its interior light had flickered and gone out and a sour-milk smell had filled the flat.

"It only needs cleaning out," I'd said.

"It needs an electrician. You're not to use any of these until I get Mick to check out the wiring."

I'd nodded.

"He can fit electric heaters while he's here, too. I'm not having you breathing in the gas from that Superser, and where's your dinner table?"

I'd pointed at the red, formica-topped table, folded up and leaning against the wall. There were three folded metal chairs beside it.

He tutted. "It'll do, I suppose, since it's just yourself."

Mick had arrived the day after I'd moved in, fixed the wiring and fit two heaters.

"Just make sure you don't overload the sockets, or you'll blow a fuse," he'd warned.

I'd painted the walls and reglued the peeling paper. I loved the high ceilings, the plaster cornices and ceiling roses that remained from the house's earlier, grander days. Every time I put my hands on the thick window frame, to look out at the busy street below, I imagined the well-to-do Georgian woman who must have been mistress of the house at one time. She'd have stood in my position, her feet on the same floor, her hands touching the same moulded wood. It thrilled me that I was in her place now, mistress of my own home.

My father had raised an eyebrow at the sight of the double bed in the bedroom. Though he passed no comment, I told him it came with the flat and it'd be a waste to throw it out and buy a single one. I was delighted with it – I bought a colourful quilt, pillows and cushions. I immediately started sleeping in the centre of it and discovered the luxury of breakfast in bed with the Sunday newspaper spread out on the quilt all around me. I felt like the queen of my own little castle, with the centre of Dublin on my doorstep.

I'd been living in the flat six months when I met Leo Hackett.

I was at a restaurant with friends from work. We'd had some wine and I was almost overcome with my own sophistication. I told the girls I needed to powder my nose, and they all laughed at me.

On my way back from the ladies' toilets, he bumped into me, his shoulder just grazing my ear. I looked up into his face and saw the most beautiful sky-blue eyes looking down at me.

"I'm so sorry, are you all right?" he asked.

"Fine, really." The words came out in a high pitch and I blushed. He briefly placed his fingers on the top of my arm, and I felt the tingle of an electric shock.

"You're looking a bit flushed Bea," one of my friends said when I got back to the table and the others laughed.

"Shut up."

When we were leaving the restaurant, he reappeared and asked if he could call me. I agreed without hesitation and gave him my number.

On our first date, he came to my apartment with a bunch of freesias. He stood in the doorway, his left shoulder leaning against the frame, with his left foot crossed over his right one, hands in his pockets. He watched as I filled a vase with water and placed the flowers in it. His gaze filled me with embarrassment and excitement.

When I sat into his car, he paused before starting the engine.

"The first thing you need to know about me is that

I'm not the marrying kind." He spoke firmly, and I felt he was scanning my face for reaction. "You should leave right now if that matters to you."

"Aren't you taking yourself very seriously for a first date? And anyway, what makes you think I want to be shackled to any man?"

He drove me to the Glenview Hotel in Delgany for lunch. I had vegetable soup and lamb. He ordered egg mayonnaise and pork chops, with apple rings. He was so relaxed being waited on. I wasn't used to it and worried I might fail some test I wasn't even aware of.

"This is a long way to come for lunch. Are you trying to hide me?" I'd been joking but he'd lowered his eyes to the table and it was then I knew there was another woman. I considered making a dramatic exit, snatching my handbag from the back of my chair, turning from him in righteous anger. But then there was the transport problem and my distinct lack of indignation. We were only having a meal, I reasoned, and when it was over I could let him leave me home and then firmly say goodbye. It'd be better than making a scene.

"I'm not married or anything, but it's complicated."

I wondered what complication there might be to prevent a man leaving someone he wasn't married to.

"Have you a child?" That would be appalling, I thought.

"God, no."

I put down my knife and fork, took a sip of the red wine he'd ordered and waited.

"We've, me and Angie, we've been together for a while and she's a really good person, but vulnerable, you

377

know what I mean?"

I said I did, and thought of my mother's friend, Louisa, a wisp of a woman Mother said would blow away in a light breeze.

"Things haven't been right between us for a while. Neither of us is happy. But, well, I'm just waiting for her to realise that . . . I don't think she could take it if it came from me." He spoke in a low voice that threatened to break at any moment.

I imagined a fragile woman, clinging to her own unhappiness and understood why Leo was unwilling to hurt her. I could see the pain in his eyes as he spoke about her and I was filled with pity for him.

"I promise after I leave you home tonight, I won't call you again – unless you want me to."

"Well, let's just enjoy our meal," I said, picking up my cutlery.

Later, when he dropped me home and whispered close to my ear that I was beautiful and made a gentle request to see me again, I said yes.